THE CABINET OF CURIOSITIES
OF BARNABY CANNON
and other stories

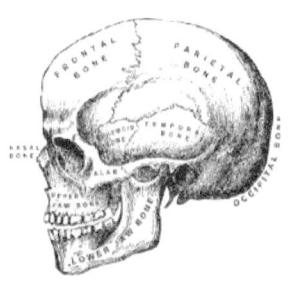

Byron Grush

Published in the United States by Broadhorn Publishing, Delavan, WI

ISBN: 978-0-9985454-4-8

Engraving from Ferrante Imperato's *Dell'Historia Naturale* (Naples 1599)

CONTENTS

THE CABINET OF CURIOSITIES
OF BARNABY CANNON

TEMPUS TEAPOTUS

THE NIGHT BIRDS OF LINCOLN PARK

THE FORTUNE COOKIE

AFTER BANKING HOURS

THE DWARVES

A BAPTISM OF FIRE

THE YEAR THE YUCCA BLOOMED

NOSTAGIA

EDDIE SUGAR

THE YELLOW KID MEETS HIS MATCH

THOMAS HARDY
AND THE BATTLE OF CHERBOURG

MUSE IMAGE, A MEMOIRE (EXCERPT)

Author's Preface

Dating back to the sixteenth century, those who could afford the time and expense of collecting objects that struck their fancy began to place these objects in what were called Kunstkabinetts or Wunderkammers: Cabinets of Wonder or Wonder rooms. These Cabinets of Curiosities were not furniture, but dedicated areas for the display and "juxtaposition of disparate objects," as Bredekamp states. Intrigued by the concept, I have penned a short story set in such a Wunderkammer, and I have taken that title for this collection—my own disparate juxtaposition of several additional stories.

Frito pies and the burning of Old Man Gloom, the fatal flight of the *Wingfoot*, Le Petit Théâtre Du Vieux Carré, the Salles des Glaces, equestrians Rose Dockrell and George Holland, the CSS Alabama vs. the USS Kearsage, Al Capone and the 226 Club, and Doc W's antique dentist's drill all come together in my Cabinet of Curiosities with as little similarity as a narwhale's tusk has to an astrolabes Islamique.

The commonality here is the quasi-genre of Historical Fiction. Some of what you are about to read happened or was reported to have happened. Some of the characters you will encounter did exist. But do not take the content of my tales as Truth. Rather, enjoy the possibilities as I have enjoyed setting them down, however inadequately.

THE CABINET OF CURIOSITIES

OF BARNABY CANNON

Any red-blooded 14-year-old boy would have been captivated by the contents of the room and I was no exception. My Uncle Barnaby was something of a recluse, living alone in a rambling old house on Mozart Street, in Boston's Jamaica Plain neighborhood. In his younger days he had traveled the world, first as a deck hand, then as a passenger on a merchant schooner. He had collected many strange and exotic artifacts during this time, and they were arranged in no particular order in the back-most room on the third floor of the house. It was a sort of private sanctuary and museum which my uncle called his "Cabinet of Curiosities."

As far as my mother was concerned, the room was off limits for me and my sister Rose on the occasions when we visited my uncle. Mother and her brother would sit in the parlor sipping port from small wine goblets and chatting about old times while Rose and I would wander through the house, exploring. Mother would, of course, admonish us to avoid the top floor and to go to the library where we might find a good book to entertain and enlighten us. Uncle Barnaby, upon hearing these strict orders, allowed a sly smile to slide briefly across his face.

Rose was four years younger than me. She wore her red hair in pigtails which, to my mind, made her look like the girl in the Swedish children's book, *Pippi Longstocking*. If I called her "Pippi" she would become furious and punch me. I couldn't resist making her furious. It was just my way of acknowledging her, but she didn't look at it that way. She would counter my taunt by calling me "four-eyes," a reference to the thick glasses I had to wear.

We soon tired of the library; my uncle had no books about red-haired Swedish girls that didn't want to grow up. There was a garden behind the house that intrigued us. Arbors choked with long neglected wisteria led down the middle of an overgrown forest of weeds where the warrens of rabbits were hidden, and errant crows alighted in a delicate ballet. The tangle of vegetation was tall enough for a short game of hide-and-seek, but the novelty dissipated as readily as our interest in the dusty tomes of Uncle's library had. Back into the house and up the stairs stealthily we went.

The creaking complaints of the old stairs betrayed us, and my mother's harsh reprimand curtailed our expedition to the realm of mysteries. This was the rule and not the exception, for my mother's hearing was uncannily acute.

I alone of we two explorers knew what lay beyond that final door. For my uncle had once, and once only, taken me there when I was about ten. My mother had left me in my uncle's care one day when it was necessary for her to drive Rose to see a specialist in Cambridge. A strange rash had spread over my sister's body. Its crimson hue rivaled her hair in a flush of coloration. A few days of antibiotics cleared up the tincture, but its origin was never discovered.

Meanwhile Uncle Barnaby, to allay my own anxiety, introduced me to an other-worldly domain, albeit a forbidden one. The Cabinet of Curiosities awaited at the top of the stairs beyond a door to which trespass had been disallowed me until that glorious moment. Even the door was miraculous: carved from some exotic wood, its decoration consisted of winding tendrils like vines from some distant planet, which, upon closer inspection, revealed curious creatures clinging by clawed appendages, whose faces flashed with dangerous looking fangs. Uncle Barnaby turned the heavy door handle which emitted a squeal as if someone had stepped on a sleeping piglet and gently pushed open that fantastic door.

"Behold" he said, "the Cabinet of Curiosities!"

There was no single cabinet—there were several. And glass cases, much shelving, and a massive wooden desk piled high with leather-bound notebooks. The entire room was filled with what Uncle Barnaby called "curiosities." The first thing that caught my attention was a large creature suspended from the ceiling by wires. It appeared to be a stuffed alligator or crocodile, or it might have been some kind of prehistoric animal for all I knew. It had very large, pointed teeth, greenish scales, and reddish eyes that stared at me maliciously. I let out a gasp.

"Don't worry," said my uncle, "it is quite dead."

Next I noticed a series of large glass jars neatly arranged on a high shelf. In each was…a thing. Sickly pinkish or pale blue with dark spots, things with tentacles or spines, things floating in translucid liquid. Things with eyes that did not blink but seemed to follow me as I walked sheepishly into the room. "Oddities," I murmured.

"Not oddities," corrected Uncle Barnaby. "Oddities are what P. T. Barnum presented in his museum. Fakes, mostly. Hoaxes. Like the Fiji Mermaid and the two-headed peacock. Nothing here is fake. Rare, yes, but real. Here is a microcosm of the natural world. Naturalia, scientifica, artificialia, exotica, animalia. Wunderkammern—miracles of the world!"

Now began a tour of the Cabinet of Curiosities. Uncle Barnaby described many strange and wonderful items as we passed among the various cases and tables and of course, the scientific names flew in one ear and out the other. I can only supply some of this esoteric information now because I obtained, after his death, several of Uncle Barnaby's notebooks. Putting together the inscriptions therein with my less-than-perfect memory has been challenging.

Stuffed animals and birds were everywhere, hanging from the ceiling on wires, perched upon tables, or arrayed in glass cases. This one, Uncle told me, was a Dodo: a flightless bird from the island of Mauritius, three and one-half feet tall and weighing almost 45 pounds. That one was a Great Auk, a large flightless kind of penguin which, like the Dodo, was now extinct. It had come from the collection of a famous 17th century naturalist and physician called Ole Worm. "Don't ask," said my uncle, "how I acquired it."

Two other large birds that I remember were a Tasmanian Emu and a giant Ivory Billed Woodpecker which had a wingspan of over 30 inches. There was also a glass case in which were pinned, like so many butterflies, dozens and dozens of hummingbirds. Their iridescent feathers sparkled in a myriad of colors, even in the dim light of the room.

And butterflies in their own case. The rarest of the rare, said Uncle. Saint Francis Satyr, Macedonian Grayling, Battus Polydamas Antiquus, Schaus Swallowtail, Palos Verdes Blue, Sapho Longwing, Sinai Baton Blue, and the exotic Question Mark Butterfly. Centered in the case was an Acherontia atropos, the African Death's-head Hawkmoth, with marks on its thorax resembling the face of a human skull.

Wall-mounted cabinets with scores of cubby holes contained every manner of small objects ranging from dried insects to wonderful gem stones, or simply unusual items like old rusted iron keys, antique spectacles, personized mustache cups, exotic sea shells, colorful mineral specimens, the horns or tusks or jaw bones of small animals, or excruciatingly beautiful feathers. Each cubby hole was scrupulously labeled and numbered on a little pane of glass that covered it.

Hanging on another wall were several round objects made of brass with moveable circular dials and long pointers, covered with numbers and symbols. Uncle Barnaby called these astrolabes Islamique; they were centuries old astrological instruments used to map the heavens by Arab scientists. Slightly more modern devices sat on an adjacent table: a mechanical equinoctial dial, an armillary sphere with concentric rings, a calendarium perpetuum, an ornate sundial of solid brass, a double framed bridge sextant, and an English orrery clock. This last device was set on sculptured legs and consisted of interlocking gears which served to rotate a series of small spheres mounted on slender posts. It was an animated model of the solar system.

"All these disparate objects, so closely juxtaposed," said my uncle, "encourage the viewer to make comparisons and to find similarities…to bring a view of the natural world as an interconnected and interdependent entity. Accordingly, I have not manipulated my displays as earlier collectors did theirs. Ruysch, for instance, exhibited the small skeletons of animals in anthropormorphic poses and placed collars or strings of pearls on them. They might be playing tiny violins or wielding weapons of war. Some collectors maintained they had the horn of a unicorn when clearly it was the tusk of a narwhale. So many Greek, Roman, and Egyptian artifacts have been faked, and so many mythological oddities have been produced to adorn the cabinets of curiosities of those dishonest folk! The monkey's paw that grants wishes, the feathers of a phoenix's tail, a piece of the True Cross, a dragon's egg! Pah! Nonesense!"

There was one dark corner of the room that my uncle didn't show me. When I asked about it, he shrugged. "Just some moldy old examples of fungi and the like. Nothing that would interest you," he said. Which, of course, made me more interested. But I would not explore that dark corner…not yet.

When Mother learned of the tour I had been given, she was livid. She scolded Uncle Barnaby and forbade him ever again to take me into that room. I didn't understand her wrath. It seemed out of proportion to what I now found to have been an exotic adventure, although a forbidden one—but why? I was very young and did not press for an explanation at that time. On the approach of my twelfth birthday, however, when asked what I wanted as a present, I replied that I wanted to see the Cabinet of Curiosities once again, The reaction to this request was an unnerving coldness and a shake of the head: no. I insisted that I should be made aware of the reason; I had come to no harm on that first expedition. I was sent to my room still unenlightened.

Later that evening Mother came to me, apologetic and consolatory. I was old enough, she said, to hear a story that might shock me. It was time to reveal an ugly truth about Uncle Barnaby and his Cabinet of Curiosities. She sat on the bed next to me, smoothed out her dress, let out a sigh, and began:

"Many years ago, before you were born, your uncle returned from one of his sporadic voyages to distant parts of the world as he often did, but this time there was a difference. As usual, he brought back a large crate filled with God only knows what awful things. There was nothing unusual about this, however, in addition to a collection of artifacts he had with him a young boy—a native boy about the age you are now. From some island in the South Seas, he said.

"There had been occasions when he had brought back living species of snakes or birds—even one time, a small monkey! But these specimens usually died within days or weeks. And never had he been accompanied by a human being. I was shocked by this and inquired just what he expected to do with the youth. 'Why, I intend at first to learn his language and to teach him whatever smattering of English it is possible to impart to him. Then I shall quiz him about his culture and the environment in which he lives…lived. I shall learn so many things!'

"I asked how the boy would survive emotionally, without his parents or others of his race. Would he not be a most unhappy being? My brother just shrugged. He told me the boy had come willingly, anxious to see the modern world and all its wonders. Barnaby had brought back samples of the food that was consumed by the boy's tribe on that remote island: fruits and vegetables and strange looking fungi. I was to observe the daily routine to assure myself that all was correct where the boy's well-being was concerned. I agreed…but I wish I had not.

"His native name was Arh-Wog-Taa. Barnaby called him Arthur. He had a tattoo on his chest which designated him as a warrior class, according to what my brother had learned. He seemed happy and had taken to Barnaby as if the white man was his surrogate father. Soon, however, the fruits and vegetables brought from his island ran out. It was impossible to find breadfruit and other exotic foodstuffs in Boston, so Barnaby tried him on what could be obtained locally. Arthur rejected oranges and grapefruit, but he seemed to like apples and pears. And there was still an ample supply of the strange mushrooms and roots that were his main source of sustenance.

"Months later it became apparent that something was wrong. Arthur acted sluggish and unresponsive. He didn't eat any fruit and only nibbled at the mushrooms. Later in the week he began throwing up and took to his bed. He was delirious and babbled in his native tongue. He was wasting away before our eyes and there seemed to be nothing that we could do to save him.

"I wanted to call in a doctor or take him to a hospital, but Barnaby refused to do so. What the boy needed was to return to the island, your uncle maintained. He determined to do this and began preparing to charter a ship. But before they could embark, Arthur died. I blamed the environment in that dusty museum-like house in which Barnaby and boy had lived. And those evil-looking mushrooms. Barnaby and I didn't talk for many months thereafter. We were becoming estranged because of the incident.

"When you came along and I saw how your uncle doted after you, I forgave him. At the same time, I admonished him never to let you enter that chamber of horrors at the top of the stairs. Now you know why."

No, I didn't exactly. What had a native island boy's death have to do with me? I wasn't going to eat any poison mushrooms. There must have been more to the story than my mother was telling me. I didn't complain or argue, since that would have been futile. I acquiesced. And I stayed away from that room…for the time being.

On that day when Rose and I had ascended the stars toward the forbidden realm and been caught, I resolved that I would eventually revisit the Cabinet of Curiosities and I would bring Rose with me. During the next few visits to my uncle's house I behaved so admirably that my mother must have become suspicious. There was nothing she could scold me for, a circumstance that was highly unusual. But I would wait until I was sure she was off guard—and then I would act!

The opportunity came that summer I had turned fourteen. Mother left Rose and I at Uncle Barnaby's while she attended a baby shower for one of her friends. There had been several of these—I later learned this was because of what had come to be called the "Post-war Baby Boom," with GIs returning from the war and making up for lost time. I was never so happy for peace time than at that moment. We were at uncle's without Mother!

The next obstacle was my uncle. I knew that no manner of persuasion on my part would cause him to disobey my mother's prohibition on Cabinet of Curiosities visits. Rose and I bided our time in the library. A mid-afternoon nap was customary for Uncle, but so far it had not manifested itself. We were halfway through a volume of bound copies of the *National Geographic* when we heard the wonderful sound of snoring coming from our uncle's study.

Up the stairs we went, oblivious to creaking or the threat of discovery, for my uncle was a sound sleeper. I paused at the door. "Rose," I said, "prepare yourself for something wonderful!" she giggled. I turned the doorknob—it was unlocked! I pushed the door slowly open, untroubled by the great squeaking it made as it swung into the gloomy chamber.

"Oh!" said Rose.

"Don't touch anything," I said as I escorted my sister through the maze of tables, pointing out the stuffed birds suspended from the ceiling, the case of pinned hummingbirds, and other wonders. The air was stale and the lighting dim. I searched for a light switch but found none. There was an antique lamp on a counter which I attempted to turn on, but it was an oil lamp and I had no matches. We persisted in our exploration and gradually, our eyes grew accustomed to the darkness.

I tried to remember the names of the various animals and the exotic devices that were on display. I might have made up some names just to avoid being found out in my ignorance. After all, this was my chance to show off and I relished it. I remembered that the astrolabe was an ancient tool for charting the heavens and navigating the oceans. I called it an astronautic compass.

Rose was fascinated by a cabinet holding many examples of rare gems and minerals. There, at least, were labels identifying the various items. A polished piece of purple amethyst sat next to a colorful serpentine rock. Flanking these were a large chunk of lapis lazuli, streaked in royal blue, and a fist-sized crystal carved into the semblance of a skull. Rose reached to examine this last item but I warned her once again not to touch anything.

While Rose remained transfixed by the gems, I wandered over to the insect displays. I was particularly fascinated by the big board of spiders, affixed by pins through their abdomens, which left their legs able to wiggle from vibrations set off by our footfalls. Here the labels identified some of the largest specimens to be found anywhere in the world. The Brazilian Wandering Spider had a diameter of nearly six inches…yet it was not, by far, the largest. That honor went to the Goliath Bird-eating Tarantula, this one a good foot in length! It came from the rain forests of South America. There was a Huntsman Spider, almost as large, and a Brazilian Salmon Pink Bird-eater, compact and ugly as they go. The very rare Hercules Baboon spider was even less appealing, bulky and hairy. But of course, I could see keeping most of these creepy crawlers as pets.

While I looked at snake skeletons and dried lizards, Rose gravitated toward the darkest section of the room. The section I had expressed an interest in back when Uncle Barnaby had shown me around. The one Uncle Barnaby had steered me away from. And now she was examining a table display of rare mushrooms. And now...incorrigible sister...she was picking up specimens and turning them over in her hands. She dropped one onto the floor.

"Rose!" I yelled. "What did I tell you?"

Yet now she had seen a door. Of course she opened it. Of course she went through it into a chamber just as dark and murky as the section of mushrooms had been. I followed. The odor that assailed our nostrils was noxious and nearly made me gag. I fumbled, running my hand along the edge of the doorway just inside the chamber. I found a light switch and flipped it on. The sudden bright light momentarily blinded both of us. But then we saw the interior—a sight I will never forget!

A fully articulated human skeleton hung from the ceiling, its yellow boned feet barely touching the floor. It rotated slowly on a wire, its empty sockets surveying room with a dastardly keenness. A glass case held artifacts from ancient civilizations, mostly tools made from bones. A table was filled with an assortment of femurs, some labeled baboon, some labeled human. An unrolled Egyptian papyrus pictured preparing the dead for the afterlife, its faded hieroglyphs adding an aura of mystery to the setting. There was a row of human skulls neatly arranged with small placards describing race and origin: Mongolian, Polynesian, Congolese, Navajo, Japanese, Bostonian—they all looked the same to me.

Against one wall stood an empty Egyptian sarcophagus. Along side of this was a mummified animal, probably a cat or a small monkey. Then, simultaneously, Rose and I saw something startling and ominous. Rose let out a shriek that nearly shook the hanging skeleton from its mounting. There in an upright box was body. It was blackened and shriveled, obviously mummified from the dryness of the chamber. I realized from its small stature that it was a boy. It had markings on its chest, lines that must have been tattooed during life. Then I knew. Out loud I uttered, "Oh my God! It's Arthur!"

Rose was taken from us one year later. She suffered from chills and nausea and her skin broke out in blotches of scarlet and purple. I was at her bedside at the end and she smiled meekly at me. "At least we got to see the Cabinet of Curiosities," she said. I wondered. The doctors could do nothing for her. In fact, they were completely puzzled by her aliment. But I thought I knew what it was. She had handled those exotic mushrooms and somehow, the spores had gotten into her body. Would she now shrivel up as Arthur had?

When I turned twenty and was no longer under my mother's thumb, I went to see my uncle. I had to know more. I found him in his study, slumped in his easy chair as usual and on the verge of nodding off. I said:

"Why did Arthur die? And why didn't you take him to the doctors?"

"You know about Arthur, eh? Well, to understand, you need to hear a story about the islanders on that small atoll where he was born. Their story is part myth and part history. So…settle yourself down in that chair while I tell it."

I sat down opposite my uncle. He reached into the pocket of his jacket and pulled out an old briar pipe that he favored, poked some tobacco into it, and lit it. He began:

"Our ship was called the *Moroccan Charger*. She was an old but sea-worthy freighter lately out of Liverpool and headed out to load up with any exotic cargo her owners could latch on to on the cheap. Nothing perishable, but teak wood, ivory, things like that. I no longer worked on ships as a deckhand, but I wished again to go to sea. The captain was happy to accept me as a passenger, once he saw the color of my money.

"I befriended a deckhand by the name of Quan. He was part Polynesian, part Chinese, and part who knows what. He had a smattering of island lingo that might get me information once we docked, so I kept close to him at each landfall.

"A few of the islands we visited were already Europeanized and proved useless for my purposes. At last we ventured further toward the edge of the charted ocean and began encountering islands less known and therefore profoundly more interesting, at least to my way of thinking. The first island we saw had no means of approaching closely as the reefs surrounding it made a formidable barrier, and the captain was not willing to risk his ship.

"Finally, we came to a small atoll with a broad, sandy beach. It was accessible via long boat and I bargained with the captain to allow me and my new-found friend, Quan, to go on the first exploratory landing. He agreed. We jumped form the boat into the gentle surf and pulled our craft onto the beach which was of a gleaming white sand strewn with empty crab shells, sea-washed twigs, and the tracks (where the sand was still wet from the tide) of large birds.

"We marched into the interior and soon found a village of thatched huts and half-naked islanders. They were friendly enough, and negotiations to trade for the abundant breadfruit that grew on the island got underway almost at once. We had brought boxes of glass-beaded necklaces and small mirrors which delighted the islanders. While much of the crew began harvesting the

8

breadfruit and carrying it back to the ship, Quan and I settled into the village. With Quan as my interpreter, I was able to gain some small insight into the culture we had discovered there. A great influence of myth and legend prevailed on that tiny island paradise.

"They had no name for their island, as they were unaware of the existence of other islands or lands and therefore simply called it Toka-Weka, which means 'world.' The origin of Toka-Weka involved two hero brothers, To-Benaka and To-Bekuyu, who fished the island out of the great ocean while using sea turtles as bait in order to catch sharks. The sea turtles discovered the island at the bottom of the sea and since it had the same shape as their own shells, brought it up to the brothers. To-Benaka and To-Bekuyu breathed on the island so that it expanded into the size it now has and it became covered with vegetation.

"The brothers were among the first men and the ancestors of the two tribes that now live on opposite sides of Toka-Weka. The people of the other side of Toka-Weka, Quan told me, were cannibals. They evolved thusly because, as the story goes, one day when To-Benaka and To-Bekuyu were out walking, To-Benaka said to his brother, 'Go, and look after our mother.' To-Bekuyu went home and thinking his brother had said to *kill* their mother, took a bamboo vessel filled with water, poured it over his mother, heated stones in the fire, and laid her on them to roast. When To-Benaka learned what his brother had done he exclaimed, 'Oh, you fool! You always do stupid things. Now our descendants will cook and eat each other.' And so he banished To-Bekuyu to the other side of the island where the prophesy came true and a race of cannibals appeared there after a time.

"As it turned out, there really were cannibals on the other side of the island. Not long before our arrival, a woman of the village had been taken by the cannibals during a raid. She had no husband, but left behind and alone her son, the boy named Arh-Wog-Taa, who we later called Arthur. Arh-Wog-Taa, because of the stigma of being alone and of being the son of a kidnapped woman, was ostracized by the villagers. In fact, an elder, one who we might call the witch doctor, placed a curse on him, saying that soon he would fall sick with illness and die.

"Quan and I took the boy into our hut to care for and protect him. We saw to it that he had food and clothing and that none of the other villagers could harass him...this displeased them and we began to fall out of favor. One night there was another raid on the village by the cannibal tribe and Arthur was kidnapped. Our distress at this was excruciating as we had grown quite fond of the boy and felt responsible for him.

"I went to our ship's captain and pleaded with him to give me some men to go to the other side of the island to rescue the boy. 'Ain't none of our business,' he replied. So it was up to myself and Quan to make the attempt alone. We secured rifles from the ship's stores and set off immediately, fearing the worst, but hoping against hope we would not be too late.

"We were able to convince one of the villagers, a young man named Ko-Tak-Ura, to guide us. Ko-Tak-Ura had been a cousin to the boy's mother and thus he went against the wishes of the villagers and helped us. Our trail led through a thick jungle of vines and exotic shrubs and I dearly wished I could have obtained some specimens of these as I had from other parts of the island, but there was not time to do so. Coconut palms towered above us and maclayana were abundant, their swollen fruit hanging sensuously. The broad leaves of the fragrant manjack, also called cummingcordia, glistened with the morning's dew, and golden cuckooshrikes flitted among the branches. We could hear the plaintiff calls of Jewel-babblers and kingfishers and the moan-like song of the claret-breasted fruit dove. But all this exotic flora and fauna would have to wait.

"Stealthily we approached the cannibal village. We were perched on a hilltop just above the circle of huts, watching in order to assess the strength of our adversaries, when we caught sight of Arthur. Two of the cannibals were leading the boy, who had his arms tied behind him, to the center of the village where a raised platform of wood and palm leaves had been constructed. They threw him down upon this, lashing him tightly to it. It looked like kindling had been arranged under the platform. To our horror, we saw a woman approaching with a flaming torch. They were about to roast him alive!

"Now what seemed like the entire village emerged from the huts and formed a circle around the platform. We were outnumbered, but we had two advantages: first was that of surprise, and second was the fact that we carried two rather lethal weapons…the loaded rifles. We wasted no time and rushed down the hill firing as accurately as we could. Three of the cannibals dropped to the ground, wounded and bleeding. The others panicked, obviously never having seem firearms before, and they ran in all directions. But now, however, the woman had lit the kindling under Arthur and it was beginning to flare up!

"Quickly we ran to cut Arthur loose from the roasting platform. This took some time as we only had one knife. Arthur was writhing from the flames that were licking at him—he was getting burned! Ko-Tak-Ura began shouting at him. Quan later told me he was demanding to know about the boy's mother. Was she still alive? Artur shook his head: no. By now the cannibals had regained some bravado and were beginning to creep back towards us.

"A few more rounds of rifle fire slowed the cannibals enough for us to break Arthur loose. Ko-Tak-Ura tossed the boy over his shoulder and the four of us clambered back up the hill and ran into the rain forest. We could hear yelling and the sounds of the scramble of pursuit. I stopped and fired into the thick forest in the direction of the village. Then I ran to the others.

"Well it was nip and tuck, but we succeeded in reaching our own village where Ko-Tak-Ura's people would surely help to turn the cannibals back…or so we thought. Instead they retreated into their own huts. There was nothing for it but to escape to the safety of the ship, and so we thanked Ko-Tak-Ura, took turns carrying Arthur, and ran to the beach where we signaled the captain. The cannibals were close upon our heel! Our shipmates came to our aid and more rifle fire ensued, accompanied by the explosive sound of the small cannon the ship carried. The cannibals turned and ran."

Uncle Barnaby tapped the ashes from his pipe into his palm and then discarded them into a waste basket next to his chair. There was more to the story, how he treated Arthur's burns, how the ship fared during the journey home, how Arthur came to live with him. He told it slowly.

"That is certainly an interesting story," I said once he had finished, "but it doesn't yet answer my question. Why didn't you take Arthur to a doctor?"

"The witch doctor's curse," he answered. "It was the cause of his illness and the only way to cure Arthur was to take him back to the island and convince the witch doctor to reverse the curse. Unfortunately, we didn't have time to make the trip before he died.

Out of politeness and respect for my uncle, I did not object to his explanation. However, I was still incredulous.

Five years later, my uncle died. In his will he left his Cabinet of Curiosities to the Boston Geographic Society, which had a small museum. He designated me to oversee the exchange of the artifacts. It would be the last time I would enter the old dark house, quiet now and perhaps even more mysterious and foreboding than I remembered. I was able, during the cataloging and crating of the collection, to procure for myself my uncle's journals. The latest of these detailed the story of Arthur—I didn't want this to become common knowledge. Curiously, when we entered the chamber of skulls and mummified remains, Arthur's body was gone. I was grateful for that circumstance, not wanting to have to invent an explanation for the macabre display.

Now, I do write the full story for the world to hear, at least as I remember and understand it—although I doubt that many will believe in its veracity. Should you visit the little museum in Boston someday where a stunning exhibit of rare butterflies and birds is on display, I urge you to avoid the collection of fungi in the glass case on the second floor. As I write this, red and purple spots are appearing on my arms and legs.

Byron Grush

TEMPUS TEAPOTUS

He woke to a cantillating of birdsong, a shrill intertwining of disparate voices competing for prominence in the dawn's early light. Light: which pierced through tiny holes in the heavy drapery—the work of persistent moths—and which peered around the fringes where the two sections had not quite met. Light that struck the painting which hung above his bed and brought alive the gilding which some artist of another age had used to indicate a golden aura surrounding the head of the figure in the painting. The figure was a young man, locks of auburn hair cascading to his white robed shoulders, eyes set in an upward, pleading glance, small droplets of crimson rolling down a furled forehead where sat a wreath of thorns. On his chest was a bleeding heart, more grim and off-putting even than the piercing thorns.

He had inherited the painting of Jesus in its ornate frame from his grandmother. It was one of the few items in her meager estate he had desired as a memento. It had hung above the stairs in her farmhouse in Central Illinois where it had stared down at a first-floor hallway with eyes now turned toward heaven, but *then* aimed downward, intent upon surveying the interior of the house. Eyes that followed you if you passed beneath their vigilance. This circumstance of the eyes that followed you obsessed and frightened him and his cousins as children when they visited Gramma Doyle. They would rush through the corridor below the painting like bugs pursued by a malevolent spider, frantic not to be trapped by the painting's gaze, and beset by nervous giggles.

So when the executor of Gramma Doyle's estate was ready to distribute the odd items left in the old house, he claimed the painting, more to overcome, through its acquisition and subsequent display in his own abode, a sort of manifest mastery over the old fears rather than an aesthetic appreciation of its artistry or a religious regard for its subject matter. None of the cousins challenged his claim.

He had meant to fix the faulty hanger which attached the painting to the wall; the thing rattled belligerently whenever a big semi roared down the street. Someday, no doubt, the thing would fall from the wall while he was sleeping, cold cocking him…or worse. He'd think about it tomorrow. Right now. some catbird or mockingbird or such was drowning out the other warblers. This was his cue to emerge from his bed and begin his day.

A day that entailed, young bachelor that he was, starting the coffee and then jumping into the shower where soap on a rope hung from the shower head and yesterday's washcloth lay, still wet and tending toward mildew, over the drain. It was a basement apartment situated in an older building with dubious plumbing and on the very first occasion of showering there he had been joined by a very large water beetle that had crawled up from that drain; the placement of the washcloth was a guard against such a recurrence.

After showering, a vigorous rubdown with a towel plucked from the clothes basket lately brought home from the corner laundromat, and then a two-minute egg. The egg, covered in cold water, brought to a boil and then removed from the heat for a period of precisely two minutes, waited patiently in an old Art Deco egg cup he had found at the local thrift shop, was beginning to cool while he buttered toast. Now he tapped around the top of the egg with a knife, neatly removing a piece of shell as if ceremoniously decapitating a miniature Humpty Dumpty. The golden yolk thus revealed glistened in the morning light. Salt and pepper completed the breakfast ritual.

It was Saturday. The alarm had not been set as there was no urgency to rush for the bus stop on the corner. The birds that had awakened him had flown away and the sounds of traffic now filtered into his room: taxis jockeying for position with horns blaring, a van filled with today's morning edition squealing to a stop in front of the news stand, a heavy garbage truck rumbling up the alley with the odds and ends of the city's cultural jetsam clattering in its voluminous cavity, the ubiquitous roar of the distant elevated train barely audible yet so ordinary and pervasive. The snorting of the city bus triggered an automatic response even though it was Saturday.

The bookstore—he thought to himself. I'll go to the bookstore. The bookstore would provide a respite from the tedium of a day off; he didn't do well when idle and had no hobbies. His life was job-centric, an existence defined by work, work, and more work, and a satisfaction when the job was well done—which was nearly always. His job, his profession, his calling in life was that of an editor in the employ of a publisher of how-to-do-it books with an inexhaustible catalog of bland subjects. It may have seemed ironic that, after working with books day in and day out, he would spend his day off in a bookstore, but printer's ink flowed through his veins, the smell of binding glue was perfume to him, and the texture of rag paper was sweet to his touch.

The bookstore was located on a shabby and trash-strewn street just across the river from the city central. The street had at one time been the location of various watering holes frequented by less than sophisticated revelers seeking entertainment in dens of iniquity or illegal gambling establishments, but had been cleared of these venues during an era of progressive city government. Said era was short-lived but somehow the rowdy and irrepressible district never completely reestablished itself. The few survivors along this section of the street included a cut-rate liquor store, a haberdashery that sold only second-hand clothing, a thrift shop that seemed never to be open, a lonesome bar, and the bookstore.

The Antiquarian Bookstore itself was as dingy as the street. It sold nothing which was new but there, in a dark interior smelling of mildew, in a labyrinth of shelves and glass-fronted counters, could be found the myriad ephemera of bygone ages: books whose titles on their spines were dust obscured, magazines with browning, mouse nibbled pages, photographs once used for publicity showing smiling actors and actresses of the silent movie age, gone and forgotten but collectable for that very reason. The covers of the magazines found in long bins had faded somewhat, but the images, painted by unabashed artists, featured scantily clad women with looks of horror on their faces, besieged by Asians drawn in racist caricature wielding long, evil-looking knives, or bug-eyed alien monsters emerging from fanciful space ships.

The green and yellow city bus had deposited him a few blocks north of the bookstore. He walked the remaining distance, avoiding the unevenness of the sidewalk which was sunken in various places, the result of a city which, built over a swamp and then tragically burned to the ground, had been rebuilt anew some eight or ten feet above its earlier level and was now, here and there, inching its way back. It was said there was an underground city below street level, long ago abandoned, and populated by ghosts.

He swung open the bookstore's door, ducking an avalanche of dust that fell from an aged yellow window shade that was pulled half way down against the glass, "Are you open?" he called to a tall, rail-thin man who was shelving books near the rear of the store. The man's posture and the limp grip with which he held a book made him resemble a giant praying mantis. A pair of bottle glass spectacles and a shiny green vest completed the illusion.

"Oh, it's you, Andrew," the man said. "Always open for you."

"Glad to hear it Mr. Hofmann. Any new acquisitions?"

Dietmar Hofmann did not look a year over forty, although he had owned and operated the Antiquarian since its inception over three decades ago. The smile with which he greeted Andrew was not given to most customers. Indeed, his normal demeanor was that of a curmudgeon, given to scowling and a reluctance to share his unique navigational knowledge of the literary empire he oversaw. His dark mood gave way to rage should a patron pull a book from the shelf using a forefinger hooked over the book's spine.

Hofmann had a soft spot for Andrew, however. He appreciated the young man's earnest interest in books. And it didn't hurt that Andrew, from time to time, brought the bookseller a box of recently remaindered tomes his company had taken off the market due to less than stellar sales. Book companies made more money writing off apparent losses than they did when profits were depleted by royalties and marketing expenses.

"There are some new volumes over in the Occult section that may interest you," said Hofmann. "Dream books."

Andrew had an ongoing interest in books about alchemy, astrology, occult magic, and especially about dreams. A whole shelf in his apartment was devoted to everything from scholarly works on the analysis of dreams to pop-culture dream books. He had the classics: Sigmund Freud's *The Interpretation of Dreams*, C. G. Jung's *Symbols of Transformation* and *Modern Man in Search of a Soul*, and Calvin S. Hall's *A Primer of Freudian Psychology*. Next to these was Madame Zolar's *Dream Book*, *The Witch's Dream Book and Fortune Teller* (facsimile edition), Dorothy Brighton's *Your Stars and Your Dreams*, and Mother Shipton's *Gypsy Dream Book*. From there on the collection diversified to include works on occult magic such as *The Golden Dawn* by Israel Regardie,

Transcendental Magic by Eliphas Levi, *The Mistery of Alchymists* by George Ripley, and a modern translation with illustrations of *De Heptarchia Mystica* (or *On the Mystical Rule of the Seven Planets*) by John Dee.

Andrew slipped around the store's two central bookshelves, towering affairs that dominated the space and sheltered an area near the back of the room where the more esoteric subjects were located. He found a number of new volumes sitting horizontally on top of the row of the occult books, there being no more room for them on that shelf. Most of these where of no interest, being popular editions devoted to horoscopes or Tarot cards. The dream books that Hofmann had referenced were drugstore pulps that Andrew considered trivial and even silly. He kept browsing.

Someone, obviously not Hofmann, had mistakenly placed a copy of H. G. Well's *The Time Machine* among the new arrivals. Andrew pulled this out to return it to the Science Fiction section. Then he noticed a small book bound in dark red leather with a title embossed in gold: *The Theater of Terrestrial Astronomy* by Edward Kelly. According to the title page it was a 19th century facsimile of the Hamburg 1678 original edition with reproductions of 16 circular woodcuts done by Kelly. Excited, Andrew began to turn its yellowed pages.

The first illustration showed a king having three faces. He sat on a gently arching rainbow, his feet resting upon a small globe of the Earth. On the globe could be seen a blindfolded man chasing a large stag. The king pointed to the Earth globe with his right hand. Above his head, almost like a halo, was a circle of light in which a triangle was inscribed. To his left was the figure of the Sun and to his right was the figure of the Moon.

Andrew flipped through the pages. The illustrations progressed through a number of symbolic scenes. A naked woman with a crescent moon on her head was standing next to Hermes. A raging stream was descending a hill while the figures of the gods of of the five planets, Moon, Mercury, Venus, Sun, and Mars, stood watching. An alchemist with a long beard placed the figures of the planets into a wide necked flask. He fitted the flask with an alembic still-head and heated this on a square furnace. In the sky above the flask was a flying dragon seizing its own tail, forming an ouroboros. On the ground below the flask were two lions. The process of alchemical transmutation continued throughout the 16 illustrations. Andrew was fascinated. As he neared the end of the book a folded sheet of paper slipped out and fell onto the floor.

Examining the paper, Andrew saw that it was a note written in purple ink with an elegant hand although hurried toward the end. A spot of ink had fallen near the signature and this had been hastily blotted, leaving a dampness that, once the note was folded, had formed a symmetrical inkblot that resembled a Death's Head Moth, or so it seemed to Andrew. It read:

Grand Hotel, Paris, May 9, 1916

Dearest Charlotte,

Already I miss our late afternoon walks and our camaraderie, our mutual acquaintanceship—what the Scots call ken. We have, I have no doubt however, made the proper decision to take holiday apart. While the separation is irksome, it may allow us a time for contemplation and, in my case, for an endeavor I believe is of a necessity to be embarked upon singularly.

We have been under a ruthless attack by our critics. Even before our publisher used our real names on the third edition of our book, they had surrounded us like wolves around two lost sheep, angry and hungry for the kill. Perhaps our story was too popular and that generated jealousy. Perhaps they simply feared what they thought we represented. It is one thing to have doubted the veracity of the experience we know must have been true. But to harass us for our friendship—calling us two old maids living together in—oh, I cannot even write the word!

Here I am in Paris, that romantic city where I first met you. You were hired to be my vice-principle at St. Hugh's College for women in Oxford. I was staying that summer in my apartment on the Rue Sainte-Sulpice. I wanted to get to know you before term started and so I invited you to come to Paris. You took the boat train. We toured the City of Light together—the Sacre-Coeur, the Tuileries, the dreadful but fascinating Pere-Lachaise Cemetery where so many important artists and literary figures are interred, the Champs-Élysées, and that fateful excursion to the Palace of Versailles.

I can see it as clearly as if it were yesterday rather than fifteen years ago. We sat in the Hall of Mirrors, exhausted after the tour. Those immense crystal chandeliers, those gilded statues gazing down at us like disapproving goddesses, the garishly painted vaulted ceiling, the beams of sunlight streaking across the polished floor like a felled forest of light. You wanted to see the Petit Trianon, Marie Antoinette's famed hideaway which had not been included in the tour.

We wandered throughout that vast place getting more and more lost. Then, in a garden, we saw two men dressed in green jackets and tri-corned hats standing by a wheel barrel. Were they gardeners or members of the Swiss Guard? A woman dressed in ballooning skirts that echoed another long-gone century hurried past carrying a jug on her shoulder. A dreamlike and oppressive malaise gripped us. I felt like I was walking in my sleep through some bizarre fairy tale realm.

Then we saw, set back in the trees, a columned building. Seated on the steps was a man with a slouch hat wearing a heavy black cloak. His countenance was evil and fear inspiring. I wished to turn back but just then another man came running up, greatly agitated. He hurried down a path around the side of the building shouting something in French which we could not make out. We followed him.

We came upon a chateau that must have been the Petit Trianon. On its terrace on a short three-legged stool sat a very pretty woman with fluffy hair wearing a broad-brimmed hat and an elegant gown that seemed too fancy for day wear. She was sketching. The excited man whispered something to her. She looked up and saw us, giving us an angry look of annoyance. The man beckoned us to follow him and soon we were back at the front entrance of the palace.

It was later that we made the connection, one we were hesitant to conclude although it was obvious. We had been transported back in time and had witnessed the doomed Queen of France, Marie Antoinette, being warned that an angry mob was coming from Paris to seize her. No one believed us. We wrote it all down and called the book The Adventure. *We used the pseudonyms Elizabeth Morison and Frances Lamont. But three years ago, that foolish publisher of ours put our real names on the cover.*

I thought I was protected, being the daughter of the Bishop of Salisbury. But I am in danger of termination from my position. The ridicule will prevent me from finding work anywhere in England, I am sure. Thus I have returned to France. I am determined to visit once again that awesome palace and to seek out the Petit Trianon. With luck I may travel back to the eighteenth century again and this time, return with proof that we did not hallucinate nor fabricate that mysterious journey of 1901.

After all is said and done, I think I may travel (in this century, however). I have a desire to see the Middle East or perhaps, America. If you would join me— but it is so unfair of me to wish it, much less to ask it. Only time will tell. Think of me fondly as I do of you.

Love, Eleanor

Andre slipped the note back between the pages of *Theater of Terrestrial Astronomy* and went to the counter where Dietmar Hofmann was dusting a green leather-bound set of the works of Miguel de Cervantes. Andrew still carried the copy of *The Time Machine* and placed both books on the counter.

"Hmm…you want both of these, Andrew? Didn't think you were an aficionado of fantastic fiction as well as fantastic nonfiction," said Hofmann.

"What? No…just the red book. The other was misshelved. Where did this come from, if I may ask?"

"An estate sale on the South Side. They bring what books and memorabilia they can't sell to me. I've a good relationship with many of the auction houses."

"Do you remember the address?"

Hofmann looked at the youth curiously. "There won't be anything left. Why do you want to know?"

"I'm not sure. Just a feeling."

Hofmann ruffled through a drawer set into the back of the counter and came up with the receipt. He jotted an address on a piece of paper and handed it to Andrew. "I hope you aren't chasing windmills." He said.

Andrew was just barely old enough to remember when the buses were electric. They loomed up and down avenues like giant insects connected to overhead wires by long whips that rode, somehow mysteriously, against the wires. Sparks would fly and a crackling sound would accompany the buses on their routes. Often, one of the whips would dislodge itself from the overhead wires and a grumbling driver would climb on top of the bus to reinstate the slender whip while giving voice to a litany of vulgar oaths. The smell the bus gave off was one of ozone, more pleasurable than today's obnoxious diesel bus exhaust.

Andrew sat on one of the side benches near the driver and watched a diverse array of neighborhoods go by, each featuring store fronts topped by signage in one language or another, rendered in color palettes that were bright but peeling. He occupied himself with trying to guess the wares or services offered by the different shops.

After buying the red bound book he had paid a visit to the library to do some research pertaining to the intriguing note he had found in the red book. It turned out that the writer of the note and its addressee were two Edwardian ladies named Charlotte Anne Moberly and Eleanor Jourdain. They had indeed written a book entitled *The Adventure* which chronicled their strange experience at Versailles in August of 1901.

Jourdain was asked to resign from the college in 1924 having wrongfully fired a tutor, not for sexual deviancy nor for publishing an outrageous account of time travel. She died of heart failure shortly before the termination could take effect. Moberly died in 1937 at the age of 90. Andrew could not learn anything about either of them living in the United States, so how the letter had found its way into the red book was still a mystery.

The bus plunged through the heart of the city and into its bowels. Then it emerged onto a corridor of neatly kept townhouses. Brownstones once the proud residences of the well-to-do, now divided into two- or three-flats, yet still commanding a pretty penny in rent. These began to be separated by grassy spaces as the avenue unfolded before the bus. Here and there an aged mansion sprouted, castle-like with turret and balustrade. This was once the realm of the rich and powerful, or at least, of those who presumed to occupy that status; an island of entitlement surrounded by a sea of deprivation.

Andrew found the address. The stately edifice sported a turret on each corner of its front elevation. It was made of yellow limestone masonry now streaked with lines of mildew running like dark tears from the sightless eyes of twin windows on the upper story. Andrew mounted the curved stone stairway to the front entrance. A mosaic of stained glass presented a scene on the heavy double doors: an armor-clad Saint George brandishing a sword on the left door and a gnarly green dragon cowering on the right. There was no doorbell or knocker so Andrew rapped on the door with his knuckles. No answer.

He tried the doorknob and found it unlocked. The door swung open easily. The entryway was tiled in dusty black and white squares of striated marble. A clean rectangular spot on the floor against one wall indicated where a chest or some other small piece of furniture had stood, perhaps supporting an urn or jardinière for flowers. Above it on the wall was an unfaded rectangle of wallpaper where a picture or a mirror had once hung. The wallpaper itself displayed a fanciful pattern of vines and limbs on which grinning monkeys sat holding what looked like coconuts.

"Hello!" Andrew called. "Anybody here?"

He entered a large room, empty except for a long table of some dark wood with heavy, ornately carved legs. The table was stacked with one half dozen matching chairs. A tag hung there which read, "Sold. Wilson." Andrew continued walking through the room and entered an adjacent sitting room which was lined with shelves. The books which had sat on those shelves were gone, sold at auction or taken to Hofmann's Antiquarian Bookstore. One or two items remained: a specimen of a chambered nautilus shell mounted on a rosewood base and a photograph in an Art Deco frame. Andrew drew closer to examine the photograph.

It was of a woman, between the ages of twenty and thirty, exact age and ethnicity indeterminate. Andrew would have said she was pretty but not strikingly so. She had a round face and closely cropped dark hair, not exactly a bob, although the age of the frame might have suggested that style, and it gave her an androgynous look. She wore round, tortoise shell framed glasses. Andrew's excitement piqued as he read the inscription on the photograph: "for Eleanor, all my love, Charlotte."

"The sale is over, young man," came a voice from behind Andrew. He was startled and almost dropped the framed photograph. He turned to find an old man, stooped and leaning on a cane, standing like a sentinel at the entrance to the room.

"What? Oh, sorry...I just...I..."

"There is nothing left to buy here. Family is moved out. Maybe you are interested in the house? I can give you the number of the real estate company."

"Are you one of the family?" he asked the old man.

"Me? No. I'm just the caretaker. Out of a job now, I suppose."

"This woman," Andrew said, showing the caretaker the photograph, "did she ever live here? Or perhaps her friend, Eleanor?"

"That's an old picture, son. Woman would be pretty old now, probably deceased. Can't say that I know anything about her."

"The family...where can I find them?"

"Only one left is the son. Don't think I ought to be givin' out that information. Why you want to know?"

"I think I may have something he would want to see. It involves the woman in this photo. Can't you help me?" Andrew attempted a look of beseeching innocence.

"Well, I should have my head examined. I'll get you the phone number. Just don't tell the son where you got it. He can be somewhat unreasonable. Wait here a minute."

Andrew was still holding the framed photograph, staring into the long dead eyes of the mystery woman (or were they long dead?) when the caretaker returned with a business card to give to him. "Take the picture too, if you like," the caretaker said.

He had already taken two personal days and work was piling up. Andrew had three manuscripts on his desk to edit: *How to Declutter your Travel Trailer, How to Survive an Atomic Attack,* and *How to Draw Unicorns.* He would have to wait until the weekend to seek out the person on the business card, the one that the caretaker had called the Son, the one that could be unreasonable. The one who, according to the business card, was named Devon Bernard Kellogg.

Kellogg was an actuary, whatever that was. It had something to do with risk management, Andrew thought. Something complicated and akin to fortune telling or gambling or clairvoyance or all three rolled together. It meant, he guessed, that the man would be analytical, cold, and unreceptive to creative ideas. But he could be wrong. Maybe that profession required a high degree of creativity. Andrew thought of his own profession, book editor. It was about as creative as line work at the Ovaltine factory—a job he had held down for most of a summer between college terms.

He had, during those college years, taken a course in creative writing and his professor had heaped compliments on his single effort at a short story. He had encouraged Andrew to become a writer. The story involved a girl, of course, and adolescent infatuation, of course, and unrequited love, of course, and was partly autobiographical. Of course. He had felt writing was too personal, too revealing. Self-awareness was not his cup of Ovaltine. As an editor, tracking down sentences that ended with prepositions, finding misplaced comas, and spelling errors was as adventurous literary-wise as he cared to get. It was safe and comfortable and easy.

He turned his thoughts to Devon Kellogg. Had Kellogg known either of the two women that Andrew was becoming obsessed with or was that notion as absurd as the idea that Charlotte Anne Moberly and Eleanor Jourdain had traveled back in time? Kellogg was his only lead, the only living link to the mystery which when solved would give credibility to the theory that Time was a dimension one could traverse as easily as walking the length, width, and breadth of a parking lot or a corn field or a geometry problem in a high school textbook (if you only knew how). He hoped that was true. He relished the opportunity of editing a book entitled, *How to Find the Best Hotels When Time Traveling.*

The man would not be in his office on the weekend so Andrew decided to call right away. After checking carefully for eavesdropping associates or the boss, he picked up the telephone and dialed the number on the card. He reached a secretary. He could visualize her: hair piled high in last year's beehive style, argyle sweater with the top three buttons undone, straight skirt riding up as she sat on the swivel chair revealing a goodly length of panty hose, comfortable flats. She would probably call him honey.

"Sorry, honey, Mr. Kellogg isn't available. He's in a meeting. What firm are you with?"

"My name is Andrew Stone and I have some information for Mr. Kellogg. Please mention to him the names, Charlotte Anne Moberly and Eleanor Jourdain. I think he'll want to talk to me."

"Please hold…"

Moments later a masculine voice came over the phone. It was a little too loud and the talker seemed stressed. "What do you know?" Kellogg asked him. "Where is she?"

Eleanor Jourdain started walking from the Salles des Glaces, the Hall of Mirrors of the Palace of Versailles and began to retrace the steps she and her companion had taken in 1901. Down the great flight of steps and past the gardens and fountains toward a long pond at the head of the central avenue. After many minutes she had the distinct feeling this direction was wrong. She cast about to get a glimpse of something she remembered but it almost seemed that the entire landscape had changed. Finally she spotted a thick wooded area that looked familiar. This she headed toward, trying to visualize the path they had taken those many years before.

They had used a Baedeker's map of the grounds back in the day, but this had proven to not be accurate. It had not shown the maze of crisscrossing pathways they had then encountered nor the little brook with its wooden plank bridge they had to cross over to reach the small glade where they had seen the gardeners. During the writing of their book, in order to clarify certain facts that had come to be disputed by detractors, they had consulted a series of earlier maps. By comparing these they could see that various features had been altered or destroyed over the years since the time of Marie Antoinette, notably the terrace in the French garden and the Queen's grotto. Although these features should have disappeared by 1901, the two women had described seeing them in their independent accounts of the adventure.

Today Eleanor had brought with her a hand-drawn map of the route they had taken in 1901 which was based on Mique's 1783 plan of Versailles. He had been the original architect that had constructed the Jardin de la Reine au Trianon, the round, wooden gallery of the Jeu de Bague, the staircase leading to Le Petit Trianon, the pond with its waterfall called Le Petite Cascade, and other features now extinct. She entered the woods and hoped to emerge near the grotto, within sight of the Temple de l'Amour, or the chapel, or the sprawling terrace by the Queen's private cottage. As she walked through the trees and overgrown brush she felt an overwhelming sense of melancholy. A vague feeling that she was sleepwalking assailed her. But by this she was encouraged; there had been similar feelings just before they had been transported into an earlier time.

When Eleanor exited the woods and her head cleared, she saw that she stood next to a wide pond. It was larger than the one she remembered from the adventure. Autumn leaves floated in little clusters and toward the far side of the pond was a bridge made of brick that arched more abruptly than any she remembered from Versailles. Reflected in the pond, the bridge formed a huge grinning mouth. Next she noticed small boats being propelled across the pond—or was it a small lake, a lagoon—by brightly clad revelers. They were too far away for her to carefully examine their clothing—would it mark them as people of the eighteenth century?

Rolling fields of close-cut grass surrounded the lagoon. There she saw children playing, throwing back and forth what, to her amazement, looked like a dinner plate! In addition, the children were dressed—or undressed—in what she interpreted as their underwear! At least, for the eighteenth century or even the early twentieth century that Eleanor knew, their attire was scandalously improper. She took herself across a narrow roadway (this paved in a smooth and seamless stone) and collapsed on a park bench.

As she sat, taking in long, slow, deep breaths, a large vehicle lumbered up the road and stopped not far from her. She heard its roar and the grinding of its brakes and turned, expecting to see an omnibus like the ones common in London in her own day. And certainly, this thing served that purpose, but it was much too large, much too streamlined and shiny, had rows and rows of oversized windows, and there was no place on the top for people to sit. It was painted green and yellow. People began pouring out of it. Their clothing, especially that of the women, nearly sent Eleanor into shock. She slumped down on the bench, covering her face with her hands.

Having abruptly disgorged its passengers, the bus snorted and whined and then thundered away leaving behind the gray haze and stench of its exhaust, the fetor and incense of the city. Eleanor moved her hands to her nose and mouth. Minutes passed. She looked up. Standing before her was a man, dressed neatly in a suit, the cut of which was unfamiliar, but at least, unlike so many she had seen today, he was respectively attired. "Are you all right. Miss?" the man inquired.

"I had the habit, whenever possible, to take the remainder of my lunch hour in the park," Kellogg told Andrew as they sat at a table near the front window of a downtown restaurant. "As I got off the bus I spied a woman hunched over on a park bench, her head in her hands. She seemed to be crying. I immediately went to her side and inquired as to her condition. Perhaps I was too bold, for she was startled and gave me a frightened look."

"This occurred...when?" asked Andrew.

"Two years ago, in September. I managed to gain her confidence by degrees and soon she relaxed enough to allow me to sit next to her on the bench. Her manner of dress was most curious...a high-waisted, pleated frock that reached well below her calf, shoes with arched high heels that were quite out of fashion...and the hat! Wide-brimmed, high crowned, and feathered! I withheld any questions or comments about her costume, hoping to learn more about her. What was the nature of her distress? What was she doing here? Where did she live...and so forth.

"Her name, she said, was Eleanor Jourdain. She was on holiday and had been visiting...and this is where I had to restrain my incredulity...the palace at Versailles! But... 'This is not France,' I blurted. 'I have guessed as much,' she replied. There was a long period of silence between us at this point, and we sat, watching children playing in the park across the road while the reality, or unreality as the case might have been, sank in.

"Naturally, the balance of our conversation centered on where and when we were on this fine Autumn day. She only stared at me blankly when I gave her the correct date. She told me where and when she had thought she was, and this evoked skepticism on my part, but I was hesitant to reveal my disbelief, not wishing to set off in the young woman any further anxiety. I approached the situation with a conviction that unconditional positive regard was the correct attitude to adopt at this juncture. She was so fragile and in need of reassurance.

"Eventually, I convinced her to accompany me to the residence of my aunt and uncle, which is the house where you found the picture of her friend. My Aunt May was a social worker with much experience in treating delusional clients, although I did not characterize her exactly as such to the young woman. I merely suggested that a conversation with an understanding female would be to her advantage. In view of the fact that she had no place to stay, I was sure Aunt May would offer her shelter of a more than adequate kind until all this could be sorted out."

"You were able to bring her to your aunt's house without her suspecting your intentions might be disingenuous?" asked Andrew.

"She had little choice," continued Kellogg. "She had nowhere to go and was, at least in her own mind, in a foreign country at some future time and that confounded her. Besides, I do not by nature present a menacing aspect."

"And she was able to board at your aunt's?"

"Freely. My aunt took to her immediately and virtually adopted her. I saw her as much as my schedule would allow. I was intrigued and, I must admit, a bit attracted to this strange visitor from another era."

"So, you came to believe her story."

"I believed there was some other explanation for her incongruity, but I believed *she* believed. She was constantly surprised or amazed at everyday modernity. Her unfamiliarity with the technology of our time did not seem specious. Her attitudes and her manner were solidly based in the era from which she claimed to be from. It was curious, but I just could not accept that she had traveled through time. Perhaps she was a sort of female Rip Van Winkle. Perhaps she had a working knowledge of the Edwardian epoch because of reading or study, and some shock had propelled her into a fantasy from which she could not extract herself."

"What about the picture and the letter?"

"It is true that she had with her the picture of her friend. This did not prove anything. The letter…I have only now become aware of it due to your showing it to me. If it is genuine it reinforces her story. However…"

"You are adamant," said Andrew, "in your disbelief in the possibility of time travel, therefore you discount the evidence of the woman's story. There is a record of her first venture through some sort of time rift in the book the two women wrote in 1901."

"But is she that woman?"

"What happened to her? Where is she now, do you think?"

Eleanor Jourdain had found the exact bench in the park after some searching; there were several similar benches in the area and little to distinguish them from each other. From this point she would attempt to retrace her steps back into the woods in the hopes that a kind of window or portal existed there which would take her back to her own time. She was homesick and she missed her companion, Charlotte Moberly. To her dismay, she had discovered the letter she written to Charlotte, stuck to the back of the picture she always carried of her friend in her purse. She had neglected to mail it before she left for France! Now Charlotte would have no idea where she had gone or why. It was painful to think of Charlotte's inevitable anxiety and this multiplied her own. She hid the letter in the back of book in the library and left the picture there too.

The woman, Aunt May as Kellogg called her, had been more than kind. Eleanor had stayed close to her new home during her stay fearing the strange new world into which she had materialized so abruptly and unexpectedly. A world too big and too noisy! And the worst was that squawking box like a miniature movie theater they called a television. She could never get use to an evil thing like that!

Now she was determined to overcome her bizarre circumstances. She had stolen away when Aunt May was out shopping and, gathering all the courage she could muster, had taken the bus to the park. As she sat on the bench she cast about for the woods, but there was nothing but the broad fields of grass, the pond sparkling in the sunlight, the gray-white strip of the road, and a few scruffy bushes around which some plantings were withering to a rusty Autumn brown.

Behind her was a child's playground with swings now empty and motionless, and behind that, across a busy city street, tall buildings rose, great edifices of stone and glass. People on the sidewalks bustled. Cars and buses roared up and down the avenue; a police car barreled by with siren blaring and red light flashing. Now she turned toward the lagoon and her eyes fell upon the bridge.

Eleanor walked around the edge of the lagoon until she reached the bridge. It spanned a narrow ditch which fed the lagoon from a canal that ran parallel to the length of the larger body of water. The canal was lined with willow trees which dipped swaying branches into the water and dropped slender silvery leaves to be washed away by the current. Trees. Not exactly a woods, but maybe it would do. Eleanor climbed up the bricked steps to the bridge.

When she reached the top she began to feel the dreamlike depression she had experienced at Versailles. She had become a somnambulist once again. The scene before her, the dipping willows, blurred briefly then resolved into a terrace of stone lined with potted flowers. A columned building sat against the terrace with steps leading up to its doors. On the steps sat a woman with fluffy hair wearing a broad-brimmed hat and an elegant gown.

Andrew Stone stood looking through the window of the pawn shop that was a few doors up from the Antiquarian Bookstore. The object of his attention was a pale green Underwood portable typewriter. The price of $25 was marked on a piece of cardboard that leaned against it. It was ribbonless, but that would not be a problem. The case showed some wear, but the machine itself appeared to be spotless. He entered the shop and enquired: "Do any of the keys stick?" "Try it for yourself." "Would you take $20?" "Twenty plus tax and its yours." Andrew lugged the Underwood home on the bus, holding it gingerly on his lap like a newborn baby.

At Walgreens he purchased a package of bond paper, some carbon paper, and a generic typewriter ribbon whose blurb on its box claimed it to fit all standard portables. Miraculously, it did. The "Q" key on the Underwood did stick when the shift key was depressed but Andrew felt he could put up with that. How many times did you need a capital "Q"? He placed a fresh sheet of paper into the machine and rolled it through to begin typing. Now he stared at the blank sheet, the bank of character keys arranged in standard "qwerty" format, the bottle of

Liquid Paper, and his half-filled coffee cup with its picture of Bullwinkle Moose and a word balloon saying, "This time, for sure!" Now what?

A woman he had never met and never would meet had become an obsession for him these past few weeks. The story, too fantastic to be true, tugged at him as if he were a fish that had taken the hook innocently, but ravenously. He had searched for some way to resolve his dilemma; the schism between wanting to believe…no, needing to believe…and the hard cold logic that pulled him away from the fantasy like a stern mother marching her child home before the last act of the circus—the one with the lions and tigers and the sequin-clad dancing girls.

He hadn't written anything since college. He hadn't had anything to say. Something had prompted him to buy the Underwood. Something compelled him to put down on water-marked typing paper words forged from the invisible emotions that would rise to the surface of his conscious mind—if only he could coax them to do so. He had needed a muse, a daughter of Zeus, to beckon, to inspire. The mysterious woman would serve. The mysterious woman was like a sketch, ready for a full rendering; like the underpainting upon which a variety of semblances might be overlaid without contradiction. She was unfinished. Her story was unfinished. Andrew began to type.

THE NIGHT BIRDS OF LINCOLN PARK

Bev imagines she is Harlow playing a platinum blond starlet in *Bombshell*, lounging in bed under satin sheets, her breasts loose in a slinky silk lingerie with puffy sleeves, nibbling bon-bons which she returns to a heart-shaped box half eaten, cuddling with her Pekinese, pink ribbons in its hair and an expression of bored disgust on its pinched little face.

Would her lover be joining her soon? She wonders. Robert Taylor or perhaps Clark Gable? As she stretches out beneath (in reality) cotton sheets, a heavy weight descends upon her: it is Bruno. Bruno is her two-year-old Staffordshire terrier, a breed most people think is a pit bull. Bev has considered drawing a circle around one of Bruno's eyes to make him look like Pete the Pup in the *Our Gang Comedies*. Bruno turns over on his back to have his stomach rubbed. It is a ritual that is repeated every morning.

After her whole wheat muffin and cup of English breakfast tea, Bev retires to the bathroom to put on her makeup. In the mirror she sees a twenty-six-year-old woman, almost pretty, with a dull fringe of burnt umber hanging in disarray around a brow wrinkling into a squint. She is squinting her grey-green eyes in order to examine a slight swelling on her neck which has been bothering her lately. She begins to apply eye shadow, her mind ruminating on an aunt who died from thyroid cancer not long ago. The phone rings. She will let the answering machine get the call which she knows is from her mother. Another ritual, one she avoids whenever possible.

Later, Bev is walking Bruno through Lincoln Park. He still pulls at the leash and she thinks it may be time for obedience training. As they pass the lagoon she notices a solitary man. He is moving slowly, his arms making gentle circles in front of him. He shifts his weight to one leg, like an archer ready to draw his bow. One arm is extended to the side, the hand forming a sort of hook, as the other sweeps out gradually in the opposite direction. As Bev watches this curious dance-like motion, it seems to her that time has been suspended. Even Bruno is transfixed. They stand, silently watching as the man seems to modulate some invisible energy. A tranquil breeze brushes across the lagoon forming faint ripples, the whispers of secrets between the water and the fragrant summer air.

Bev and Bruno have seen the man before during their early morning sojourns. At first, Bev thought he was exercising, but after talking with her friend Florida (who likes to be called Flo), she now knows he is practicing a form of martial arts called Tai Chi. This seems very exotic to Bev, very extraordinarily unconventional and daring. The dog tugs, they move on along the edge of the lagoon. Bev's thoughts turn to her friend, Florida, who is going through a nasty break-up. She feels badly for Flo, but at the same time believes that Flo is lucky to be rid of Roger who she has always believed to be a misogynistic brute. Flo couldn't see it, but wasn't that always the way? Bruno has left a neatly stacked pile of dog poop next to the sidewalk. Bev retrieves a plastic bag from her purse but the breeze picks it up and carries away.

It is early evening of the same day, a Friday. Bev and Flo are having a cocktail in Bev's apartment. Bruno is curled up under Bev's feet, snoring loudly. Flo is an African American woman who Bev met when they both attended the University of Wisconsin in Madison. Bev thinks Flo is strikingly beautiful. Her parents named her "Florida" because her great great grandfather had been a slave in Tallahassee in the 1800s. Flo tells everyone it is because her family lived in Orlando, by Disneyworld, and that she was conceived when her parents rode on The Pirates of The Caribbean ride during a power failure. Flo is drinking a "dirty martini" which Bev has made by adding some olive juice to the drink. Bev is sipping a reasonably good Malbec from a long-stemmed wine glass.

"Roger is such an asshole," says Flo.

"I always thought so."

"I know you did. I should have listened to you. Instead I let that rat bastard live with me, eat my food, drink my booze, and what does he do? He goes two-timing on me."

"He's an asshole. You've kicked him out, right?"

"Well…"

"Flo! You have to make a clean break or he'll keep abusing your good nature."

"But he's my manager, Beverly. I need him." Flo sings at a bar on North Broadway, Lulu's Lounge. She does Lena Horn and Billie Holiday covers and has a good set of lungs. Bev goes to Lulu's to hear her sometimes. She likes the ebony and chrome bar and sits on one of the swivel stools near the band stand like a femme fatale from a 40s noir movie, legs crossed, one stiletto-heeled foot bobbing to the music, elbow on the bar with wine glass raised statue-of-liberty-wise, her inscrutable smile reflected in the mirror behind the bar—a smile that seems to say, I know a secret, I know THE secret.

Bev and Flo were roommates when they first moved to Chicago after college. There was a constant flow of men attending Flo, and Bev felt awkward, isolated in her own room while Flo entertained. Eventually Bev broached the subject and Flo, concealing her chagrin, valiantly suggested a separation. Separate living arrangements cemented their friendship in a way close proximity could not and now the two share feelings instead of closet space.

Flo curls her feet under her. The two women are sitting at opposite ends of the couch, a flowered affair cast off from Bev's mother which, although it is supremely comfortable, irks Beverly when it reminds her that she is not yet completely independent. Bruno lets out a fart, an apt comment on the conversation so far. Flo appears to take the hint and changes the subject.

"You really should do something about your hair," she tells Bev.

"I know. I have an appointment at Ruby's on Thursday."

"Well, get it styled this time. It would help your love life."

"My love life…what love life?"

"Well, that's what I mean. You're smart, attractive, fun to be with. You just have a bad hair-do."

"And a bad attitude?"

Bev is referring to a general dissatisfaction with male suitors she expresses when she and Flo discuss dating. Flo admonishes her for what she characterizes as a negative attitude toward men on Bev's part. Bev, on the other hand, believes she invests bona fide regard in her approach to relationships but is uniformly betrayed and deceived by the opposite sex. Flo would say she protests too much. Bev would say throwing caution to the winds leaves one vulnerable and exposed.

The telephone is ringing. Bev ignores it. The answering machine clicks into action and they hear:

"Beverly? Beverly? It's your mother. Pick up, I know you're there. Are you there? Where are you? Are you out with that…that girl friend of yours? Probably at a bar I bet. Call me when you get home, Beverly. I worry about you. Goodbye. Oh, don't forget it's your father's birthday next Tuesday. You could send him a card. Or call. Call me, Beverly. I'm your mother, you know. I love you. Goodbye."

There is a long beep following the message. Flo says, "Your mother hates me, doesn't she?"

"No, she doesn't hate you. She's just overly protective of me. It drives me crazy! I'm a grown women for Pete's sake!"

"She thinks we're lesbians, doesn't she."

"No, Flo, she doesn't. She just doesn't want me to have my own life. She's controlling…clinging…smothering!"

"I could smother her!" Flo says. Bruno starts barking crazily at something out the window. They are on the third floor but he is uncanny at perceiving dog oriented disturbances outside the building. It is a secure building, however, with a buzzer system being the only access to the lobby. The lobby is a wannabe Art Deco wonderland, checkerboarded with tiny red and white floor tiles and featuring a chrome edged, black faux marble topped desk where the now absent doorman never seems to be sitting. As Deco, it is a far cry from the real thing.

After Flo leaves, Bev takes Bruno down in the elevator for an evening 'round the block walk. Nearby Clark Street is always choked with people even late at night so Bev is never nervous about walking there. Besides which, she has faithful Bruno at her side who at least looks like a vicious pit bull. After their circuit of down Clark and back up Lincoln Park West to Belden where her building is, Bev stops to get the key out of her purse. Bruno starts to growl as a tall man approaches her. She recognizes the man: it is Roger, Flo's ex-boyfriend.

"You bitch!" he shouts. "She kicked me out."

"Good for her," Bev answers.

"It's your fault, you bitch. What did you say to her? You talked her into kicking me out."

"That makes me even happier!" says Bev. Roger takes another step toward her. Bruno is barking furiously, straining at the leash. Roger backs away. "This isn't over," he shouts, and then disappears into the darkness.

"Good dog!" Bev tells Bruno. "Good dog!"

Tuesday she calls her father to wish him a happy birthday. There is the usual father daughter banter, the small talk (which includes the weather, the price of gasoline, and his conservative politics verses her liberal views), the large talk (which today consists of his complaining about her mother and Bev actually taking her mother's side—imagine that!), and the requisite do you need any money question which, although the answer is yes, Bev replies in the negative. Her father then informs her that Mom wants to get on the phone but Bev insists the dog is peeing on the carpet and she has to hang up.

On Thursday she keeps her appointment at Ruby's Hair Salon and Day Spa on Milwaukee Avenue. She loves the smell of the place, a distinctive mix of stale shampoo and old plastic combs clogged with hair. She takes Flo's advice and has her hair styled: short, but cute in a sort of Louise Brooks bob. Irene, her stylist, turns her chair around to face the mirror, points with a wicked looking pair of scissors and asks her does she like it. Bev is elated and over tips.

It is Friday. Again. Today she is in the waiting room of the clinic where she will have a blood test. She has just seen Dr. Amanuliah Shakir about what she perceives is a lump in her throat. Dr. Shakir has ordered a blood test for thyroid, calcium, phosphorus, and various three-lettered abbreviations that send her head swimming when she looks at the order form. She waits, a patient patient, sorting through rumpled magazines, apprehensive and needle shy. There is a Christian magazine in the stack. As she looks through it her mind wanders through half-remembered bible stories. She thinks about Genesis.

Apparently, she remembers, God made humans last. He made a man, because 1) He was bored, 2) He was a man himself so it was easy to copy the format, and 3) women hadn't learned to write until well after the Bible was published. What Bev wonders is, how did He dream up the idea for a woman? She doesn't remember reading about a Mrs. God. There was no prototype. Had God ingested too much Welsh rarebit and been visited with a weird dream? And why was Adam fully equipped with male apparatus before Eve's arrival? After the expulsion the pair did a lot of begetting, she remembers, but wasn't paradise a place untroubled by fleshy concerns? Pre-snake, of course. Bev comes to the conclusion that God must have been a woman; Eve another soul sister; Adam just an afterthought—a rarebit dream gone wrong.

A man's body—was that *really* attractive? Some argument could be made for the appeal of the erected penis, once you got over the strange parts: the wrinkled skin like an old man's neck, the large vein running down the middle of it, the funny cap on top like a warrior's helmet. It had all the maleness you could wish for, the sturdy, sweaty, ostentatious presence of it. Nothing good could be said, however, for the balls. Odious, bulbous encumbrances. Dead weight wrapped in more wrinkled flesh.

A woman's body—that was source of poetry and art, a landscape lithe and yielding, yet mysterious, seductive. Its secrets hidden away to be discovered only after determination and a lengthy concerted effort. Bev was reminded of the old children's nursery rhyme:

> *Snakes and snails and puppy dog tails*
> *That's what little boys are made of.*
> *Sugar and spice and everything nice*
> *That's what little girls are made of.*

She is sitting on her couch, stroking Bruno's ears, a Looney Tunes band-aid holding a small piece of cotton against the purple and blue-black bruise on her arm pit where the technician stabbed her numerous times trying to find a vein. She had nearly fainted watching the blood filling the syringe and now, as she muses about recovering the couch with a leopard skin pattern, she realizes she requires some chamomile tea to sooth her jangled nerves. The telephone rings and she thinks, oh what the hell, I have to talk to her sometime.

"Hello, Mom."

"Beverly! You're home!"

"Yes, Mom. How are you?"

"Oh, don't get me started on my arthritis, dear. How about you? What have you been doing? You're never home."

"I got my hair styled today, Mom. It's really cute."

"That's nice, dear. Did you know your Uncle Al is thinking of moving to a condo in Sarasota? Way too hot and buggy down there for me. Why would anyone want to live in that humidity?"

Bev decides not to mention that Flo has gone to Florida to visit her parents. Florida is in Florida—that's funny, she thinks: Florida going to Florida. "He'll probably have air conditioning, mom."

"I hope so."

"Mom, tell me about Aunt April, the one that died."

"What do you want to know about her for?"

"Just curious."

"She went into the hospital for an operation on her thyroid. They did something wrong during the operation. Poisons got into her system. They couldn't save her."

"Was it cancer?"

"I don't know, Dear. That was a long time ago. Why do you want to know about Aunt April?"

"Just curious."

"Are you eating enough, Beverly? You know Mrs. Hoffmeyer's daughter, Roberta? You used to play together when you were kids. She's as thin as a rail. Eats like a pig and then goes to the bathroom to throw up. Anorectic, poor dear."

"Bulimic, Mother. Bulimic is when you eat and purge. Anorexia is when you starve yourself thinking you're too fat."

"Whatever. You're not that, are you honey? You're just skin and bones. You need some good red meat."

"Mom, I got to go. I hear the tea kettle whistling in the kitchen."

"You should get an extension phone in the kitchen, dear. Honestly, I don't know!"

"Goodbye, Mom."

There is no kettle cooking on the stove but Bev starts some water boiling, filling a battered old pot with cold water and placing it on the back burner. She rummages through the cupboard looking for the chamomile tea but can't find it. "Shit!" She twists off the burner and heads for the door. Maybe she can go up the street to Barnaby's Coffee Shop and get her mother off her mind. Bruno excitedly wags what little tail he has, his large tongue drooping almost to the floor. "No, no, Bruno. You wait. I'll be right back," she tells the dog.

In the elevator she pushes the button marked "L." It is capped in mother of pearl, one of God's details, she thinks. The elevator has one of those accordion gates, crisscrosses of brass-colored metal that creak and clank as the dwarf-sized box slowly descends to the lobby. She pulls back the gate and pushes the heavy door open, still fuming at the thought of her mother's self-absorbed attitude. She's wearing clogs which slap sharply on the lobby floor.

Outside it is a moonless night, the only illumination a dull haze of city lights conveyed by humid air that hangs ominously at the rooftops. It is this dim phosphorescence that renders the sky fluid, as if it is an ocean bottom filled with luminescent one-celled animals, faintly glowing sea worms, and alien looking crystalline fish that has been fastened upside down over the city by some ancient and gigantic deity. Through this effulgent liquid nocturne fly the birds of night: black crows barely seen against the shadowy buildings, starlings sitting in trees and rubbing their tired heads against their wings as if emulating crickets singing sorrowful songs, and the occasional and inevitable pigeon, inheritor of all this at the end of time.

The rustling of the birds is equally as loud as the din of traffic noises from Clark Street. All of it fuses together into white noise: a kind of sonic blur that can't be easily deciphered. Thus she doesn't hear the footfalls behind her. A hefty arm encircles her. Something cold and metallic presses against her neck. She can smell bad whiskey and rancid tobacco in the hot breath striking the back of her head. She barely registers the gruff vocalization of "Gotcha, Bitch!" nor does she give herself time to be terrified. She automatically activates the self defense class routine she learned long ago and stomps hard against her assailant's shin bone but her flimsy clog flies off and her bare heel slams harmlessly onto his shoe. He tightens his grip. Bev twists and turns wildly trying to dislodge him but the knife at her throat traps her as surely as a snare catches an unwary rabbit by its unlucky foot.

"I'm going to cut you," he whispers and she understands that this man is Roger, drunk or on drugs or both. Coupled with this realization is the knowledge that she is about to die. A strange calm comes over her. She is beyond fear, beyond terror. There is only an empty, quiet darkness that expands, becomes solid and envelops her, sucks in her soul the way a black hole eats everything around it. Time has stopped. Then there is a sudden jolt as if something has pushed against her and her attacker. Roger loosens his grip and spins around. She turns as well and sees that another man has come up behind them.

"Leave the lady alone," says the man.

For a moment, nothing happens. Roger seems temporarily frozen, stunned by the strike to his shoulder and perplexed by the bravado and chutzpah of this interloper. Incredulous that someone would try to stand off a man with a knife, his machismo erupts and a broad grin forms across his face. There is no more talking, only action. Roger swings the knife in an arc toward the man to slash and gouge across his chest. The man sidesteps, reaches toward Roger's arm, gripping it with one hand near his wrist and the other on his upper arm, He guides Roger's forward momentum so that he is thrown downward and leverages the arm against its natural angle, causing a loud snapping noise. As Roger hits the sidewalk he yells, "You bastard! You broke my arm!" The man sees the knife lying on the sidewalk and puts his foot over it. Roger struggles to his feet, has just enough time for a "You fucking bastard!" and then stumbles off into the night.

The few minutes this has all taken seem like hours to Bev as she watches in disbelief. "I know you," she says, "You're the Tai Chi man," The man is clearly amused by this description of himself.

"Yes, I've seen you walking your dog in the park when I do my form," he replies.

"That was... that was wonderful! I think I owe you my life."

"Possibly. You never know with these drugged out types. They're crazy."

"I know that guy. He used to date my friend. He's a real asshole."

"Do you think he'll be back?"

"Oh, I don't think so."

"Just the same, is there any place I can walk you to?"

"I was just headed to Barnaby's for some tea. Let me buy you a coffee or something."

"I really like your hair," he says.

It is a week later. Friday night again. Bev has covered the couch with a leopard skin patterned throw. Flo has returned from Florida and the three of them (Bev, Flo and Martin, the Tai Chi man) are having cocktails while Bruno is curled up under Bev's feet, snoring loudly. Bev is tipping a long-stemmed glass of a remarkable Malbec to her lips while Flo and Martin swirl the liquid in their dirty martinis. Bev has just finished telling them about the long, verklempt heart-to-heart phone call she has had with her mother. This was prompted by her need to share the results of her blood test—that ironically wonderful word, "negative" —with the woman she used to talk openly to when she was a child. Mom was shocked that she hadn't anticipated Bev's concerns about her health. Bev began to realize that some things never change, that understanding and acceptance are a two way street that must be traveled at least in one direction and sometimes alone.

Martin raises his glass and does Mel Blanc doing Bugs Bunny doing Humphrey Bogart as he says, "Here's looking at you, kid!"

Bev shakes a non-existent lock of hair from her face and flashes Martin a Lauren Bacall knowing smile. (She always daydreams in blond.) Flo tries to work up a Dorothy Dandridge gesture but finds she doesn't remember any so she opts for a little Billie Holiday pout. Flo then begins a narrative of applying for a restraining order to keep Roger, the wolf, away from her door. It's a shame, she says, that Bev wouldn't prefer charges against the bastard and throw his ass in jail. There is a hurt Lena Horn look (Flo) being cast at a "Dah-ling, I could care less" Betty Davis (Bev) demeanor. Martin, sensing the ensuing collision, decides to change the subject.

Martin tells them about the new friend he has met in a bar on Rush Street: "He reminds me of a young Cary Grant." Oh great, thinks Bev, I meet a man I could love and he turns out to be gay! Outside, the night sky, still asparkle with light pollution, produces half-hearted shadows where buildings block the dazzle of the city streets. The night birds of Lincoln Park are flocking.

THE FORTUNE COOKIE

That day, Vera Blaine combated boredom in an unusual way: by house cleaning. Husband Raymond at work, children at school, her neighbor friend Dorothy Gimble on vacation to Florida with her hubby and brood, the television uselessly and static-wise flip flip flipping no matter which way the rabbit ears were twisted, Vera had few alternatives. She could have laid out cards on the dining table in a pointless game of solitaire or baked cookies or gone walking up Avery Street toward the little strip mall where she could get her hair done and her nails polished, or, at the drugstore at the end of the mall, she could spin the wire rack of romance paperbacks and fantasize herself onto one of those lurid covers with their beefy, long-haired, bare-chested, mysterious men (perhaps sporting an eye-patch) pawing her (she with flimsy negligee ripping seductively), and thumb the book to the last chapter where...

But no, those usual methods of coping just raised her anxiety. She needed to apply herself to something utilitarian, to gain a sense of satisfaction for tackling a job. A job not particularly crucial, a job with procrastination written all over it, a job that nonetheless was doable and mindless enough to distract from that depression that ebbed within her—a job to be well done. So, with dustpan and broom, cleaning rags and bucket of Spic and Span, the big kitchen waste basket lined with a brown paper bag from the A&P, and an unshakeable resolve, Vera tackled the hall closet.

She found something pushed way toward the back. There, behind a worn-only-once floral-decorated hat, an unstrung tennis racket, a shoebox of birthday cards and Christmas cards (from grandmother and still smelling of toilet water), a cigar box filled with seashells, odd buttons, single earrings, and other junk jewelry intended for never-begun craft projects, Raymond's wool muffler wound tightly in a ball (she knitted but he never wore), and a stunning collection of dust bunnies, was a simple metal box. Nondescript and slightly rusty, its hinged cover was latched and locked with a small padlock, the type that came from the Five and Dime and could be opened with a hairpin. Vera went to look for a hairpin.

It was a relic from preteen years that held secrets and treasures and which she had revived for that same purpose her senior year in high school. The old treasures dumped and forgotten made way for the new. These consisted of keepsakes and mementos relating to fun times with best girlfriends collected especially at sleepovers and outings and mall visits. There would be dance cards and notes passed during English class and pictures of heart throbs torn from fan magazines and plastic hair barrettes shaped like squirrels or bears or bunnies.

The lock presented little resistance. Vera dug in, nostalgia superseding melancholy. Under the artifacts of adolescence, near the bottom of the box, twisted around an adjustable Crackerjack diamond ring, was a small, long strip of paper. Vera spread this out smoothly on the kitchen table with nervous fingers. The strip of paper was precisely half of a fortune from a fortune cookie. A fortune cookie shared, she now remembered, with someone from the distant past. Someone no longer in her life. Someone not easily forgotten.

She was Vera Henriksson then. Blond hair done up in French braids, peasant's blouse and jumper like Shirley Temple in the Corliss Archer movie, *Kiss and Tell*, which had just opened at the Arcadia. She and her best friend, Lucy Carr, had gone to see the movie despite her mother's objections. The plot centered on two teenage girls, Corliss and Mildred, who were not so unlike Vera and Lucy, who decided to sell kisses at an USO bazaar. Mildred married Corliss' brother, a returning soldier, and became pregnant. The town's gossip saw Corliss and Mildred visiting an obstetrician and assumed that Corliss was pregnant out of wedlock. Comedy based on the tantalizing prospect of teenage sex was not something Mrs. Henriksson wanted her daughter to see.

The drugstore still had its soda fountain in 1945. Vera and Lucy, fresh from the Arcadia, migrated to its counter of round, swiveling seats and shiny chrome. Towering spigots dispensed phosphates and a mirror behind where the soda jerk stood reflected the rest of the interior of the store. Lucy giggled and elbowed Vera when she saw in the mirror the approach of the boy. He was just as handsome as Dexter Franklin, Shirley Temple's love interest in the movie. He headed straight for Vera and sat next to her, spinning the seat first by way of introduction.

Sometimes a fantasy experienced through the suspension of disbelief lingers to merge with reality. Vera became Corliss and Robbie, for that was the boy's name, became Dexter. Robbie Peterson was two years older than Vera. In two weeks he would be reporting for active duty even as the war in Europe was beginning to wind down. Vera/Corliss and Robbie/Dexter would make the most of those two weeks.

Mother did not allow Vera to date boys so subterfuge was necessary to bring the lovers together. Vera walked to Lucy's house where Lucy would cover for her in case Mother called. Robbie would meet her halfway there and the two of them would walk to the playground in the park, sit on the swings and talk. Two days later Robbie arrived behind the wheel of his father's Buick. Vera slid across the seat to lean against him as he drove out to the forest preserve. There they engaged in an activity that girls her age were warned against by mothers and prudent gym class teachers: they petted.

Vera thought the term "petting" was a bit misleading. What they were doing involved open mouth kissing and very little of what you might do to a dog or a cat with your hands. That is, until Robbie asked Vera to use her hand in a certain way. It was sizable, the thing he wanted her to pet. She hadn't seen one before, much less touched one. At first he guided her through the proper rhythms. Later she became quite expert at evoking the response that showed how much he loved her—such a surge of emotion could not be trivially spent. Soon, he was reciprocating, pushing his hand under her skirt along her thigh and exploring her. Vera wondered if Corliss Archer ever did things like this with her Dexter.

Father brought home chop suey from the Chinese take-out restaurant one evening, to make up for a spat between Mother and him. Vera held the noodles in her mouth, savoring their slippery texture and their exotic flavor. It was a welcome change from the usual meat and potatoes Mother usually fixed. The take-out package had included three sets of chopsticks, but these had been discarded in favor of forks. The Henrikssons could take the novelty only so far.

Three fortune cookies had been added to the big paper bag with its cardboard containers of food. Vera slipped a cookie into her pocket. Tomorrow was a special day for her as it was Robbie's last day before boot camp. She would bring the cookie with her on their final date and together they would read the fortune. Father broke open his cookie and glanced at the slip of paper that fell from it to the table.

"Aren't you going to read it?" Mother asked.

"Foolishness," he grunted.

"Well, I'll read mine," she said. She did not read it aloud, but she smiled. Vera guessed it said something like, "You will meet a tall, dark stranger."

Vera also wondered what Father's fortune had said and so as she cleared away the dinner dishes, she scooped up the paper and placed it in her pocket to examine later. When she finally had the chance to look at it, she was surprised to find that it said, "Disbelief destroys the magic." That seemed to her to be more profound than one might expect from a mere fortune cookie. And such a fortune for Father! She found it hard to believe that her father, so self-absorbed and, well, frankly boring, would ever recognize magic if he saw it. Real magic. Magic such as she had with Robbie.

The Buick was waiting down the street from Lucy's as Vera came up the sidewalk. She had told her mother that she needed some notes for her homework and had to go to Lucy's for them. And yes, she knew it was a school night, and no, she wouldn't be out too late. And so what, she would like to have said, if I stayed out *all night*? If Robbie asked, she might just do that. She still had the fortune cookie in her pocket.

Now at the forest preserve, with no other parked cars around with other lovers to see them, Robbie did ask. It was his last night. He might be overseas tomorrow. He might be killed in action. He wanted something to remember…something special. He fumbled with her clothing. She turned to make it easier and smashed the fortune cookie in her pocket. "Ouch!" she said.

"What's the matter?" he said.

"Nothing. Oh, I brought this," she said, extracting the broken fortune cookie from her pocket. "Let's read the fortune. It will be *our* fortune. Our special memory. We'll save it and treasure it."

Vera read the fortune to Robbie and then tore it in half, giving one half to Robbie. "You keep yours and I'll keep mine," she said, and kissed him full on the lips. Robbie's hand completed the unbuttoning necessary for *his* idea of a special memory to take with him into battle. The reality of the romance descended upon Vera, a consequence of heavy weight.

Vera was lucky and did not share the fate of Mildred of the movie. Which is to say that she did not get pregnant, although she was grounded for staying out late on a school night. That was of little consequence compared to the separation from Robbie. Now she waited for a letter.

Every day she read the newspaper for news of the war. She read that 25,000 American troops and equipment had crossed the recently captured Ludendorff Bridge over the Rhine; was Robbie among them? She read that B-29 bombers had dropped incendiary bombs on Tokyo killing 100,000 civilians. My God...the cost of winning the war! No, Robbie wasn't in the Airforce. Japanese planes had devastated the USS Franklin, an aircraft carrier. 800 service men were dead. No list appeared in the paper. Where was Robbie? There hadn't been a letter from him.

On April 12 Vera saw the shocking headline that President Franklin Roosevelt had died at Warm Springs, Georgia. Harry Truman was now the President of the United states. By May the news came that Adolph Hitler and Eva Braun had committed suicide. US troops were liberating Nazi concentration camps. Still no letter from Robbie. More news: Joseph Goebbels, Hitler's chief of propaganda and one of the orchestrators of the Holocaust, had killed his six children before he and his wife committed suicide in Hitler's bunker. He hadn't wanted them to someday learn what a monster he had been. May 8 was VE Day, but still the war with Japan went on and on and on. And still no letter from Robbie.

What Vera didn't know was that Robbie had never shipped out. He hadn't liberated any concentration camps or raised the flag on Iwo Jima. He had become a MP, a Military Policeman. He had been stationed at a base near San Francisco. And no, he didn't write. He was too busy chasing GIs out of bars and brothels. He came to know a lot about bars and brothels. After the war was over, Robbie stayed in California, moving to Los Angeles, and finding employment there as a security guard at Columbia Pictures, ironically, the same studio that had produced *Kiss and Tell*.

She would see him one more time. She was attending a small

Lutheran college in the Midwest when her father died suddenly of a heart attack while coming home from work on the commuter train. She came back to town to be with her mother during her time of grief and did not return to the college that term. While she was home she saw Robbie crossing the street by the corner where the Red Cap Tavern was located. This establishment was rumored to have a house of ill repute upstairs but this did not occur to Vera at the time. She waved to Robbie, then, as he apparently hadn't seen her, she called out to him.

He turned and looked at her for a moment, a puzzled expression on his face, then he entered the Red Cap. Vera followed. She had never been in the bar before. It was often described as "old-timey" by locals who frequented it only when they were in the mood for "slumming." Vera was apprehensive but determined to catch up with Robbie. She walked the length of the old oak bar with its brass fittings and worn upholstered stools, its rows of dusty and half-empty bottles on shelves handy for the bartender to reach, and past the few drinkers who sat on the stools at odd angles as if they were birds trying to take flight with broken wings. She reached the back of the barroom where booths lined the walls and searched these but all were empty. Tables placed randomly beneath green-shaded chandeliers were also devoid of customers. There were two doors at the back, one labeled "Setters," and the other labeled "Pointers."

Once she got the joke she figured that Robbie was indisposed, having had to use the john. She wanted to wait for him to come out, but the bartender was eyeing her in a way that made her uncomfortable. She left to wait outside. After fifteen minutes and strange looks from strange people passing by, she gave up. Well, he knew where she lived. He'd come by later, she supposed. But he didn't.

Vera ran a finger along the length of the half-of-a fortune cookie fortune she had retrieved from the treasure box. Her half read, "Be true to each other," and the half she had given to Robbie had read, "and all will turn out well." Perhaps she had kept the wrong half. She placed the paper strip back in the box and picked up the diamond ring. It was garish, with a faceted piece of glass like an over-sized diamond, and it was adjustable. It had come from a Crackerjack box Raymond had bought for her at the county fair. That had been the year before she met Robbie.

She had found Raymond quite boring and his constant pursuit of her all through high school quite annoying. But he was steadfast and always there just at the periphery of her life. It wasn't until after they were married that she realized how much Raymond reminded her of her father. Steady and boring. Their lovemaking never brought her to the heights of passion she had experienced with Robbie, but it had resulted in two children.

Twin tornados, ripping through the environment of her life with boring Raymond. A delight, a distraction, a dreadful responsibility. Timmy was a few minutes older than Tommy, but Tommy was the alpha dog. Tommy led his toddler brother on many a hunt for mischief, climbing the backyard fence, tormenting the neighbor's cat, hiding from their mother's frantic calls. Gradually they mellowed from tornado to thunderstorm to mild gale. School provided a modicum of discipline.

School began at five years-old with half-day kindergarten. Now, to Vera's great relief the twins spend most of the day in the stuffy third-grade school room at Saint Steven's Elementary where a frightening figure of Christ on the Cross hung in bloody anguish over the front entrance. Nuns did for the twins what Vera had never been able to accomplish: put the fear, if not of God, of Sister Ruth in them. Still, once home and safe from the threat of yardstick against buttock, they were free to resume their childhood. Which meant mischief now fine-honed to a degree that eluded maternal discovery.

Things disappeared. Things changed positions. Things appeared from…where? It was a fun game, especially watching the frustration appear on their parents' faces. But so far, they had not set fire to anything. So far.

On the day that Vera discovered the fortune cookie fortune and the Crackerjack ring, the twins had been introduced to phonetic spelling at school. They were delighted with this new type of learning and invented many unique sounds of their own to express letters. Sounds that involved the kind of dexterity of tongue that only eight-year-olds can produce. Sister Ruth was not pleased. A note came home with them.

Vera thought, what if I give them the box of mementos to play with…taking out the fortune and the ring first? That should give them new material to hide or alter, and I really couldn't care less what happens to that stuff. She thought, I'll keep the fortune and the ring somewhere they can't find them. A strange sense of nostalgia linked with a slight rush of eroticism came to her when she held those items in her hand. She closed her hand to a fist around the ring and the fortune. That amplified the feeling that a kind of magic was initiated through the touching.

Thrusting the magical objects into her pocket she called to the twins: "Look boys! Look what Mommy found in the hall closet today." That was the last she would see of the box. Just as well.

At dinner (the twins had gone to play in their room) she asked, "Ray, do you ever think about the old days when we were dating? You know, teenagers learning about…things…for the first time?" Of course, Raymond hadn't been her first time, but he didn't know that.

"Um, no Dear. You know I sold a really big policy today to Bruce Overcash. He's at Rotary most of the time and I trapped him after the meeting. Convinced him he needed the best coverage money can buy. Sure did."

Raymond finished his mashed potatoes and pushed his dish away. He continued talking *at* her: "Gonna go watch the news now. Eisenhower made a speech today. Something about the military industrial complex. Everybody was talking about it at Rotary. The new guy…I don't know about him. Kind of a socialist, I heard."

The new guy, Vera knew, was John F. Kennedy, the newly elected 35th President of the United States of America. Vera had voted for him. Raymond had not. They had canceled each other out at the poles, she figured. Kennedy would be sworn in in a few days from now and a new era would be ushered in—an era of enlightenment and progress. And people like her husband could just lump it!

That night she came to bed later than usual, waiting until she heard Raymond snoring like a wounded elephant. She could not face the prospect of "cuddling," even though it never progressed beyond a grapple and a pinch. She slid into bed and plucked the copy she had been reading of Elizabeth Spencer's *The Light in the Piazza* from the night stand. It fell open, not to where she had left her bookmark, but to where one of the twins had hidden the dance card from her high school prom, an item that had been in the secret metal box they had played with. Damn. Something about this intrusion into her ritual escapism really bothered her. Now tonight she would not follow Clara's exploits with Fabrizio. Instead she would fantasize about taking the twins deep into the woods and leaving them there.

The nightmare woke her, sweating, around 3 AM. It wasn't about stranding the twins in the woods or setting them adrift in a leaking rowboat. It was about Raymond. In the dream, Vera was driving a Ford 150 pickup that was more rust than metal. It clattered down a country road kicking up gravel and dust that was rendered blood red in the dwindling sunset. In the bed of the pickup was Raymond, bridled and bound like a young hog for slaughter.

She pulled off the road and drove across a landscape of dead vegetation until she reached the edge of the forest. It was late fall in the dream and moldering leaves of hemlock and ash made a crackling sound as she trudged through the putrescent underwood. The garden spade she dragged with her knocked against unseen things below the thick carpet of decay, sending furry shapes scampering. A lone crow eyed her from a tree branch, shaking its beak at her in criticism of her invasion.

Hole dug, blackened sweat running down her face, she returned to the truck for Raymond. She got the shotgun that hung in the rear window, a rural status symbol handy for the job. She unbound Raymond's feet and gestured with the shotgun for him to jump from the truck bed. She then marched him without ceremony into the forest. At the freshly dug grave she stopped, considering. This was extreme cruelty but warranted. Passion won over logic as she leveled the 12 gauge at his midsection. Squeeze, don't jerk…she knew this. Gradually, with the man shaking with fear and hatred in his eyes and the crow taking flight in anticipation, she pressed gently against the trigger as if it were a blister or a wart. She squeezed…

Midweek following the nightmare, Vera's friend, Dorothy Gimble, met her at Kay's Kozy Kafe for lunch and catching up. The clatter of cutlery and the aroma of French fries sizzling in day-old oil was a familiar balm that soothed the soul and whet the appetite. The waitress wore a blue and white striped uniform, stiffly starched and almost spotless as she brought glasses of water with slices of lemon to the women's table.

"Ready to order?" she asked. "No? I'll give ya a coupla minutes," she said and whisked off to attend to the coconut cream pie ordered for another table.

Dotty was aflutter with tales of beaches (and beach boys) on the East Coast of the Sunshine State where she and family had just vacationed. There were Portuguese Man-O-War washed up on the sand and you couldn't touch them...not that you'd want to...for fear of getting stung by their dangling tentacles. It was like something out of a science fiction movie. They had to keep yelling at the kids to stay away from them, she told Vera. Vera told Dotty about her nightmare.

"We've been friends for...how long?" Dotty asked.

"Oh, ages."

"You know I don't believe in gossip. Don't like to hear things that concern my friends. But sometimes...well, you know...sometimes one just *has* to blurt it out. Get it out in the open. You know...as much as it might be hurtful."

"Why, Dotty! You think I've done something dreadful?"

"No, Vera. Not you. Raymond. Mrs. Daniels heard it from Sara Magaly who..."

"Just get to the point, Dotty. What did he do?"

"He's been seen, a number of times, mind you, with that Victoria Greenly. That woman is a homewrecker, you can be sure."

"I'm sure it was innocent, Dotty. Ray was probably trying to sell her insurance."

"At the Pine Tree Motel? Both their cars were parked alongside each other at the motel. And not just once."

"How do you know this? Somebody has been spying on my husband? And it's all over town now?"

"I'm sorry to tell you this. But Mrs. Daniels heard it from Sara Magaly who heard it from..."

"Dotty, what am I to do?"

"Why, anything you might dream up, love."

Now what? Confront him? Go home to Mother? Vera was in a quandary. Action, of any kind, was scary. Inaction would only foment her disgust and anger to a curdled and caustic contempt—a loathing that would eat away at her self-worth until...? Until she snapped. She *would* snap. That was what the dream was all about. An intuition, a warning. Had she suspected his infidelity? Not really, not on a conscious level. Then there was the fortune cookie: be true and all will turn out well. That hadn't just applied to her romance with Robbie it appeared.

Running on automatic pilot (she was still dazed by the revelation of Raymond's affair), Vera decided not to cook and went for takeout.

She hadn't planned to pick up Chinese (she wasn't prone to irony), but somehow she found herself at the drive-up window of Chen's Golden Dragon where a bag full of little cardboard boxes was handed to her. General Tso's chicken, Szechuan beef, chow mein, and pot stickers for the children who wouldn't eat the spicier food, fried rice and wantons, and, of course, a fortune cookie for each of them.

Raymond was reading at the dinner table again. Not the sports page, but the advertising flier, the one with the checkerboard of colored ads for aluminum siding companies, garage door companies, sales on lawnmowers (it was winter, for Pete's sake!), specials at the A&P (sirloin 89 cents per pound, frozen chicken pot pies 29 cents each, carrots 9 cents per bunch, Land O Lakes butter 67 cents per pound, Wrigley's Double Mint gum 5 cents, oranges 89 cents for 2 dozen). There was a big gun sale at the Farm and Fleet, and…oh, here it was: State Farm Insurance, Raymond Blaine Agent, call Harrison 8-9767. *His* ad.

Vera dipped a wanton in Chinese mustard, the hot sweetness burned her tongue and perked up her senses. She had made a decision—of sorts: she would not leave Raymond nor would she confront him about Victoria Greenly. She would do nothing. Live, but not forgive. Endure with the grace given to those who are betrayed. Embrace the oh-so-human tendency of denial—it worked for religion and politics, why not for her? Maybe later in the summer, however, she would take a separate vacation. Raymond could not mind as it would give him more time with his mistress. She would travel. Perhaps to California to look up an old friend. Did she have his address? His parents still lived in town. They would know how to find him.

The cardboard cartons were empty now; just a little sticky sauce left in the bottoms. Vera distributed the fortune cookies. Raymond pushed his to one side. Vera frowned. "Read your fortune, Ray. It might make your day," she scolded.

"If you insist," he said. Breaking open the cookie he pulled the narrow strip of paper out as if he were unreeling a metal tape measure. He laid it on the table next to the cookie pieces.

"What does it say?" asked Vera.

Grumbling, Raymond read: "A good friendship is often more important than a passionate romance." He smirked and crumbled the fortune into a little ball. Vera now opened her cookie.

"Be true to *yourself* and all will turn out well," the fortune said.

Tommy smashed his on the table with his fist, found the fortune in the fragments and popped the paper slip into his mouth. "Tommy! This is not good for you," shouted Vera. Tommy grinned. Timmy put his cookie in the pocket of his blue jeans. "I'll put it under my pillow, he said, "for the tooth fairy."

"That's not...oh, all right, Dear. You do that. Run along now, you two. Play in your room until bedtime."

"TV!", said Tommy. "I want TV!"

"Oh, let the kids watch a little television, Vera," said Raymond. I think *Gunsmoke* is on about now."

"I wish they'd watch something educational. All those cowboy movies are so violent."

Off the children went to turn on the big 21-inch Admiral. Vera cleared away the table and started loading the dishwasher. When she entered the study to send the twins to bed they were watching *Peter Gunn*. She liked the handsome actor who played the detective, and the show's cool, sophisticated style. But it was too grown-up for young children. She stood in front of the screen and reached behind to switch off the set. "To bed, now," she ordered.

Vera did not sleep well that night. She had another nightmare. In this one she was relaxing on a sandy beach under the blazing Florida sun. Sea gulls flew in intricate formations overhead, swooping down occasionally to pluck a morsel of something pink and slimey and dead from the beach. Suddenly she noticed the beach was covered with dead and dying jellyfish. Translucent purple, sickly pale blue, or nearly colorless, they were impossibly tentacled, gooey, and shimmering. She wondered how she would be able to walk across the beach without stepping on them.

She looked up in horror as a huge Portuguese Man O War floated toward her in the sky. It was as big as a blimp. Its inflated, sail-like upper body was the color of a long-rotted corpse: putrid purples and bloated blues with a tinge of fleshy pink. A large black spot in the center of the sail made it look like a giant eye in the sky. Its long tentacles dragged across the sand, leaving ruts as if it were plowing a field to plant the dead bodies of its cousin jellyfish. It made a sucking sound as it came. Vera leaped to her feet and tried to run. This was one of those dreams in which the dreamer cannot move their legs. Try as she might, she was in a state of paralysis. Slowly the tentacled monster approached. She could smell it now, the smell of death. Something began to wind around and up her leg. The sting of the tentacle sent her into shock.

She woke, breathing hard and sweating profusely. Her legs were wrapped in the twisted sheet, hence the paralysis. It was always some trivial thing that stimulated the sleeper and influenced their dream world. A bit of General Tso's chicken. Chinese mustard. She crawled from the bed and went to the kitchen where she took a glass from a cabinet and filled it with water from the sink. She gulped down the cool liquid and began to settle down from the frightful dream.

On the counter was a butcher knife she had forgotten to put away into the drawer with the other knives. She picked it up and examined its long metal blade, felt its sharp edge (Raymond had bought one of those electric knife sharpeners and used it religiously). What an interesting object, she thought. So useful. The way it slices into meat, cleanly severing membrane from fat. So beautifully designed, so elegant and slender, yet so strong and inevitable.

When she returned to the bedroom Raymond was snoring as usual. In one hand she held two small strips of paper: one, the fortune fragment which read, "Be true to each other," and the other, which she had gotten that night which read, "Be true to yourself." She placed the former on Raymond's heaving chest. In her other hand she still held the knife from the kitchen. The blade caught a beam from the nightlight in the hall and flashed briefly.

Vera watched Raymond sleeping. Slowly she positioned the butcher knife at the place on his neck where his juggler vein bulged a little as he snored. Was he dreaming of *her*? The knife rested against his throat with the slightest pressure: don't want to wake the sleeper, spoil his dream. With an expertise worthy of a sushi chef, Vera drew the knife across Raymond's throat, slicing open his juggler. The dark red fluid of his life gushed out, soaking the bed clothes. She paused to admire her work, then, knife in hand, Vera walked down the hallway toward the children's room.

Byron Grush

AFTER BANKING HOURS

The half-block in the heart of Chicago's Loop that was bounded by Jackson, LaSalle, Quincy, and Clark Streets was the site of a two-story granite building. Although towered over by Art Deco skyscrapers, it could not be overlooked nor could it be characterized as diminutive element of the City of the Big Shoulders. Its elegant neo-classical design featured a colonnade stretching its 100-foot length. This had eight Corinthian columns topped by a cornice of off-set blocks which repeated the rhythm of the columns. Heavy bronze doors over thirteen feet high guarded the entrance to the Illinois Trust and Savings Bank. Its outer façade enticed visitors and predicted its unique and spacious interior.

Adel Claiborne, Addie to her friends, began working at the bank on 16 April 1918. She had joined an army of bookkeepers, most of them women, who occupied the inner sanctum of the bank, a great open space, 27,000 square feet, nearly the entire first floor. This was surrounded on three sides by the public areas and separated from those marbled corridors by bronze screens. The corridors had richly paneled ceilings supported by marble pilasters. In the main banking room, a rotunda stood on Doric columns and ran along the second story. The ceiling of the main room, sixty feet above the heads of the workers, was coved and fitted with a broad skylight. The skylight filled the room with daylight.

Addie never lost her awe of that space, an exhilaration which she had initially experienced on her first visit to the bank: the day of her interview with bank president John J. Mitchell. She had mounted the grand marble staircase that led from the main entrance to a mahogany-wainscotted reception room where wall panels imitated a Gothic tapestry. She waited to be summoned into the private office beyond. Inside, Mitchell had quizzed her as to her marital status, informing her of the prohibition he observed in his hiring practices of women. Male suiters were not allowed on the premises and it was assumed that female employees would stay single during their tenure with the bank. Addie assured him she had no intentions toward matrimony, nor suiters of any description.

She didn't tell him about Danny, however. Daniel Morrissey was the one. Addie and Danny had known that they were meant to spend their lives together since their high school days in East Peoria, Illinois. Only Danny had entered military service after graduation and was now stationed at Base Hospital 13 in Limoges, France. Addie waited for his return. There was talk of an armistice. This war couldn't last forever, could it? They would marry and as far as Addie was concerned, the bank's President Mitchell could go jump in the lake.

Danny's letters hadn't mentioned very much about his war experiences, just how much he missed her and missed home. He only hinted at his duties at the hospital. He assured her he was not there because of an injury. He was happy to be away from the fighting and took seriously his interactions with his fellows, those who were recovering from wounds or amputations and needed cheering. The worst were the unfortunates who suffered from the inhalation of mustard gas. Danny tried to help as best he could.

Addie came to work on Monday morning on the eleventh of November 1918, to find her workmates in jubilation, hugging each other and raising their voices in a merry clamor that was certainly inappropriate for such a dignified bank. She quickly learned that, after three days of negotiations at a secret location in Northern France's Forest of Compiéqne, an armistice had been agreed upon. The treaty was signed at 11:00 o'clock Paris time, about 4 in the morning by Chicago's clocks. The war was over! Danny would be coming home!

She saw Clara Gaines in a group of revelers and ran to her; Clara was her best friend—perhaps her only friend among her co-workers. She cried out to her:

"Oh Clara, isn't it wonderful? The war is over! Danny will be coming home!"

Weeks went by but there was no word from Danny. No letter saying when he was being shipped home. Nothing. Addie and Clara watched the victory parades down State Street: troops of young men in uniforms and tin hats, rifles shouldered, with flags waving from the curbs—women and children cheering. Brass bands. But the excitement about the end of hostilities began to dissipate in the following months. Veterans returned from combat to find there were few good jobs available. An atmosphere of unrest pervaded the country.

Toward the end of January of 1919, a letter arrived from France for Addie. It was not, however, from Danny. It read:

Dear Miss Claiborne:

I obtained your address, I'm afraid, by sorting through Dan Morrissey's kit bag. I felt it was crucial to do so, as Dan has been unwilling to communicate with you in recent weeks—indeed to communicate with anyone, friends or parents alike. I am one of his friends here at the hospital, and also a patient. Dan has often spoken of you with great affection and thus I deemed it important to make this contact and let you know how he is faring.

Dan is suffering from what is termed "shell shock," for lack of a better description. He has no physical injuries but is subject to periods of depression and even suicidal tendencies. This is the result of a traumatic experience on the battlefield many months ago. Dan was in a trench very near the front when a grenade or a bomb rolled into it and exploded with an impact that knocked him senseless for some time. When he awoke it was to find a heavy weight pinning him to the muddy floor of the trench. He extricated himself to find, to his horror, that on top of him had been the body of his sergeant, one Travis O'Hara, now a bloody corpse riddled with shrapnel and undoubtedly the human shield which had protected Dan from a like fate.

His time at the hospital was well spent in recovery and it seemed that the instances of staring blankly into space or cowering in a corner were now so few as to indicate his emergence from that self-imposed terror. Only when the armistice was announced and we were told we were going home, something snapped in the poor man and he regressed into an almost catatonic state.

Soon, the hospital will be closed and all patients and staff will be returning to the States. How Dan will deal with this is uncertain. When you do finally meet up with him again, I hope you will take all this into consideration. Be kind and tender and understanding.

Sincerely, Private Anthony Determann

Addie dropped the letter, looked around the room at the other bookkeepers hard at work at desks strewn with leger paper. Shards of sunlight falling from the skylight formed a mosaic of odd shapes; her eyes were blurred from the tears she sniffed back. She had to walk. She threw her coat over her shoulders and exited the bank building, walked through the Loop, through jostling shoppers, across busy thoroughfares, and soon found herself at Grant Park near the lakefront.

New snow had fallen during the night and it covered the landscape with a crystalline whiteness as yet unsoiled by the city's soot. The lake beyond surged with white-capped fury spattering the breakwater rocks with spears of ice. She saw children, tarrying on the way home from school, engaged in a riotous snowball fight. Frozen missiles flew from opposing sides of the fray often finding their mark on the foreheads of the boys. Cold wet snow found its way through loose collars to melt on backs or chests. Laughter mingled with mocking and rude taunts.

Boys will be boys, thought Addie. Yes, boys playing at war. And so it begins.

Milton G. Norton had worked on the *Chicago Herald and Examiner* since its inception as *Hearst's Chicago American* in 1900. He had lived through the so-called newspaper wars, when the *Examiner* and the *Chicago Tribune* had vied for distribution rights and violence, perpetrated by local gangsters, Dion O'Banion, Vincent Drucci, Hymie Weiss and Bugs Moran, had been the result. Those were tumultuous times for the newspapers, times happily beginning to ebb.

Norton was one of the new breeds of journalists: the photojournalist. While steel engravings had dominated the visual representation of news events dating back to the Civil War, as early as 1914 new printing techniques allowed actual photographs to be reproduced. Photos were now beginning to replace illustrations to draw the public's attention to the front pages.

Norton's expertise with the technology was in demand. Setting the focal plane shutter of his Kodak-made Speed Graphic press camera was a slow process and it required precise calculation to achieve proper exposures, but Norton was adept at this. He loaded half a dozen double-sided 4 by 5-inch film holders with Kodak's new panchromatic film in the total darkness of the newspaper's darkroom, then waited patiently at his desk for his editor, N. M. Meissner, to give him an assignment. He was looking forward to the coming baseball season when he could cover the home games of the Chicago White Sox and the Chicago Cubs. Fate, however, would not allow him the opportunity to photograph the final World Series game between the White Sox and the Cincinnati Reds; the game the Sox would throw in what would come to be called the Black Sox Scandal. Fate had other plans for Norton.

Meissner called Norton over to his desk. "Get over to White City," he said. "They are going to launch a new dirigible for a test flight. You may be able to get some great shots of the city if you can wangle a ride on that blimp."

White City was an amusement park located at 63rd Street and South Parkway on Chicago's South Side. It had opened in 1905, perhaps catering to public nostalgic for the now defunct White City midway of the World's Columbian Exposition of 1893. It had a tall "electric tower," an illuminated structure that thrust skyward near the center of the park, a giant Ferris wheel, reminiscent of the 1893 original although much smaller, roller coasters, a shoot the chutes, a penny arcade, a ballroom, a roller rink, a fun house, and many other attractions. Entrance to White City cost only a dime.

White City was also the location of one of the few airship hangers used to build dirigibles for the U. S. Government's war effort. Now that the war was over, the Goodyear Tire and Rubber Company was still constructing airships there and had just completed their latest C-class blimp called the *Wingfoot Air Express.* It would be used to transport passengers between the White City Amusement Park and a landing field downtown at Grant Park. Today, July 21, 1919, it would take off on its maiden flight over the city.

Milton G. Norton arrived at White City early that morning, before the crowds. He showed his press pass at the entrance gate and strolled through that great arched edifice. It was startling to see a sleeping park without throngs of revelers, young children scampering hither and thither, the elderly (or just the lazy) pushed along in wheeled wicker chairs, escaping balloons blown away into the city's dusty skyscape. He passed the Midget Village, its inhabitants not yet costumed but relaxing with large mugs of coffee. He saw rows of idle paddle boats docked along the small lagoon rocking gently in a bit of breeze—a whisper of the breath of the Windy City.

Finally, he found the airship hanger. He entered but to his dismay, it was empty. The *Wingfoot* had already left. A man approached him, dressed in suit and tie, clearly not a worker. He identified himself as Earl Davenport, publicity director of White City. Norton told him of his intension to photograph the city from the blimp. He could get some shots of the amusement park as well, he said. Davenport was pleased that the photographer had taken an interest in the *Wingfoot*'s first flight. It would be landing around noon, he told Norton, at Grant Park, and that would be his only opportunity to hitch a ride on the blimp. Sensing that a photo coverage in the Examiner could result in priceless free publicity for White City, Davenport offered to drive Norton to Grant Park.

Later that same morning, the Twentieth Century Limited pulled into Chicago's LaSalle Street station at Roosevelt and Clark, clouds of gray-black smoke billowing from its smokestack. It was considered a luxury train with its red carpet service and deluxe Pullman accommodations, the preferred way to venture from New York City to Chicago and stops in between. The War Department had commissioned the train for a special post-war service: the transportation of veteran soldiers, and especially, the wounded.

Private Anthony Determann sat next to Private Daniel Morrissey as the train jerked to a stop and let out a squeal of steam. Their uniforms were the cleanest they had been since before deployment, shoes polished like mirrors, brass buttons shining like stars, and crisp seams on their trousers legs you could cut your fingers against. Determann pulled their duffle bags down from the overhead rack. He said to Morrissey:

"You've come a long way, Dan, both figuratively and literally. You've beat that shell shock, I've no doubt."

"As long as there aren't any loud noises," answered Morrissey, "I'll be just fine."

"Are you off to East Peoria now? To see your family?"

"I've got one stop to make first, here in Chicago."

"Going to see Addie, I suppose. You never did write her, did you?"

"I didn't know what to say. I do now."

"Going to pop the question?"

"I...I'll have to see how she reacts. I'm not the same person I was last time I saw her."

"You'll do fine. And here," Determann said, holding a piece of note paper out for Morrissey, "is my address. Please keep in touch."

Daniel Morrissey stowed his duffle bag in a locker at the station and stepped out onto LaSalle Street in the cool Chicago mid-morning air. Overhead the shadowy form of the Goodyear blimp hovered, on its way to land at Grant Park on the east side of the Loop. Dan shielded his eyes from the sun with his hand as he looked up at the airship. Now he would walk up LaSalle toward the Illinois Trust and Savings Bank where he hoped to find Addie Claiborne. He hoped he would be just in time to take her to lunch.

LaSalle Street ran north along side of the train tracks which extended to a commuter substation just south of the Loop. Locomotives steaming by so close made Danny nervous. Yet he had, he believed, worked out his fear and anxiety to the point where his shell shock was manageable. It simply required understanding that the stimulus, in this case, the rumbling of the trains, was not a lethal artillery shell plummeting down upon him to blow him and his companions to Hell. Too many times had he witnessed the real thing. It was nearly impossible to shake the sensation of impending doom or the aftershock of survivor guilt. But he had made remarkable progress, or so the doctors had told him.

The smell of coal smoke from the locomotives mingled with the odor of fresh droppings from the few horse-drawn wagons that shared the street with Mr. Ford's Model Ts. Scores of pigeons descended upon the pavement searching for anything edible. Danny passed men huddled in doorways, dressed in rags that might at one time have been uniforms. Some of them stretched out hands; Danny gave them what coins he had.

It was a much longer walk than Danny had anticipated, and he reached the bank well after the traditional hour reserved for lunch. He managed to find one of the bank tellers who was willing to summon Addie from her desk on the main floor. "Be careful," the woman told him, "there are rules against meeting boy friends and lovers at the bank during working hours." Danny hadn't needed any additional worries— he was already concerned about this reunion. Would she be disappointed in him for not writing? Would she even want to see him again? The war changed one so! But:

"Danny! Oh, Danny...is it really you?" she called out to him, still half-way down the hallway. She rushed to him, embraced him, and cried in his arms, a hopeful crying like lovers long separated give when words fail. He hugged her so firmly he was afraid she might break. The moment expanded to an immeasurable time, then it was broken by:

"Addie!" the woman who had helped Danny earlier called. "Addie, remember you must be careful."

"Danny…we can't do this now…here. It's against the rules," said Addie. "I could be fired. But wait for me until after banking hours. Oh…we have so much to catch up on, so much to say to each other…"

"Of course. I understand, I'm disappointed though. I want to take you in my arms and carry you away from here. But I'll wait. When does the bank close?"

"At five o'clock, but we usually have to work later. To close up the books and so forth."

"I'll wait as long as it takes. There is a hotel in the next block. I'll wait there in the lobby. Come to me as soon as you can!"

She was nearly 200 feet in length and 42 feet in diameter. She was nothing like the hot air balloons he remembered from circus or carnival venues he had visited in days now long gone by. Not at all colorful; just a plain gloomy gray like the color of a darkening sky before a storm. A long gondola hung from her belly in front of two 150 horse-power engines. Through the windows of the gondola Norton could see her four-man crew as she came to a rest at her docking area at the Grant Park Air Strip. A large crowd of on-lookers was gathered around the blimp in a wide circle. Norton snapped off one or two photographs of the *Wingfoot* holding his camera over the straw hats of the men and the feathered hats of the women.

Norton and Earl Davenport, the White City's publicity director, pushed their way through the crowd. When they reached the gondola, the pilot, Jack Boettner, was conversing with W. C. Young, the manager of the blimp. The engines had operated smoothly and the rudder had responded accurately, Boettner reported to Young. He was however, said the pilot, still getting used to some of the eccentricities of the airship, how it handled in the stronger winds that came off the lake, the little tremors the superstructure made on occasion, how the changes of temperature affected the buoyancy of the hydrogen gas. Hydrogen gas. It wasn't explosive, as long as it didn't get mixed with oxygen from the atmosphere. As long as it wasn't exposed to a flame.

Norton readied his camera, pulling the slide from the film holder he had just inserted into the camera's back. "May I get a shot of you and the crew in front of the blimp?" he asked Young. The pilot and the crew were busy checking the rigging and priming the engines for the return flight. Mechanic Carl Weaver was burning oil off the propellers with a blow torch. Norton wondered if that was dangerous. Young called them to stand at attention for the photographer.

After the photo session, Davenport informed Young of their intention of riding in the *Wingfoot* in its flight over the city. "Norton will get some wonderful photographs of Chicago from the air and the park will get the publicity it needs and deserves," he added. Young was not happy about the request. "It is still in the testing stages, he complained. "It may not be safe." Jack Boettner, the pilot, interjected with his own concern:

"We've released quite a lot of hydrogen on the flight over. The ship won't carry more than five people now."

The men argued some more but ultimately, Davenport won. The pilot picked two of the mechanics, Carl Weaver and Harry Wacker, to crew the blimp and soon five men were seated single file in the gondola, outfitted with parachutes which were attached by a rope to the outside of the gondola. If something happed and the men were forced to jump from the blimp, the ropes would cause the parachutes to open. Davenport joked to Norton that he was glad he had worn his tennis shoes in case he needed a running start before jumping. They both laughed.

They flew up along Michigan Avenue, past the imposing Blackstone Hotel and the decorative Auditorium and Fine Arts Buildings, unique facades of the Boul Mich. Norton leaned over the side of the gondola with his camera. They turned up Adams Street where the Art Institute of Chicago maintained its prominence as the sole structure on the east side of Michigan Avenue. A canyon of skyscrapers beckoned the eager photographer.

Norton would capture an aerial image of the Rookery and the Marquette Building as the blimp approached the inner Loop. He could see people on the street below looking up at the *Wingfoot*, gesturing. An American flag was flapping from the stern of the airship. And a wisp of smoke was beginning to coil out from the top of the blimp.

The Grand Pacific Hotel once occupied the entire block.

Destroyed in the Great Chicago Fire, it had been rebuilt in 1873 in a style known as Palazzo, with ornate decorative elements, crystal chandeliers, and 15 dining rooms. It was one of Chicago's most prestigious luxury hotels and had attracted the wealthy and the famous, including Oscar Wilde and James A. Garfield. In 1895 the western half of the rambling edifice had been torn down to make way for the building of the Illinois Trust and Savings Bank, where Addie Claiborne now worked. The remaining half of the hotel had been remodeled in a more contemporary, blocky style, and it now featured stores and restaurants on its ground floor. This third iteration of the Grand Pacific, it had just been announced, would soon be demolished and a modern office building would take its place. Such was progress in the City of the Big Shoulders.

In the hotel coffee shop Danny Morrissey sat nursing a cup of mocha java, now as black and cold as an artic night. Several times the waitress had approached him, expecting him to order something more; several times Danny had waved her away. He gazed into the dark mirror provided by the coffee, saw reflected there a vision of the past, a past so distant, so dislocated from the present by the intervention of a war, a past so sweet it hurt to revisit it. He saw *her*. Her auburn hair done up in a pile of tresses, coming undone as she lay back on the moss-covered bank of the Peoria Lake where they had picnicked one summer. Addie. Addie of the smiling eyes and soft laughter. Addie who vowed to wait for him, the warrior. Addie—had she waited?

Danny looked at his watch, the one his father had given him just before he shipped out, the one that had been with him through chaos and catastrophe, the one with the cracked crystal: it still worked. It was after five o'clock, after banking hours. He would go to see if Addie had to work late. He had an important question to ask her.

When he emerged from under the coffee shop's green awning, he saw a commotion on the walk ahead. People were looking up at the sky and pointing. As he rounded the corner, he saw it. The *Wingfoot*, low in the sky, smoke rising above it. It was descending rapidly, headed for…the bank! He ran to the heavy doors of the bank; they were closed and locked. He pounded on them, bloodying his fists.

In the *Wingfoot*, the pilot, J. A. Boettner, saw smoke and a lick of flame. He called out to the others, "Jump, or you'll burn to death!" The others were shocked, not believing something like this could happen. But it had. Mechanic Weaver was the first to act. He leaped from the gondola. His chute opened, perhaps too soon for as blimp plunged down past him, flames caught his parachute. Burning, he fell through the bank's skylight, landing in a broken heap on the floor.

Earl Davenport then jumped. He had slid his legs over the side and dropped, not heeding the instructions he had been given earlier to jump clear—ironic after his joke about wearing tennis shoes for a running start. His parachute became tangled on the edge of the gondola. Frantically he tried to tear it loose but he was unable to free himself. He hung helplessly from the airship as flames rose above him in a boiling ball of heat. Trapped, he rode down with the burning airship as it crashed through the skylight.

Norton jumped next. He flung himself far out into empty space and his parachute opened automatically. He managed to clear the edge of the bank building and land in the street below. But being inexperienced in the art of parachuting, he broke both his legs. He had left his camera in the gondola. Mechanic Wacker and pilot Boettner both parachuted to safety with minor injuries. Wacker landed on a roof top while Boettner landed in the center of LaSalle Street. By now a crowd had gathered and soon the pilot and Norton were rushed to a hospital.

Addie Claiborne was carrying a heavy ledger across the main banking floor to place it in its storage cabinet when she heard a crash above her. A shower of glass shards began hitting the floor around her and some landed on her head and shoulders. A trickle of blood ran down her forehead. Her cheek was bleeding. She froze in place. Suddenly, the body of the mechanic, Wacker, struck the floor mere feet from where she stood. She screamed and dropped the ledger.

The next thing that dropped through the skylight was one of the massive engines. This fell into a cluster of desks, shattering them and trapping hapless workers under the rubble. Some struggled to get free; some lay still, for it was too late for their salvation. There were perhaps 150 bank clerks and bookkeepers in the big room, mostly women. There was only one exit as the room was surrounded on three sides by the bronze screens. In the pandemonium that followed, there was a rush toward the exit. Most made it into the corridor. Some were injured in the crush. Others were left in the big room as a huge ball of fire erupted above the broken skylight and fragments of the burning blimp fluttered down upon them. Then the *Wingfoot* fell into the bank.

The aviation fuel ignited with a terrible roar. The room was filled with burning, blistering gasoline. The stragglers were instantly incinerated. Miraculously, when it was all over, only eleven people had died. But eleven was too many. Outside of the bank, Danny Morrissey was still pounding on the bank doors. Suddenly they burst open and people began pouring out. Danny looked frantically for Addie but could not find her in the exiting crowd. He was not fully aware of what had just happened, but he knew that the blimp had been burning overhead. He wanted to rush into the bank to search for her. But just as this resolve for rescue came to him, he heard the explosion of the burning gasoline. He froze.

He was back on the battlefield. The smell of the burning fuel and the screams of the running women catapulted him back in time. Fear paralyzed him. He could not move forward into the bank nor could he turn and run from the scene. He stood helplessly as people pushed past him. The sound of sirens as fire engines rushed toward the bank could be heard above the cries of the survivors. But still no sign of Addie!

It was an hour before the valiant fire fighters could quench the blaze. Some of the tellers whose injuries were minor returned to drag the books with the bank's records in them out of the building. Firemen soaked the books with water, damaging them greatly. The main room of the bank was a heap of charred and smoldering fragments that had once been desks and tables. $50,000 in government bonds had burned but beyond this, the cost of the catastrophe would be estimated at only about $15,000—not counting, of course, the loss of life. The bank reopened the next day.

The City of Chicago took action to ban the flight of aircraft over the city proper and closed the airfield at Grant Park, eventually building a more proper airport farther south. White City Amusement Park, not owning the *Wingfoot*, claimed they had no liability for the accident. The Navy canceled several future orders for the airships that Goodyear and Goodrich had been building in Chicago.

The day after the fire, in an unrelated incident along Chicago's Lake Michigan south shore, Black teenagers migrated over from the exclusively Negro 24th street Beach to the exclusively white 29th Street Beach. This initiated an ugly ruckus which resulted in a Black youth named Elliot Williams being struck in the head with a rock. The youth subsequently drowned. Riots raged through the city. 38 people died.

Three weeks after the *Wingfoot* crash, Addie was released from St, Luke's Hospital where she had been recovering from second degree burns on much of her body. Fleeing from the burning debris, her clothing had caught fire. Thankfully, there was no scarring from the burns, just a bit of discoloration on her arms and legs. The only disfigurement she suffered was a nasty-looking scar on her left cheek where the falling glass had cut her and the deep wound had failed to properly heal. Clara Gaines had been to visit her at the hospital and had brought her up to date on who had died, who was injured, and who had escaped unharmed. This did little to raise her spirits.

There was now something that she understood more fully about Danny and his condition of shell shock. She thought she could talk to him at last in a way she had not been able to before. Her ordeal, she knew, was nothing compared to Danny's, but she shared with him an experience of unrealistic anxiety and survivor's guilt. She decided to return to East Peoria to find him.

At Danny's parents' house she talked to Danny's mother. No. Danny wasn't at home...he left the house every day and stayed away until evening. No, she didn't know where he went or what he did...he wouldn't talk about it. She didn't think he was drinking though, she'd have smelled it on him. "I think he goes somewhere it is quiet and just sits," his mother said.

She found him on the bank of the lake, in a shady spot near the big willow where they had picnicked so long ago. He was sitting, staring, rocking ever so slightly back and forth as if the wind that rustled the willow branches was pushing, then releasing him. When she approached he didn't look up. She touched him gently on the shoulder. He jumped.

"You scared me!" he said.

"I'm sorry, I didn't want to startle you. But...can we talk?"

"I thought you were dead," he said.

"Almost," she answered. "Oh, Danny, I'm so sorry."

"What do you have to be sorry for?"

"The day you came to see me at the bank, just before the accident...I shouldn't have sent you away. I should have gone with you right there and then. It would have solved a lot of problems, I think."

"It would have kept you from burning up, for one," he said. "I'm sorry, I didn't mean that. I really did think you had died in the fire."

"I understand now how you feel...what you feel. How the world has beaten you up, let you down, given you nothing but despair. I feel that way too, to a degree. I've lost friends. I've lived through a horrible disaster. It wasn't fair I lived while others died."

"No…you can't say that. You can't think that. I wasn't your fault. It was just…fate."

"But now, Danny, we are both alive. You came back to me. Now I've come back to you…if you'll have me. You don't mind, do you? This…" She touched the scar on her cheek.

He kissed her then, a kiss he had waited for so long. He kissed her lips, then he kissed her cheek, where the scar was. "What do you think?" he said.

The healing would have to take place over a lifetime shared without fear, without pain, without regret or guilt. They returned to that place under the willow many times and watched the mallard ducks swimming up and down near the bank and the long dripping branches of the willow tree caressing the water with pale green fingertips. They never again talked about the war or about the *Wingfoot* disaster. But the bliss was not to last. The bad dreams returned. The old, unreasonable fears haunted him. On July 10, 1924, the same day that the Scopes Monkey Trial began in Tennessee, Danny Morrissey took his own life.

THE DWARVES

In Horton Park along Highway 11 in Delavan, Wisconsin, stands a historical marker. One may stand in the shade of ancient willow trees that line the bank of the nearby creek and read these words:

In 1847 two New York brothers, Edmund and Jeremiah Mabie, toured Wisconsin with their United States Olympic Circus. The circus stopped over in Delavan and the brothers took time off to hunt prairie chicken near Delavan Lake. They liked the area so well that they purchased 400 acres of land and established winter quarters for the circus here. Because this circus was the largest and most profitable in existence, circus performers and other show personnel flocked to Delavan. Twenty-six circuses winter-quartered here between 1847 and 1894, including Harry Buckley's National Circus and Roman Hippodrome, W. C. Coup-Dan Castello's Egyptian Caravan, Holland and McMahon World's Circus. The colorful days of the circus era in Delavan ended with the E. G. Holland and Co. Railroad shows. In 1871 the idea for forming the P.T. Barnum Circus was developed in Delavan by W. C. Coup, who also was first to put a large circus on rails and introduced the second and third ring to the performance. Delavan reached its peak as a "circus town" during the 1870's. About seventy members of the "circus colony" are buried in Spring Grove and St. Andrew's cemeteries.

Buddy Hannigan loved the old man and could spend hours listening to his stories. He had first encountered the old man last summer in the Tower Park, downtown, where Buddy ambled, attempting to wander away his teenage angst. The old man had been sitting on a bench, tossing bead crumbs to an odd collection of urban birds: a sea gull and two crows. The old man didn't look like a street person—Delavan didn't have any of those—just a nice old soul who probably was lonely and had nothing to do. Just like Buddy. So he struck up what would be the first of many conversations; many ventures into an enchanted world of the past as exotic as the Arabian Nights.

A native son, born into a circus family, George Holland was nearing the mid-point of his octogenarian decade. He had joined the John Robinson Circus in 1889 at the age of fourteen and followed in his father's profession as a bareback rider. He and his wife, equestrian Rose Dockrell, had traveled and performed with the Sells Downs Circus, the Norris and Rowe Circus, the Seils-Sterling Circus, the Frank Hall Circus, and others, and had played the New York Hippodrome as a featured act. Their last performance came in 1937, at the Police Circus in Saint Louis. They retired to a farm near Delavan, bringing with them their team of four snow-white horses to romp in its meadows. George had lived through the glory years of the circus colony and had seen its decline.

Now that so many of the old troupers were gone, this young boy, curious and attentive, was the only remaining sounding board for the old man's steadfast memory. He looked forward to their meetings in the park. Together they fed birds. Buddy listened while George reminisced. Sunlight was modulated through maple and oak fronds and dappled the park and the two friends. Other park strollers passed by, unaware of the sequins and bangles that danced in the boy's eyes or of the hesitant tears almost formed in the eyes of the old man.

Buddy was at an age when romance was a notion projected by the female sex in response to…well…to the lustful longings of the male adolescent. Yet when the old man talked of those first years on the road, meeting the beautiful and talented Rozelle Dockrell—his Rose—Buddy's resistance to the notion slackened. He could picture her poised to pirouette on the back of her horse, Dolly, bespangled in stiff linen tutu and white tights, her chestnut hair in curls and a golden cape fluttering out behind her.

When he met her, the old man said, her parents, who were themselves famous circus performers, had left Rose with her grandmother in order to protect her from the drudgeries and sometimes tragedies of circus life. But Rose and George soon developed an act that brought them fame in the center ring as "Holland and Dockrell, the World's Greatest Riders." George stood on the back of his horse and lifted Rose to his shoulders. Later in the act George began a series of somersaults while Rose danced in toe shoes on her own prancing horse.

"I could do a backward-facing forward somersault," the old man told the boy. (Buddy marveled at the perplexing term.) "I stood on the horse's rump facing backward and did a series of flips. My father taught me that move. You'd think you would fly right off the back of the horse, but the momentum of the horse stays with you in the air and you land perfectly…or maybe not. There was a time when my father had this friendly rival…Stickney was his name. Stickney challenged him to see who could do the most backward-forward somersaults before falling off. Stickney fell off at 18 while my father did 44. I later got up to 56. It was and still is the record."

Buddy could practically taste the sawdust flying up from the horses' hooves. He could almost smell the cotton candy and wipe the sweat on his brow from the heat under the big top. He had been to the circus—one returned to Delavan about once a year even though the venue here was not lucrative. But that was nothing like the spangles and tinsel and three-ring extravaganza that the old man described. The caged lions, the performing Russian bear, the clowns…

"Rose's father, Richard Dockrill, was a great equestrian too," the old man was saying. "He was the ringmaster for the Barnum show in London soon after Bailey came in and until about the time John Ringling took over. Dockrill had a 60-horse act that was really something."

"If there were so many circuses here in Delavan, asked Buddy, "where are they now? Why did they leave?"

"Because of Coup, mainly. Coup got the idea to put circuses on trains. That meant they could get around the country better. Didn't need to winter in their territories no more. Some left for warmer climes, some got swallowed up by bigger outfits, some just folded."

"Coup? Who was Coup?"

"W. C. Coup. He got started back in the 1850s working for P. T. Barnum. Barnum didn't have no circus then, just a museum of oddities. He got up a traveling menagerie and Coup worked for him as a roustabout. Later Coup joined Mabie's circus that wintered here in Delavan, then partnered with Dan Castello. At one time he had a fish aquarium, but I guess he got bored with that. Then he ran what he called "W. C. Coup's Monster Four-Ring Circus and Paris Hippodrome," which featured "Lulu, the Man-bird." Lulu was hurled from a catapult across the length of the tent and was caught in a net. Most of the time. Coup then came back to Delavan and opened a cheese factory, of all things. By 1870, Barnum had retired, what with his museum in New York City burning and all. Coup talked him out of retirement. Barnum's Museum, Menagerie, and Circus was born. That had the first side shows featuring freaks and the like. Giants and midgets and bearded ladies."

"Midgets? I'd liked to have seen that. Were there very many midgets in the circus?"

"More'n you can count on all your fingers and toes. Barnum had General Tom Thumb and Mrs. Tom Thumb, of course. Also Commodore Nutt who worked with Colonel Goshen, the giant. There was Commodore Foote and Peanuts Genimal…Peanuts was Japanese and worked as a clown. They came from all over the world. Lady Little and Princess Marguerite were born in France. There was a troop of 23 Russian midgets that performed for the Romanoffs. Some of them, you know, worked at the Midget Village at the Chicago's World Fair and Century of Progress in '33 and they was also in the Wizard of Oz movie. But the circuses was their best way to earn a steady living. Well, more or less steady, I suppose. They liked to be called 'little people,' by the way."

"Did you work with any little people, Mister Holland?"

A glassiness crept over the old man's eyes as he stared across the park toward the old Park Hotel. It was as if he could see the specters of people long passed away, dancing in a last waltz to a music so faint and so hollow and yet so compelling that he could not look away. It was...

A crisp autumn afternoon in 1919. The circus had crossed the Missouri River ten miles south of Sioux City, Iowa, on its way from the small towns of Nebraska to an engagement later in the week in Des Moines. A ferry boat had taken most of the wagons across and returned for the caged and uncaged animals. The elephant, a female named Dorothy, bulked at climbing aboard the ferry—a circumstance for which the ferry driver was thankful, given the pachyderm's weight, but which perplexed the circus manager, Herman Wilkins.

"She'll have to swim it," Wilkins told Sam Cooper, the elephant's handler. "Can elephants swim?"

"We'll find out," answered Cooper, and he calmly led Dorothy to the water. Again the animal bulked. Cooper slid into the cold muddy water and beckoned. "Come on, sweetheart," he called. Miraculously the elephant followed Cooper into the Missouri and, reaching a depth which lapped at her shoulders, began swimming.

Only she swam downstream with the strong current and soon was out of sight of the circus crew. Cooper crossed the river and mounted one of the ponies. He rode along the bank of the river for several miles, trying to find any evidence where a large animal might have climbed the muddy bank and taken off into the woods, but he found nothing. He stayed behind as the circus moved on to the next town and renewed his search on the following day.

As he crossed some bottomland that stretched out for about one quarter of a mile from the bank of the river, he saw large tracks in the mud where Dorothy certainly had wandered, probably now lost and hungry. The tracks disappeared once they encountered firmer ground. After an exhausting day of searching with still no sight of the elephant, a discouraged Sam Cooper finally gave up and returned to where the circus was to pitch its main tent, at the small hamlet of Mapleton.

The ring was laid out with precision and skill by tent-men plowing furrows in the dirt. It was a circular arena which the French called the Cirque, thus giving the name "Circus" to the great traveling outdoor shows that followed in later years. Other tent-men raised the poles which would hold up the large canvas roof of the tent. The sound of hammers driving stakes into the ground rang like church bells in the air. Other tents sprouted like mushrooms: the stable tents, the food tent, the dressing tents, the sleeping tents; the circus was like a small town—one that would appear, and then vanish in the blink of an eye.

Small boys from the town came to watch and marvel at the camels, the lone zebra and the cages of spotted monkeys, striped tigers, and an elderly lion. "That's an old donkey they painted to look like a zebra," taunted one of the town boys. "Ya," said another, "and them tigers is just old dogs they painted up too!" One of the roustabouts eyed the boys with disdain at the insults, but he did not chase them away. They might return tomorrow with their parents who would pay the price of admission.

In the food tent that evening, a bizarre assortment of humanity (some might say, barely human humanity) sat elbow to elbow at the long table. Terisa the Bearded Lady, Gordo the Giant, Hilda the Fat Lady, Dondo the Dog-faced Boy, Jack the Legless Wonder, Princess Babette the midget, and several lean and muscular men and woman who were acrobats, trick riders, and aerialists, chattered as a platter of baked chicken was passed around followed by a basket of biscuits and a jug of fresh milk, all obtained from a local farmer (who received free tickets to tomorrow's matinee).

Babette Géroux, known as Princess Babette, had been born in Barritz, France, twenty-six years ago. She was 29 and one-half inches in height and weighed 27 pounds. She and her two siblings, an older sister named Marie and a brother named Josué, had been part of a troupe of performing midgets in France called Les Colibris Barritz (the Barritz Hummingbirds). Being underage when she arrived in America, Babette was adopted by the manager of Midget City at Coney Island so that she could be exhibited legally. One day, after bemoaning the sparse pay and long hours, she and Gordo the Giant determined to leave Midget City and join a traveling circus. They had been with circuses now for nearly eight years.

There was another long table for the tent-men, the drivers, the trainers, and the roustabouts. And another for the ring master and the clowns. The clowns were the most important performers of the circus, more important even than the high-wire acts or the trick riders. It was the clowns that brought in the crowds, especially the children. And this small circus, so poor that it could not afford to travel by rail as the bigger shows did, kept an even dozen of the funny men on salary, no matter what.

Of course, none of the clowns were in costume and makeup tonight. It was a time for relaxing, comradery, and later, a little boozing. Tomorrow they would put on the grease paint and break out the carefully performed acrobatics, antics, and hilarity that entertained and amazed the masses. Among the clown contingent were twin brothers, Jan and Norbert Kasprzak, little people originally from Strusina, Poland. Their normal-sized parents had immigrated to Chicago at the turn of the century. Once they became of age, the brothers could find employment only in a side show or a circus. They trained as acrobats and made themselves available to the score of circuses that still wintered in Wisconsin. Jan was 31 inches in height and weighed 29 pounds. Norbert was 32 inches in height and weighed 30 pounds. Their specialty act involved being tossed through the air by the other clowns or jumping from a spring board and somersaulting onto the back of the elephant—the elephant that was now roaming the country side.

Wind against the sides of the food tent flapped the canvas making sounds like clapping—an anticipation of tomorrow's applause. Accompanied by the clatter of silverware and the blabber of raised voices, the clapping became a drone of monotonous rhythm—the rapid heartbeat of a circus unable to properly rest. The technical subtleties of trick riding were analyzed and refinements discussed. New jokes were proposed and passed from clown to clown. A certain trainer was given a dressing-down for the loss of a very expensive elephant.

Then a voice rose above the clamor: "Anybody here lose an elephant?"

The man, a local farmer, had heard banging coming from his barn. Upon investigation, he had discovered a large gray elephant lying on a pile of straw, shivering from cold and anxiety. He quickly covered the elephant with some of the straw and hurried into town where he had heard a circus was setting up. He poked his head into the food tent.

"Figured it must be you folks was missin' an elephant. Nobody else 'round here have one."

Dorothy was returned, happy to be reunited with her trainer. The shackle and chain which attached her firmly to a stack in the ground was unnecessary as her adventurous romp was unlikely to be repeated. The circus manager, however, was taking no chances. The Kasprzak midgets were glad of the return of the elephant. They had a new twist on the spring-board vault to the elephant's back which they wanted to try out. It involved a hoop which would be set on fire.

Twins, especially those with nearly identical physical resemblances, are said to have nearly identical personalities, each arriving at the same thought at the same time, choosing similar clothing, similar diets, and similar professions even if separated by great distances. This was not the case with the Kasprzak midgets. Jan was strong of body and of composure. Quiet, but although this made him seem shy, he was not reluctant to voice dissatisfaction at any injustice levied at him; he was the twin who had stood up to the circus manager when that spendthrift of a man had shorted the Kasprzaks' salaries one month. Most of the time, however, Jan Kasprzak was docile and polite, and usually ignored by the other circus folk. Norbert was just the opposite. It was he who brashly belted out a ballad as bawdy and irreverent as they come during drinking bouts in the evenings. It was he who boasted of abilities far exceeding those of men of normal size. It was he who had thought of setting fire to the jumping hoop. But it was Jan who would be the one to jump through it.

The Kasprzaks did have one thing in common: they both had designs upon Princess Babette. True, she was the only female little person at the circus. But little people were not obligated to mate only with their own kind. It was not unheard of to witness the union in marriage of a little person with a normal-sized lover. Princess Babette represented an ideal to the brothers: she was beautiful, smart, and talented. She was not relegated to the world of clowns, not her! She rode bareback on sequined ponies and could pirouette in her tiny toe shoes while the pony galloped and trotted around the ring. And she could do a somersault while on the pony's back.

The old man paused in his story and sniffed. Was that a tear? No, just allergies of the season, Buddy supposed. The old man wouldn't say where Princess Babette had learned to somersault on a horse's back. He wouldn't say who it was that had taught her those moves, or what kind of relationship had existed between teacher and student. Or how he knew the bittersweet story of the midgets. But he continued.

The circus reached Des Moines, Iowa, the next day and the tents rose in a field just outside of town. The advance man had already pasted posters on every available pole and wall throughout that burg and a parade was planned for that afternoon. The wagons, pulled by draft horses now decorated with sequined drapes and feathered headdresses, formed behind the camels and the zebra, tended by ladies dressed in tights and more sequins and more feathers. In front of these was Dorothy, the once rogue elephant, now docile but deliberately intent on lumbering, a circumstance which would cause Cooper, her trainer, to coax her on with a wicked-looking prod. The trick horses were in front of these, dainty Princess Babette astride her pony and a family of equestrians mounted on their own white steeds, all splendidly attired in exotic costumes. The clowns were set to weave in and out of the ensemble. Then the parade moved forward toward town led by a brass band and a prancing ringmaster in red coat and black top hat. The circus had come to town.

People lined the streets, filling the sidewalks. Small boys hung from street lamps or crawled upon the roofs of automobiles to leer at the scantily dressed ladies. There were cheers at the antics of the clowns and applause for the equestrians who rode bareback and then stood up on their horses. But the largest response, and this did not go unnoticed by the circus manager, was for the tigers in their cage as it rolled up the avenue. The two great cats paced and growled and occasionally a clawed paw appeared swiping through the bars. The circus manager, Herman Wilkins, now had an idea.

During the rehearsal period before the first show of the day, Wilkins talked to the ringmaster who talked to the lion tamer who agreed to the idea. And so the ringmaster went to Princess Babette and made a proposal:

"A new wardrobe and fifteen dollars for you if you will go into the cage with the tigers," he had told her. "You can carry a whip for show, but I urge you not to brandish it at the tigers. Otherwise, I assure you they will be bored with your presence. If this is successful we will bring the tigers into the big cage during tonight's performance and you will accompany Mr. Jordan, the lion tamer, as he puts the tigers and the lion through their paces. And fifteen dollars extra a week as long as you do this. What do you say?"

Jan happened to be standing nearby and heard what the ringmaster had said. "Don't do it," he told Princess Babette. "Those tigers are unpredictable."

But fifteen dollars was fifteen dollars, and so Babette agreed and the experiment, to see if the tigers would accept her, commenced. Into the cage she went.

"Jordan bends over and makes them jump over him," said the ringmaster. "See if you can make them do that."

Babette stooped down, but the two tigers simply sat at the other end of the cage and stared at her. Perhaps they were bored. Now the ringmaster pushed a tin pan filled with small pieces of raw meat through the bars. Babette took the pan and approached the tigers, offering one piece to each. Eagerly they gobbled. She gave them the rest of the meat and then patted them on their heads. They licked at her hands. It was not, perhaps, an affectionate act.

"Get out of the cage, now!" shouted Jan. The ringmaster echoed the command. Babette backed slowly toward the door at the other end of the cage. One of the tigers raised up and crept toward her. When she reached the cage door, Jan was ready with an iron bar to jam against the door once it was shut. Babette opened the door and Jan pulled her out of the cage, slammed the door and barred it, just as the tiger leaped. She fell into his arms.

"I guess you have decided not to do the act," said the ringmaster, looking dejected.

"You owe me fifteen dollars," answered Babette.

"So did Babette fall in love with Jan, Mr. Holland?" asked Buddy.

"I think she loved both of the brothers," answered the old man, "but neither of them to the point of marriage or an affair. You know what I mean by an affair, don't you?"

"I'm not a child. You mean they didn't do *it*."

"Well, who knows? But picture Babette and Jan walking away from the tiger's cage, holding hands. And picture Norbert watching them, wondering what they were saying to each other. She: 'You saved my life, now it belongs to you.' Him: 'I will never let anything happen to you. I adore you.' And Norbert: 'I could kill him! I could kill both of them!' Of course, we'll never know for sure."

"He didn't kill them, then?"

"There is more to the story. Much more…"

The show had begun with a burst of clowns coming through the flaps of canvas that hid backstage from the audience. Cartwheels and the tossing of the little people in the air delighted the crowd. Then the band came, leading a half-dozen snow white horses and a pony, all with riders costumed in brightly colored spangles—of course, it was Princess Babette on the pony. Dorothy entered the arena led by Cooper, her trainer. She stopped in the center of the ring and knelt down to allow a female performer dressed as a ballerina to climb up to the top of her head, then stood and swung her trunk as if to say, "look at us…look at me!"

A performance on the high wire, trapeze artists, jugglers, and trick riders followed while vendors hawked peanuts and cotton candy to the crowd. Then the big cage was wheeled out and a wagon deposited two angry tigers and a tired lion down a chute into the cage. Henry Jordan, lion tamer extraordinaire, entered the big cage, whip under arm. The crowd roared even louder than the big cats.

Meanwhile, the Kasprzak midgets in full clown makeup began a parody of the lion tamer's act. It was Norbert who held the whip and Jan who played the lion. As Jordan caused the tigers to rise up on their hind legs, Norbert cracked his whip at Jan who disobediently rolled over on the sawdust and kicked up his feet. The crowd laughed. The whip was coming a bit close to Jan but the crowd didn't seem to mind.

Jordan leaned over and the tigers took turns jumping over him. Norbert and Jan pantomimed this act but with Norbert suddenly standing up, sending Jan sprawling. Jordan made the tigers leap up onto painted wooden pedestals; their roars delighted the crowd. Now it was time for the Kasprzak's specialty: the spring board leap. Dorothy was led back into the ring and she knelt down once again next to the midgets. Jan stood on one end of the spring board while Norbert ran and jumped onto the other end, catapulting Jan into the air where he did a flip and landed squarely on Dorothy's back. It was a sensation.

What was good the first time needed to be even better the second. Now, as Jan slid from the elephant and took his place again on the spring board, a large metal hoop was put in place between him and Dorothy. They had practiced the routine only once or twice, but it seemed workable. However, they hadn't tried it yet with fire. Norbert had seen that the hoop had been wrapped with cloth soaked in kerosene. There was drum roll, and Norbert struck a match and held it to the hoop which immediately burst into flame.

Dorothy panicked. Just as Norbert landed on the springboard and Jan flew through the air, Dorothy bolted. Jan had hit the side of the hoop and his costume caught fire. He hit the elephant just as it charged past the clown midgets. Jan grabbed onto the elephant's harness. The hoop fell from its stand and rolled across the sawdust ring setting it on fire. The elephant trumpeted and ran through the backstage entrance, dropping Jan, whose flaming clothes set fire to the canvas.

A common practice in those days was to waterproof the canvas tents by coating them with a solution of paraffin wax dissolved in gasoline. No one apparently thought the resulting material, being extremely flammable, would be a problem. Once the flames started to climb up the canvas sides, the rising heat stopped under the top of the tent and super-heated the ceiling. The result was that a huge ball of fire exploded above the center ring. Posts and ropes were set aflame and the ceiling threatened to collapse. Hot burning wax dripped down on the audience.

Other than the performer's entrance, there was only one entrance/exit to the big top. The crowd yelled and screamed in pandemonium, and many jumped from their seats to run for the exit. Some fell from the bleachers, some were trampled. No one seemed to realize they could simply crawl under the canvas sides of the tent to escape. Circus workers who were outside of the big top began to cut through the canvas with knives. They were able to pull many spectators to safety in this manner. Others were not so lucky.

Horses and the zebra still in the arena escaped without injury, led out by the performers. Henry Jordan left the tiger's cage in a panic, leaving the big cats to the mercy of the fire. Babette saw him leave. She feared an impending tragedy as smoke thickened and more flaming hot wax dripped from the ceiling. She ran to the cage door and flung it open, calling to the tigers and the lion to come to her, but the animals were afraid of the rushing crowd of spectators who had to pass the cage to get to the exit. Into the cage she went. Picking up the lion tamer's discarded whip she moved to the back of the cage to get behind the big cats. She yelled and cracked the whip at them. They began to move slowly toward the cage door.

Norbert Kasprzak was paralyzed with fear, unable to flee or to help others to escape. He had watched his brother fall from the rampaging elephant with his clothing burning, but he was unable to move to save him. All around him people were pushing and shoving each other; he was at the center of a cyclone of terror. Then he saw Babette enter the big cage. Still he was frozen in place, a stark statue of uncertainty and graceless shortcomings. Today he would lose a brother and a potential lover, and his entire world would be swallowed by a maelstrom of hell-fire, an inferno from which there could be no return. His jail term in a purgatory of his own making (for it was he who had thought of the hoop of fire) was just beginning.

"Well," said the old man, "there's Rose with the car. I guess that's all for today. Back to the farm for me…gotta fed them horses."

"But Mr. Holland, you haven't finished the story! What happened to the little people? Did Babette die?"

"It was a terrible fire. Something like 40 people perished, and many were injured. Jan and Babette didn't survive. All the animals got out, though. Circus never started up again and the circus people had to find other positions or take jobs like normal people."

"What about Norbert? What did he do?"

"Oh, he drifted from circus to side show to the Chicago World's Fair where he lived in that Midget Village for a while. Couldn't take the guilt, I guess. Killed himself there in Chicago. Slit his wrists in the bath tub. He heard it was less painful that way."

"You knew him, huh?"

Holland waved at his wife who had brought the car up to the curb. "Be there in a minute," he yelled.

"Take care, Buddy," said the old man. "I'll be seeing you."

That fall Buddy began his college career by entering the University of Wisconsin at Madison. The campus, situated along Lake Mendota, was a stimulating venue for a young man intent on conquering the world. He elected history as his major and literature as his minor. Someday, he thought, he might write about the circuses that wintered in his home town of Delavan those many years ago.

In December, his mother wrote him a letter which included a newspaper clipping. The clipping was an article about Charles Holland, the old man, who had died that week. He was interred at the Spring Grove Cemetery there in Delavan, where many of the old circus folk were also buried. His widow, Rose, was moving from the farm to a house in the nearby town of Darien. The horses, who were the offspring of the couple's trick riding steeds, had been sold.

Byron Grush

A BAPTISM OF FIRE

Excerpt from the brochure, "Visiting the Land of Enchantment"

There was a time when the Santa Fe River was fed by wetlands where the town of Santa Fe would one day appear. Its tributary, the Rio Chiquito, flowed from a spring where Bishop Lamy would one day plant his garden. A series of ditches crisscrossed the community with gates which could be opened or closed according to the wishes of the Mayordomo, the water master who controlled irrigation and who would divvy out allotments for the parciantes, the water users. One of the major ditches, the Acequia Madre, or "Mother Ditch," still flows down from the Upper Santa Fe Canyon, bubbling richly during the infrequent rains.

This intricate water system is gone now, like the numerous pueblos that lined the river in the thirteenth century. The river's importance began to disappear in 1610 when Santa Fe became a town. The once bustling stream which helped to irrigate the many farmlands along its journey southward toward the Rio Grande cut a channel in the dry earth becoming a deep arroyo with long periods of low water between the seasonal monsoon rains.

These days, tourists, wandering off the Plaza, stare at the riverbed during the dry season and wonder why no one has filled in the unsightly gash. When water does flow, however, it rushes robustly; a brilliant deluge sparkling in the ever-present New Mexico sun. And woe be to any homeless being who takes shelter under its bridges. One such being, a boy of perhaps seventeen from somewhere in the Midwest, watches as his knapsack and blanket are torn away in the tumbling torrent; he is unsure where he will sleep this night.

He drifts towards the Plaza, the center of downtown. Native Americans have spread blankets under the portico of the Palace of the Governors for their wares: an array of hand-made items to be perused, and hopefully, purchased by the incessant procession of vacationists that flow past. On San Francisco Street, in front of the entrance to a shop selling turquoise jewelry made of plastic, he sees a boy not much older than himself sitting hunched against the wall. Next to the youth is a mangy dog upon whose back sits a scraggly cat which, to complete the curious pyramid, has upon its back, a small brown mouse. The boy's hat, containing a few coins, is on the sidewalk. Passersby add to the treasury infrequently but are not disinclined to exclaim their surprise and amusement at the sight of the dog-cat-mouse miracle.

A few doors down is an ensemble of South American musicians in colorful woolen attire. A guitarist accompanies a man playing a pan pipe, expertly rendering *El Condor Pasa*, an eerily beautiful Peruvian tune. An open guitar case is used to collect contributions; here paper bills and coins have accumulated in greater abundance than in the hat of the dog-cat-mouse youth. The wandering boy thinks, "If only I had a talent, I might earn some money!"

He is hungry. His total wealth, some $34.65, was in the knapsack now half-way to La Cienega, swept away in the rushing river. He enters a restaurant across from the Plaza called, fittingly enough, the Plaza Restaurant. He sits at the old chromed diner-like counter and looks at the menu. He hasn't had breakfast although it is almost noon. The huevos rancheros look good: two fried eggs on blue corn tortillas, topped with red or green chile and cheese, and a side of pinto beans and hash browns. Or perhaps a stuffed sopaipilla, or an Indian taco, which (according to the menu) is fry bread topped with your choice of calabacitas, chicken, camitas, or carne asada, and beans, cheese, chile, lettuce, tomatoes, guacamole, and sour cream. His stomach begins to churn.

The counter man asks, "What are you having?"

He answers. "I haven't any money. Lost it in the arroyo."

"You want a job?

"What do you have?"

"You wash dishes?"

"I can do that."

"I suppose you want to eat first. I have pozole and tortilla soup. Which?"

"What's pozole?"

"It is hominy cooked slow with maybe pork or menudo. I like to add some red chile."

"What's menudo?"

"Where are you from?"

"Illinois."

"Figures."

It is a dry heat. Visitors to the Southwest are told this when concerned that temperatures in the 90s here are common. You don't feel it the same way you do in the East. Drink lots of water. But the boy, bent over the stainless steel sink, scrubbing a battered pot with an SOS pad, is breathing in steam from the hot water spray and sweating like un cerdo. His t-shirt is soaked and the baseball cap he wears backwards on his head is stained with a permanent sweat band. He has been working at the Plaza Restaurant now for a week. Apparently, the owner is pleased with his diligence in showing up for his shift on time. There are many out of work who would gladly grab his job were he truant.

It is a long walk from the hostel on Cerrillos Road where he stays. The counter man set him up with the first overnight, loaning him the money. Ordinarily, the people at the Santa Fe International Hostel, do not accept New Mexican residents or people working in the town. He got lucky; his luck stemmed from a good friendship that existed between the counter man and the operators of the Hostel. He has been asked to find another venue, however, only just this morning. As he wipes the sweat from his brow he worries about this.

There are two perks to working at the Plaza. The first is the free food. Usually this consists of whatever the cooking staff has prepared too much of for the day's turnover. There is always an abundance of chips in the bowls cleared by the busboys, and plenty of red and green chile to dip them into. Because of the owners' ancestry, besides New Mexican favorites, the restaurant also offers Greek food. Lamb sliced from the vertical rotisserie (intended for gyros) is always available to the dish washer as long as it is surreptitiously obtained.

The second and most wonderful factor of the boy's situation is the phenomenon, the happenstance, the fortuitous occurrence of a walking dream: Cassie. Cassandra Constanza Santos is a waitress at the Plaza Restaurant. She courses between the tables adeptly balancing a tray laden with slices of tres leches, the traditional three milk cake. She is, to the boy's estimation, sweeter than the cake. But unlike the cake, she may be off-limits for him.

Certainly, Cassie flirts with the cooks and the busboys, and right under his nose! His nose, which is out of joint because she ignores him.

He has learned that she is originally from a small town up in the mountains called Chimayó. She moved to Santa Fe, which she thinks of as the "big city," last year after graduating from high school. She is working to earn enough money to attend college at New Mexico Highlands University in Las Vegas, New Mexico, where she wants to study to become a teacher. The boy has no such desire to attend a college; another barrier between him and the girl.

No girl, no place to live, no prospects for much beyond the drudgery of dish washing. He is done with his shift and crosses the street to sit on one of the benches in the Plaza. A lone crow lands on the grass before him, delinquent from its murder. A bus pulls up; painted blue and white, the Gothic lettering on the side identifies it as belonging to Grace of God Gospel Camp, Colorado Springs, Colorado. A gaggle of teenaged boys and girls, splendidly outfitted in matching blue and white shirts flits out from the bus. They head for the Gap store on the other side of the park.

"May I join you?" she says as she sits beside him: Cassie.

The shock of having the object of his closeted desire not only talk to him (the first time ever), but being now so close, so almost touching, renders him speechless. Sends him spinning into a limbo world where he vegetates, like the blind, deaf, and dumb boy of the Whos' *Tommy*. See me, feel me, touch me…heal me…

"Oh, I…yes, please," he manages to croak out.

"Bruce said you're being kicked out of the hostel. That's a shame. Do you have a place to go?" Bruce also works at the restaurant, another human being for whom the boy is anonymous.

"Ah…no. I have to look around. Places are so expensive."

"Oh, I know! I stay with two other girls to make ends meet."

"That must be nice. I mean…"

"You could crash on our couch for few days until you get something."

"Oh, I don't…I think…I could do that? I couldn't put you out, though."

"It would be fun to have a man around the house. Angélica and Marisa won't mind. They bring boys home all the time. It's my turn."

He is wedged between Angélica and Marisa in the back seat of Bruce's 1969 Camaro. The restored muscle car is a two-door, four-seater and quite cramped for the three sweating bodies in the back.

Bruce is driving, Cassie sits shotgun, her arm hanging out the window as they drive up the main drag of Espanola. Bruce, kitchen staff and sometimes cook at the Plaza Restaurant, has offered to take the girls white water rafting down the Rio Grande. Cassie has insisted the boy be included. Bruce has agreed, although reluctantly. He senses the boy's interest in Cassie; it conflicts with his own.

They will be taking Highway 68 up toward Taos, passing Verlarde and Embudo and Dixon, to their destination at Pilar on the big river. Still in Espanola, Bruce stops at Saints and Sinners, a drive-through liquor store. At the window he orders a quart bottle of Budweiser. "And would you open that for me?" he asks. 'I've got no church key."

Just past Verlarde the road skirts the river. The river begins to fall away into a gorge on their left while steep rock walls rise on their right. It is a misconception that the river has carved the gorge from the bedrock over unimaginable millennia—not so. New Mexico is split down the middle where tectonic plates separated during ancient periods of intense volcanic upheaval; the rift was filled in with sand and debris, making a soft bed for the river to further erode. Miles upriver the gorge drops to a depth of 800 feet. There it is spanned by the Taos Gorge Bridge, a spectacular landmark much visited by the curious, and the suicide inclined.

As they approach Pilar the road and the river share a common elevation for a brief time. Just before the turnoff to Pilar there is small parking area. It is next to part of the river known as "the Karnic Wave Rapid." Bruce tosses his empty beer bottle out of the window and pulls into the parking area.

"Shoulda got a six pack," Bruce says. "Jeffy ain't here yet." Jeffy is Bruce's long-time buddy. He is important mainly because he is the one with the rubber raft. An hour passes and the entourage strolls along the river, watching kayak runs and the occasional commercial rafting company boat filled with eager tourist families, their skin shining from sunscreen and their straw hats wobbling in the wind, about to take wing in the breeze. Finally, Jeffy roars into the parking area in a vintage Ford pickup, the rubber raft secured in its bed with a tangled forest of bungie cords.

The boat is unloaded and dragged to the water's edge. Jeffy drives away. "Isn't your friend coming with us?" Cassie asks Bruce. "He'll pick us up at the bottom of the rapids and bring us back to the car," he answers. "Aren't we supposed to have life jackets?" the boy asks.

"Can't you swim?" is Bruce's response. All in all, the boy is not happy with the prospect of white water rafting. The boy examines the rubber raft and cannot overcome his apprehension upon viewing the many ragged patches on what is clearly an army surplus craft. The only question is, from which war?

Bruce throws an oar at him. "Make yourself useful," he taunts. The oars are not for propelling the craft, the river with take care of that. They are for steering. Avoiding sharp rocks and low bridges is essential on this stretch of river called The Racecourse. Cliffs of shining quartzite on one side, impossibly black basalt cliffs, the vomit of ancient volcanos, on the other. This rushing deluge of bone-shaking white water called the Racecourse, is what is termed a Class IV run. Waves thrown up higher than the boat and "holes"—dips in the water where a drop is treacherous. All of it is well known to rafting and kayaking aficionados: Saddle Rock, the Mile Long Rapids, the Souse Hole, the Sleeping Beauty, the Cheese Grater, the hazard at Glen Woody bridge, the narrow channels at low water, the Slot at Big Rocks, the Final Drop. It is a good place to get wet.

"Really, Bruce" he says, "aren't we supposed to have life jackets? Isn't it a law or something?"

Bruce scoffs; the roommates, Angélica and Marisa giggle. The boy has been staying with Cassie for one week now and has formed an opinion of Angélica and Marisa. Although in their mid-twenties, they are callow and petty—over-ripe adolescents; he might use the word, "featherbrained" to describe them. And yet, their amusement at his treatment by Bruce reinforces his self-doubt and his disconsolate state of being. Cassie, at least, takes his side with a demure smile. This is fleeting, however, as Cassie turns her attention to Bruce's bravado and boasting—he is a seasoned expert, he says, at this boating business.

They are afloat. The current seizes the rubber raft and twirls it into midstream like a lonely leaf in an autumn rainstorm. They are facing backwards. "Row!" commands Bruce, and after a few ill-fated attempts at turning the boat around, they manage to point the bow downstream. Angélica and Marisa giggle.

The river doesn't care if it sweeps them away riding on top or beneath its furious foam; they are just so much flotsam to the river. They are random rocks to roll along, to etch round and smooth as a baby's ass. The river whips, leaps, thunders, slaps. The little boat bobs and threatens to topple but somehow stays on top of the foam. The argonauts are holding on to a rope attached to the raft's edges, fed through rubber loops like a belt on a fat man. A flat fat man. Now and then Bruce makes feeble attempts at steering with his oar—until it slips from his grip. The oar rides the rapids alongside of the raft. Father and child at odds with the elements.

Water. The planet's life blood. Flowing by gravity from mountain to ocean. Collected from sky and aquifer. It could be placid; it could be furious. It could be the Racecourse, pushing along toward the Gulf of Mexico so far away. Pushing along a little rubber raft containing arrogant humans (rulers of the planet? —a delusion.) Consider sister water carried by wind across the ocean, rotating at impossible velocity, making landfall, flattening cities—who is the ruler now? The river, by comparison to the hurricane, is just a small squirt of fury. But big enough to taunt, to cause the foolish to challenge it. Perhaps the river laughs. Perhaps it cries.

Bruce stands in the bow, arms stretched out like a Captain Ahab embracing the sight of a Great White Whale. He lets out a whoop. The roommates giggle, all except Cassie. Cassie yells over the roar of the river—get down, get down! The boy, secretly hoping Bruce will take a well-deserved plunge, twists the rope more tightly around his own free arm. The raft collides with a large rock protruding, as rocks will do, from the shallows before a big drop. The raft flips, tumbles into a hole—holes are a dangerous feature of white water, caused by water pouring over submerged rocks or dead trees; the river flows backwards here, toward the rocks, a cycling turbulence to trap the unwary.

Everyone is thrown from the boat into the hole. The boat frees itself and is carried down river, dragging the boy who is still tangled in the rope. The others fight to gain the surface, swallowing the river water, thrashing arms against the current. Angélica pops up, gasps for air, treads water as she tries to orient herself. Marisa has dog-paddled to shore and pulls herself up to safety. Bruce is upside down under the surface, kicking in the wrong direction. His head hits bottom. He is lucky not to have knocked himself unconscious. He manages to right himself and swim to the surface. He sees Angélica reaching shore. But where is Cassie?

The boy, dragged behind the rubber boat like a sea anchor on a ship of the realm, is buffeted by the river's shallow bottom. He twists trying to free himself, manages some crucial gulps of air. He passes closely by a sweeper, a fallen tree; the turbulence tosses the boat and its reluctant passenger violently. Now swift current, a turn in the riverbed, and two great rocks directly in his path. The obstructions cause a sieve, a narrow channel where the water is funneled into a raging pressure wave. Sucked against the rocks, the boat hangs as upstream water slams into it. He flails hopelessly, battered by the relentless boil of angry water.

Ironically, he still holds the oar in his free hand. He thrusts this down against the riverbed; it gives him enough leverage to gain access to the jammed boat. Now he can pull his bleeding arm from the rope. He jumps, the current carries him around the side of the sieve and sends him on a new journey of pain. He is exhausted. It is a struggle just to stay afloat much less to swim to the river's edge. He considers letting the river take him to a peaceful eternity—to simply let it fill his lungs with liquid death.

There is a shout from the bank: "Someone's in trouble in the river!" The river drowns out further human noises. He loses consciousness as strong hands, the end of a human chain that has waded to his rescue, clamp on his leg, pull him ashore. The mighty Rio Grande will not claim another victim this day—at least not at this bend of the river.

He wakes in the day ward of St. Vincent's Hospital in Santa Fe. He has three broken ribs and is bruised raw and feels like a recently skinned rabbit, only bigger. The two giggling roommates are visiting although he will be released later today. They have brought a few sprigs of Russian Sage they have stolen from someone's garden. It is now that he learns that Cassie won't be coming home. Her lifeless body must have floated right past him when he was hung up on the rocks. He wishes he had died as well.

Angélica and Marisa tell him he can still stay with them, at least until he is better. They need the money. He is not convinced he wants to go back to work at the Plaza Restaurant. There is too much pain associated with it now. His broken ribs will heal but his broken heart will not. And then there is Bruce. Of course, it was just an accident. An accident caused by Bruce.

One week later he still hasn't returned to the restaurant. He loiters daily on the Plaza, Santa Fe's city square, beneath tall cottonwoods and oaks. Today he ventures across San Francisco street and enters the F. W. Woolworth store. He sits at the lunch counter and orders a Frito pie. Some say this strange dish was invented here at Woolworth's by Teresa Hernandez in the early 1960s. Others point to a recipe printed on a Fritos bag in 1962 or to that company's 1949 recipe cookbook which touted items like Frito meatloaf and salmon croquettes made with Fritos. Teresa's pie is unique, however, and consists of an orange, snack-sized bag of Fritos sliced longways, drenched with New Mexico red chile (not chili, which is a meat dish found in Texas), sprinkled with grated cheese, and topped with sliced onions. There is no meat offered here, unless the diner wishes to add sliced hot dogs. The boy skips the hot dogs and savors the hot, spicy pie, scooping it up with a plastic spoon.

A man sits next to him and orders a cup of coffee. The boy senses that the man is eyeing him, and this makes him uncomfortable. There are all sorts of predators out there, and Santa Fe is no exception. The man smiles and says, "What happened to you? You look like death warmed over!" referring to the still healing abrasions on his face and arms.

He forces a laugh. And: "You should see the other guy!"

"You a local? Looking for a job, perhaps?"

"Well…"

The boy considers the man's appearance: neat in dress shirt and tie (loosened), but no sport coat. Recent haircut, manicured nails. Some sort of businessman—a realtor? But that doesn't preclude the possibility that this is a come-on. One incongruity: Adidas running shoes with those little half socks the boy thinks are creepy. Still, a job?

"My name is Sidney Bertrand…Sid for short. I am with the Kiwanis Club of Santa Fe. I'm currently trying to round up a crew to help build Tico Coco."

"Tico Coco?"

"You know about Zozobra, certainly." The man waits for the affirmative nod. "Every year we burn the 50-foot puppet of Old Man Gloom that we call Zozobra over in Fort Marcy Park, right? Fire dancers and fireworks and big crowds yelling 'Burn him, burn him!' and all that."

"Yes…I haven't been to one, but I know about it."

"So, Zozobra was originally started by Will Shuster back in 1924. Gave the rights to the Kiwanis in '64. Back in 1940, they had a movie premiere here for *The Santa Fe Trail*. Errol Flynn, Olivia de Havilland, and Ronald Reagan were in that. Shuster built another big puppet to celebrate the event. Called it Tico Coco, Zozobra's cousin. This one was only 38-feet tall. We want to bring Tico Coco back. He'll burn a week or so before Zozobra and we'll have children for fire dancers. It will get Fiesta off to an even bigger start than usual!"

"How much does it pay?"

"Twelve dollars an hour, but it's short term."

It is more than he makes at the restaurant. Any qualms he might have about Sid Bertrand disappear. "When do I start?"

He starts the very next day, working on the big puppet in the back yard of Bertrand's compound, a mini-estate on Camino Pinones near the Old Pecos Trail. Tico Coco will be built in sections, then transported by truck and assembled for its first and last stand later at Fort Marcy Park. He is working on the wooden frame where the arms will be attacked with large hinges and manipulated by pulleys. Next to him another young man is covering a roundish wooden frame with chicken wire, which will eventually, through the medium of papier-mâché, become Tico Coco's bulbous, scrap-paper filled head. There are several boys about his age in the compound working on Tico Coco.

The older Zozobra, was at first modeled to appear as a Spanish Conquistador, in parody of the Fiesta celebration held each year commemorating Don Diego de Vargas reconquering the territory of Nuevo México in 1692 after the Pueblo Revolt of 1680. (Those wacky collaborators, the Society of Quien Sabe, drinking bubbies including Will Shuster Jr., Gustave Baumann, and others, styled the first Zozobra with goatee and flopping mustache, but over the years, this has given way to a more clownish countenance, albeit grotesque and purposely frightening.) Tico Coco will be almost a parody of Zozobra—a parody of a parody. Bug eyes, bushy eyebrows, bow tie and tuxedo will be there as inherited. The ritual, the music, the fire dancers, and the shouts of "Burn him!" will also prevail, or so it is hoped.

Two days before the big event, Tico Coco's elements are completed. It is a hot July afternoon. A lone raven sits on the adobe wall squawking congratulations. Sid Bertrand summons the boys into the main house for lemonade and celebration of, he says, a job well done. The boy has not been inside the house before. There are shelves built into the stuccoed walls upon which sit very old pueblo pottery from San Ildefonso, Santa Clara, Acoma, and Zia, together with Hopi and Navajo Kachinas. The Saltillo tiled floor is covered with a scattering of Navajo rugs. A long table of heavily carved wood is set with bowls of tortilla chips and salsa. Sid moves to an elaborate hi-fi system occupying the top of a rustic pine sideboard, places a record on the turntable, and carefully lowers the needle onto the vinyl platter's surface. It is a memorial edition of the best of Judy Garland. *Born in a Trunk* begins to play.

As the boy munches chips Sid comes over to him and places an arm around his shoulder. Does he want to stay over, Sid asks. The boy replies that he has to be somewhere tonight. Thanks, but no thanks. He makes a hasty retreat as soon as he sees that Sid is not watching. Obviously, his first instincts had been correct. He had come to admire the man for his generosity in giving him a job and for the brief environment of camaraderie Bertrand created of boy-help, albeit suspect for potential debauchery. This is not for him; it is unsettling, frightful.

Back at the casita where he is staying, he tells Angélica about his experience. Is there something about me, he wants her to tell him, that made the man think he could…

"Well," says Angélica, "you are sort of…mild mannered. In a manly way, I mean. But you're not aggressive. You know, you've lived with three woman without ever…"

"It's not that I didn't want to," he answers. "I just…"

"You are a good person. And if it turns out that you're queer, I'll still like you."

"But I'm not!"

Marisa has been listening to this exchange between her two roommates. She beams a meaningful smile at Angélica. "You know what?" she says. "I think our boy is a virgin. I think we are obligated to do something about it."

What follows will remain in the boy's memory as a milestone of the first degree. The hasty shedding of clothing tossed about like jetsam from a storm-lashed ship. His inept struggling soon abandoned, and deservedly so, as hands and lips explore and skin touches skin and the weight of first one, then the other, presses on him. And the rhythm of their lovemaking transports him to a place of unimagined sensation.

The following day he goes to Fort Marcy Park to help assemble the finished sections of Tico Coco. The park sits on a hill overlooking the City Different. In 1846, when the territory was still part of Mexico, the United States declared war and marched into the city of Santa Fe, liberating it (another liberation in the city's history of Indian to Spanish to Indian to Spanish to Anglo occupation). A fort of adobe walls was constructed on the site but abandoned in 1868. In 1887, a tourist from Silver City was exploring the old fort and discovered a catch of gold coins hidden in one of the walls. The ensuing frenzy of searchers, digging and tearing down the remaining walls, effectively destroyed the fort. Now the site is a city park.

The boy is no longer afraid of Sid Bertrand. He approaches him as the man oversees the raising of the giant puppet. He explains that he appreciates the kindness he has been shown, but he is not gay. He knows he is not, and makes this clear to Bertrand, not expecting the man to feel rejected, nor for that rejection to turn into hostility. But Sid answers, "You may go now. Your assistance is no longer needed here." Another lesson in life for the boy.

He decides to return to the Plaza Restaurant to see if he can get his old job back, or perhaps, a better position as busboy or waiter. He is ready to confront Bruce. There is the clatter of dishes and the roar of steam from the big sinks in the kitchen as he walks in to find his old supervisor. There is a new boy scrubbing pots and pans. He learns there is no opening for kitchen staff at the present time. So sorry, come back real soon. Bussing? Waiting? He still looks too beaten up to be a waiter. Maybe busboy if he'll work the late shift. He takes the job. There is no sign of Bruce, for which, at this moment, he is glad. One thing at a time.

The next day is the newly initiated, first annual burning of Zozobra's cousin, Tico Coco. It will commence as dusk gives way to darkness. He asks if he can quit work early to attend the burning and is given permission once he agrees to a double shift tomorrow. When he arrives at Fort Marcy Park there are already a few hundred people there, blankets spread, beer coolers open, and cans of Dos Equis XX lager and Pepsi Lite dispensed. Eager children run through the labyrinth of folding chairs and blankets waving sparklers or whip-like things of glow-in-the-dark plastic. Some of the spectators have brought boxes of paper consumables to place at Tico Coco's feet: old receipts, paid bills, junk mail, advertising circulars, unpaid parking tickets, divorce papers.

He sees Sid Bertrand in a last-minute organization of the fire dancers, all of them young boys. Unlike at the Zozobra burning, the fire dancers will not sport flaming torches. The music starts, blaring from loudspeakers, accompanied by terrifying growls from Tico Coco. The puppet's long arms raise and lower and the crowd begins their chant: "Burn him!"

He moves closer to the front of the crowd to see better. There is a rip in the cotton covering near the hinge for the left arm; he had worked on that part of the puppet, and now he sees what might be a fault in the construction: splintering wood. No matter, he thinks, it's going up in flames in a second or two. Now a lone female dancer, dressed in the diaphanous garments of a young sprite (although she is a woman well past her forties), comes carrying a lighted torch. She dances around and around the puppet, taunting it with the flame. The puppet roars. The crowd yells, "Burn him!" Then, a pause in the music, and she touches the torch to Tico Coco. Bottle rockets go off behind him. Flames lick up the sides of the puppet.

He sees Bruce in the crowd. Bruce is coming toward him. Now is not the time he would prefer for confronting the man about the drowning, but there will be no choice in the matter. Bruce calls out something to him which he cannot hear clearly over the crowd's chanting. It is an ugly face turned toward him; no doubt ugly words issue from the twisted mouth. The devil is attending the incineration of one of his minions. Flames from the burning puppet alternately illuminate and cast shadows on the ugly face—flickering light and dark making the approaching devil resemble Bela Lugosi, bent on mayhem. The music, the dancers, the spectacle, all contribute to a hallucinatory state. Bruce now reaches him. He reaches out—it is only a friendly gesture, but...

The boy pushes at Bruce and retreats backwards, falling over the platform on which the conflagrated puppet sits flaring like a beacon (Earth to stars; City Different to cities ordinary). His impact against the hastily built platform jiggles lose the faulty arm, now high on its arc. It falls, spilling kindled wooden structure, blazing cotton covering, and waste-paper stuffing in front of the audience. It lands squarely on the boy.

Bruce does not hesitate. Bruce springs into action. Bruce pulls the boy from the burning puppet parts, rolls him over and presses down on him with his own body, smothering the flames. Both have serious second-degree burns. Both are medivacked to the University of New Mexico Hospital's Burn Center in Albuquerque.

Some days later the shades have been cracked open enough to allow splintered light to dance across their faces. They wake. The boy and his rescuer are roommates, an ironic turn of events by way of the boy's thinking; a satisfactory vindication as Bruce would characterize it. Slowly recollection of events creeps into the boy's as yet fuzzy consciousness. He remembers the Bruce-wise threat coming at him, but beyond that...nothing.

"What did you do to me?" he asks Bruce, convinced that the villain of the Rio Grande had attacked him.

"I saved your fucking ass! You knocked over the damn puppet...don't you remember? I pulled you out of the flames and we both got burned, I guess."

The boy smolders silently, considering this. If it is true...

"You saved my life! Why did you do that?"

"I couldn't save her. I had to save you." This confession (of sorts) is uttered painfully—both through the pain of emotional conflict and that of the rending of bandaged facial tissue.

The boy settles back, seeking oblivion and release from this new reality. It is difficult to rid oneself of hatred, envy, and sublimated guilt. Now there is silence. Quietude and peace most dearly needed. Peace of mind as old resentment dissipates. Peace of body as medication flows through IV into blood stream.

Many days later they sit in obligatory wheelchairs in the lobby of the hospital, having been discharged and loaded up with bags of ointments and pain relievers while they wait for the shuttle which will transport them back to Santa Fe. Visiting ladies in print dresses carry bouquets bought at the gift shop toward the elevators. Nurses in stiff-starched uniforms hustle and bustle, opening and closing doors to green-painted corridors. The smells of antiseptic scrub-downs linger and will haunt their memories in the days to come.

"Coming back to work at the restaurant?" Bruce asks.

"Dunno," says the boy. "I think I might go back to Illinois."

"What's in Illinois? Family? A girl?"

"I left there because of that. I did a girl wrong. We were young...thought we were in love. You can figure out the rest. It's kind of funny, Angélica and Marisa thought I was a virgin."

"Why you sly old fox. I thought you were pretty much of a dork."

"A sorry one. A repenting one. A born again one...now that I've had a baptism of fire."

THE YEAR THE YUCCA BLOOMED

When he was a village dog he was called Penguin—if anyone referred to him at all. He liked to hang out on the boardwalk, begging scraps from tourists exiting the ice cream parlor, or to wander down the middle of the road in defiance of progress—the tourists' cars were unable to achieve much progress with an unruly dog in their path. Penguin was the color of New Mexico dirt with patches of a variety of unidentifiable substances rolled-in and matted. His chin whiskers stuck out at odd angles and his stubby tail kept time with the squawking of the myriad ravens that incessantly circled the small village of Margarona, New Mexico. He didn't belong to anybody. He was his own dog; a dog's dog with an independent soul. The village belonged to Penguin, not the other way around.

Things weren't so good around Margarona in those days. Not for people much less for dogs. Some of the locals from the town saw that Penguin wasn't going to make it through the oncoming winter. That's when they took him up the mountain to Paul's place where he would join Paul's pack of eight or nine dogs, six cats, a donkey, three goats, and six horses. When Jenny and Mandolin Dan dropped Penguin at Paul's Tarantula Ranch off the Placerville Road, the man and the dog stood still and studied each other as if waiting for some great truth to be revealed. Nothing presented itself. But nothing was good enough for the man and the dog.

"They call him Penguin 'cause he walks funny," said Jenny. Her battered Stetson was wrapped with some dead animal, Davy Crocket style. The gap between her front teeth reminded Paul of the joke about Margarona: What is a pretty woman in Margarona? One with all her teeth.

"I'll call him Gris because he looks gristly," replied Paul.

If Penguin/Gris could have understood what was being said he might have thought, "You should talk, you old coot." But the Tarantula Ranch dog pack had begun their investigation of him, sniffing and poking cold noses at his belly as he flopped over in a submissive posture intended to assure his admission to the canine social order.

Paul had been a rodeo cowboy in the Texas and Oklahoma panhandles until a bronco threw him coming out of the gate. After that his right leg had never been strong enough to ride anything with a wild disposition. His affinity for horses led him to Hollywood where he became a trainer and extra in western features. Some say the novel, "The Horse Whisperer," was based on Paul. He could calm a spooked colt and lead it through fire if need be. He was still in demand after he retired to New Mexico and occasionally worked when westerns were filmed locally, but he preferred to hang at his Tarantula Ranch where he boarded horses and donkeys for other people.

Paul loved horses so much he had built an addition onto his trailer with wide doors and a gravel floor so he could bring them indoors when his bad leg restricted his own movements. He had opened up one long wall so his living space, elevated four feet above the gravel floor, overlooked this combination indoor corral, barn and tack room. Adorned with old rodeo posters and a battered guitar, Paul's digs suited his minimal and peaceful life-style.

With her long graying hair hanging loose to her shoulders, Jenny sometimes seemed like an over-the-hill earth mother to Paul, but he knew she had a good heart. After all, she'd rescued that mangy dog. In fact, most of Paul's pack had come up from the village as rescued dogs brought by Jenny and her friends. Paul even thought she was pretty good looking. Even she hadn't all her teeth.

"You need to come down to the restaurant, Paul," said Jenny. "We haven't seen you in a while." Her eyes reminded Paul of Elizabeth Taylor's: deep violet and luminous as if lit from within.

"Aw, that lout-tay is too rich for my blood."

"Latte, Paul. And that's for the tourists. I've got some good old chicory I can trot out for you."

"Yeah, your place is real good for local gossip, Jenny. What do you hear lately?"

Mandolin Dan, who had been quietly studying a huge candelabra cholla cactus that served as a key element in Paul's landscaping, or lack thereof, suddenly spoke. "Did you see some fool is looking for water down in the gulch?"

"I thought old McKennedy had water witched all over down there and found nothing."

"He's never wrong," offered Jenny.

"Oh, yeah, he told me this place was haunted with the ghost of Indians that the Spanish massacred way back when. Only I ain't never seen no ghosts here."

"Your place has a good vibe, Paul," said Mandolin Dan. Paul knew this was quite a compliment, coming from Dan who rarely contributed to conversations unless they were about music. He played a mean Mandolin and could keep up in the blues, funk or even minor classical pieces but otherwise he didn't say much.

"Well," Paul replied, "Whoever it is will be drilling for a long, long time before they get water down there. It's nothing but shale."

That night, as Paul lay in bed with Gris curled up at his feet, he was awakened by the loud braying of Moses, the donkey. He shook out his boots in case some critter had crawled into them in the night, pulled them on and hurried outside with Gris at his heels. The sky was solid with blackness even as the first few stars pricked through with an impossible brilliance. Ordinarily, even the distant whining of coyotes couldn't break the heavy silence of the New Mexico night, but Moses was braying and kicking the wooden corral fence, making commotion enough to wake those Native American ghosts.

"Whoa there, boy," Paul said as he stroked Moses' neck. As the donkey began to settle down Paul became aware of a faint noise. Sounds carried for miles in the high desert, even up here on the mesa, and at first he couldn't determine its direction. Then, as he realized what it must be, he turned toward the gulch and held his breath. A steady ca-chunk, ca-chunk met his ears.

Gris added to the surveillance with his own acute dog sense of smell. The various horse and other animal odors overlaid with the rich sticky sweetness of juniper slowly gave way to another scent he didn't recognize. A harsh, metallic aroma not unlike the underside of Paul's pickup truck but with an added ingredient: something ancient and dead. Paul and Gris exchanged quizzical looks. Now why would those fools be drilling at night?

In the morning, the chores involved feeding and watering of Paul's resident menagerie. Corn meal mush and fried ham with hot coffee for Paul, timothy and oats for the horses and donkey, alfalfa and sweet feed for the goats and kibble for the dogs and cats to supplement their usual diet of pack rats and jack rabbits. Gris followed along, helping by growling and snapping at the cats trying to steal the honey-coated oats from Jules, Jim and Juliette, the flop-eared French mountain goats.

Most days Paul would ride Brown Beauty bareback out onto the mesa with an entourage consisting of the dog pack and Moses the donkey. Brown Beauty was a three-year-old mare named after the horse Paul Revere rode on his famous midnight ride. Although not mentioned by name in the Longfellow poem, Paul had read somewhere that the "steed flying fearless and fleet" was borrowed from a neighbor and most likely was named Brown Beauty. The name fit the horse well with her shining dark coat and long flowing mane.

Today, however, Beauty got a saddle. The saddle blanket with its Navajo design Paul had picked up in El Paso one winter. He pulled the cinch tight and checked the length of the stirrups. Satisfied, he buckled the holster to his belt that would hold his single action Ruger Vaquero, a .357 magnum "six-gun" modeled after the famous Colt Peacemaker revolver popular over a century ago. He checked the barrel and slid five rounds into the cylinder. Although this gun had been designed not to fire unless fully cocked, he didn't like to have a live shell under the hammer while it was in the holster. There was plenty of time to pull back the hammer and aim if he encountered a rattler.

And today Moses and the dogs would not be invited. Gris emitted a mournful noise that made Paul think he could almost talk. It sounded like "Take me along," or at least Paul thought so. The scruffy mutt had a bum leg like his new master and Paul knew he couldn't keep up with Brown Beauty.

"Oh, Hell's bells," said Paul, "See if you can jump up here."

Bending down to receive the excited dog with one arm, Paul placed one hand on the pommel and one foot in the stirrup, then swung up on Beauty, dog in tow. His bad leg ached with a sudden sharp pain. With Moses complaining from his corral and a few of the other dogs following tentatively, Paul, Gris and Brown Beauty headed down the mesa toward Dolores Gulch. One by one, the dog pack gave up and returned to the ranch for their morning naps.

The Ortiz Mountains, of which Paul's mesa was a foothill, were once the scene of the first gold rush in the new West. Some twenty plus years before the California gold rush, a mining town sprang up there called Real de Dolores. Now virtually disappeared, Dolores was once the center for thousands of placer miners, hungry to extract the glittering metal from the dusty soil. Because the gold was deposited as small flakes and particles, the miners needed water to separate it from the soil. Water was scarce and the going was slow. The inventor, Thomas Edison, came to the Ortiz to attempt to remove the gold electrically with a process he had invented. He lost half a million dollars trying.

There was no trail from the Tarantula Ranch to Dolores Gulch. Paul wound his way through twisted juniper and piñon until he came to the arroyo. Following this and carefully avoiding the loose rocks and small boulders, he traveled gradually downhill. He knew about the ghost town of Dolores and its history. He knew also that Native Americans had lived here and done their own mining for centuries before the Europeans came. The silver and gold they found didn't interest them much. But they treasured the shiny blue stones they found as they dug for lead which they used to paint their pottery. And faces. And they probably died young of lead poisoning.

There was a rise ahead. Paul could see the top of the drilling rig just above it. "Big rig!" he thought. A red-tailed hawk drifted lazily across the sky, a small furry creature in her talons. Paul eased Brown Beauty up the rise. The noise level increased. Gris began to squirm against Paul's legs. A view of the valley below met his eyes. He saw a huge impact drill pounding viciously away at the hard earth. Surrounding it were half a dozen men, their faces gaunt, their shirts soaked with sweat. "What the hell?" He saw that the men carried rifles slung over their shoulders. He saw a tall barbed wire fence surrounding the rig. He saw one of the men turn and look up.

The sun, El Ojo Rojo, is rising blurry-eyed over Margarona, New Mexico. A tiny dust devil swirls down the partially paved main street, dancing to the discordant harmony of a braying cloistered goat and llama. In the bed of an old rusting Toyota pickup parked at a no-parking sign lies a bedraggled dog, chin on paws, stubby tail slowly undulating, his eyes gazing at nothing in particular, his ears perked for deciphering distant noises only he can hear. Down the street, scooting on a skate-board, comes a young girl, a baby clutched tightly in her arms. She rolls past the Turquoise Gift Shop, past sway-backed miners' cabins, past slag heaps and old mine tailings, past the Camposanto Viejo, the old Spanish cemetery. A few chickens wander cackling down the road as the musty village wakes.

Margarona, once a booming coal mining town, nearly died a ghostly death when the railroads turned from coal to diesel fuel. Miners' cabins, a boarding house, a bar and a company store were cheap to buy or rent and so became populated by hippies and burned-out Vietnam vets in the early 1970s. Artists, musicians, and expatriate stockbrokers trying to write the great American novel reversed the slow death threatening Margarona, retaining the "ghost town" essence while eager to earn visitors dollars from tchotchke gift galleries.

As the skateboarding girl makes her second traverse of the town Jenny is sitting across from Paul and Mandolin Dan in the back of her restaurant. Jenny's idea of marketing is to change the restaurant's name every so often so folks will think it is a new place. It has been known variously as Quagmire Café, The Poets and Peasants, The Last Chance Café, The Silence of the Yams, Betty's Boop-a-teria, The Tattooed Lady, Trippers, and The Turquoise Goat. This week it is called The Bum Steer.

Paul is poking at the remains of his Huevos Rancheros while Dan devours a breakfast burrito with chorizo and red chile. Jenny is nursing a non-fat raspberry yogurt.

"Why were they guarding that well with rifles?" asks Jenny.

"Well, think about it," Paul replies. "Remember I said there wasn't any water there. Water is found in sandstone. That place is all shale."

"Then you mean they were drilling for…"

"Yes, oil! Black gold."

"But back in the '80s they dug some wells but they abandoned them."

"It was too expensive," interjects Mandolin Dan, wiping a dribble of chile from his chin. "The oil embargo had just ended and it cost more to get it out of the rock then it was worth on the market."

"So what's different now?"

"I think I can answer that." The three look up to see a thin young man wearing a Milwaukee Brewers sweatshirt and a baseball cap with a White Sox logo on it. He has a small, neatly trimmed goatee and steel rimmed glasses a few years out of style. He is edgy but steadfast in his approach, capturing three sets of eyes with an unwavering gaze. "I'm sorry, but I couldn't help overhearing your conversation. Maybe I can clear something up for you."

Mandolin Dan scowls, being the curmudgeon that he is. Paul simply stirs his huevos, his dead pan expression revealing no interest at all in this young interloper. Jenny, ever gregarious and at times almost bubbly to customers, gives him a gap-toothed grin, pushes an extra chair out from the table using her foot, and says, "Have a seat, partner. What's your name?"

"I'm Randal Wainwright the Third." Some huevos leave Paul's month during a muffled burst of incredulity.

"I'm Jenny, this is Dan and this is Paul."

"Let me ask a question," says Paul. "Why are you advertising two different baseball teams? Isn't that a conflict of interests?"

"Ha. No, you see, I was born on the south side of Chicago and I went to school in Madison, Wisconsin, where I now live when I'm not traveling. I'm loyal to both teams. Besides, they're in different leagues."

"You on vacation, then?"

"Business, actually. That's sort of what I wanted to talk to you about. I work for an organization called Concerned Citizens for a Peaceful Environment. I'm here to monitor oil drilling in New Mexico."

"That sort of like Green Peace, then?"

"No, they work at sea. We take on big environmental offenders on land."

Jenny can sense the words, "tree hugger," beginning to form on Paul's lips and seizes the conversation. "So you think our area is at risk from oil exploration?"

"You live in a beautiful and fragile environment with limited resources. Damage from drilling can be irreversible. I can cite many cases in the Western states where landowners have lost livestock from polluted water tables and ecosystems have been disrupted by impact from heavy truck traffic, noise, road building and laying pipelines."

"Well they can't come on my land," says Paul.

"Yes and no. New Mexico has split-estate ownership of property. You own the surface but not the mineral rights. The state can lease whatever may be under your property to anyone. In Colorado, mining rights were even sold to foreign countries who aren't required to uphold our laws and regulations."

"Why would they do that? Certainly not in New Mexico!"

"New Mexico has already sold millions of dollars of leases for oil exploration in your county. Even though there are some regulations in place to protect the environment, the truth is, the companies doing the exploring only need to find oil, not extract it. They then sell the wells to the big companies like Shell or Exxon and move along, often without cleaning up their messes"

"Certainly they aren't going to find much oil here. That's been tried before."

"This area is very rich in what is called shale oil. You usually think of an oil well as tapping into an underground reservoir of a big pool of liquid oil. Here the oil is trapped in the rock. They used to use strip mining techniques to get and crush the rock. It required great quantities of water to extract it not to mention the impact on the environment. Now they have new technologies to obtain gas and oil from shale. They force liquid chemicals into the well to open cracks in the rock. It's called fracturing, or frac'ing."

"Ah, they're trying to frack us over!"

"Exactly. The fluids contain toxic chemicals like carcinogen benzene and neurotoxins like toluene and xylene which can remain underground long after fracturing is completed and can find their way into the water table."

"Where do they get the water?'

"Once they use up your water, they'll truck in more. Also, they reclaim the water by storing it in huge pits above ground but it always ends up unpotable. And when they leave, they leave the pits. Frac'ing can also cause seismic events and even if they aren't drilling on your property, because they can drill down, turn 90 degrees and continue at an angle…they can affect the very structure of the ground you live on."

The three listeners are somber and suspended in muteness. Randal Wainwright the Third is surprised at the transformation he has caused but pleased with himself for his effectiveness. The silent interval finally becomes uncomfortable so he stands.

"Let me leave you with a flier for a presentation we'll be giving next week in Santa Fe. Trying to stir up some awareness. Well, nice meeting you," he says and exits the Bum Steer.

Jenny retreats to the kitchen to check on her staff, returning a few minutes later with a basket of sopapillas and a plastic squeeze bottle of honey.

"What do you think?"

"I think people that don't take off their hats indoors are exceptionally rude," answers Paul.

"I mean what do you think about the drilling?"

"It makes me mad. I wish we could do something."

"Maybe there is something we can do." The characteristically quiet Mandolin Dan seems awakened from a long hibernation. Something about the assuredness in his voice causes Paul and Jenny to attend to his next words. "Have you ever heard of the Monkey Wrench Gang?"

"Isn't that a novel by Edward Abbey about a group of hippy eco-terrorists?"

"Yes it is, but it just might have been based on some real people. And I just might have known a couple of them. Anyway, in the book, they decide to blow up the Glen Canyon Dam by floating a boat full of explosives down the Colorado River."

"Ha," says Paul. "We'd have to wait for the arroyos to start running to float anything down to Dolores Gulch. "

"But maybe we could rig something up."

"Are you serious?" asks Jenny. A twinge of fear flows through her followed by the sensation of excitement as she realizes what the three conspirators are contemplating. She wonders, could she do it? She can visualize the pristine high desert spotted with monstrous metal pumping stations, vast storage tanks and waste-water pools. She can also picture herself standing on the bluff above the drill site with a bottle, appropriately filled with gasoline, a cloth stuck down its neck, a match touched lovingly to the cloth, an arm cocked. She can feel the warmth of the missile as it passes close to her cheek, can see it arc majestically through the air, smash brilliantly into the derrick. She can see the flames leap high into the air....

Outside of the Bum Steer the tiny town of Margarona is coming to life. The dog, finally bored with his lot, jumps over the gate of the Toyota pickup and walks freely in the street, excited to be visiting his old haunts. A tour bus will soon be winding down the narrow road. The skateboard girl will be heading back toward the cemetery. Later, a journalist filming a documentary about the former ghost town will notice the stillness of the baby she carries and will discover the horrible reality, not only of its death, but of its death, burial and subsequent resurrection by the mother.

That was the year all the yucca bloomed. Their pale white forms seemed like delicate blossoms dancing on slender stalks. Rising high above sword-like leaves, they were, ironically, hard and brittle shells that rattled with tiny bullet-like seeds in the wind. Such an abundance of blooms only happens when the conditions are just right in the high desert. Either more rain than usual or less. Up on the mesa there was a white dotted landscape, no longer so brown, so dry, so desolate. The field of yucca gave way to scraggy chamisa and prickly pear. Beyond that was the oil rig. On the bluff above, Paul squatted secure behind an outcropping of rock, covering Jenny and Mandolin Dan with that cowboy gun of his; what he could have hit with it God only knows! Jenny and Dan crawled through the brush keeping low and out of sight of the guards. What a glorious day! Placing the bomb, setting the fuse. Watching the pandemonium after the blast.

Later at the Tarantula Ranch, Paul broke out a bottle of Patrón Añejo he had been saving for a special occasion and the three amateur eco-terrorists toasted their success. No one hurt. No one killed. And most importantly, no one caught in the act. They knew then they could do it again. And again. And again and again and again.

"Someone might have been hurt," Paul said.

"They weren't, though," Jenny replied. When Paul pointed out that it was only one well from many that would be drilled, Jenny's jubilance surrendered to an uncharacteristic seriousness.

"We need to find out where they're drilling next," she said.

"How do we do that?" Paul asked.

"I think I know how to find out. Remember that young boy from the environmental group? I bet he can tell us."

"Jenny, I hope you're not just looking for a left-handed monkey wrench," said Paul. At the quizzical glance Jenny aimed at him Paul continued. "It's a fool's errand. You'll be looking for something that doesn't exist."

"Information on oil drilling?"

"No, a way to stop it. They're bigger, richer, they have the establishment behind them, and they will counter attack."

"Paul, you're an old woman!"

Randal Wainwright the Third lay on his back in bed staring at the rough worn vigas on the ceiling of his short-term rental casita in the bario on Santa Fe's West Side. It was early afternoon and the soft sounds of children playing rode in on a silent breeze through the screenless window. He still had several hours before he would have to leave to pick up his supervisor at the Albuquerque Airport. Concerned Citizens for a Peaceful Environment, the organization he worked for, became nervous when things started going downhill—like when oil wells exploded and you had just given a somewhat rabble rousing speech about the evils of big oil companies. Still, Randal's conscience was clear—for that one anyway.

Why was he so attracted to older women, he wondered. When Jenny had offered to buy him lunch earlier that day he had thought, sure, a free meal would be nice. He hadn't counted on her deep violet eyes or her beguiling manner. As they had sat on the patio outside the Zia Dinner sipping margaritas and munching chips and guacamole he was seduced by her smile and her lighthearted banter. If an occasional reference to special knowledge he might have about the oil company slipped into the conversation, what was the harm?

He knew about the bombing of course, but he couldn't connect such a violent act with someone so soft, so sweet, and so sincerely interested in him. If he bragged about the intelligence gathering which was so crucial to the operation of an activist organization, so necessary for fund raising and establishing credibility for its constituents, well, perhaps that made up a little for his youthful self-consciousness and the transparency of his enthrall.

So when, after chiles rellenos for him and a bowl of posole with menudo and red chile for her, they had walked up toward the plaza. He had begun a free-wheeling dissertation on all aspects of the drilling company's plans to decimate the pristine South West. He knew, for example, not only where the designated drill sites were to be located, but where Toxacon, for that was what the evil oil exploration company was called—where their local development headquarters, and hence their maps, manuals and computers had been squirreled away out of sight and out of mind to the general, sometimes apprehensive, public. Wouldn't it be too bad if that were bombed!

"So tell me," Jenny had said, "what's so special about this secret headquarters?"

"It's not really secret, it's just that they want to remain incognito while they hatch their devious plans. They don't want demonstrators storming the portals of industry."

"How would you find it?"

"Hmm, well, you go out of town toward Agua Fria and keep going across the river and up toward the foothills. There's an old deserted ranch out there. You'll see some newer buildings with green metal roofs. Then you'll see an old adobe building. But if you are planning…"

"No, I'm just curious. What did you think about the bombing?"

"Not my style. If fact, it's the sort of thing we worry about. We don't want to be blamed for the acts of a few lunatics."

Jenny's voice lowered a pitch or two. "You have to understand, these lands have been fought over for hundreds of years. The Spanish fought the Indians for them and then the Americans fought the Spanish. They've been mined for silver, gold, coal and uranium. They've been paved over and sprawled upon by the homes of movie stars and what we call 'Republican Boat People'. Water has been pumped out of the aquifer to spray on golf courses. There's still a few hardy souls that take exception to the destruction of what's left."

"We are trying to stop that. Through political activism. Not with violence."

"Could be too little too late," replied Jenny.

Back in his casita, Randal reflected upon his tête-á-tête with Jenny. Why would a woman old enough to be his mother take an interest in a punk like him? Almost as if in answer to his question there came a knock on the door. A very loud knock. And several more. Randal rolled off the day bed and strolled across the Zapotec rug to investigate the clamor. Opening the door, he found himself staring up at a tall figure dressed in suit and tie. That's odd, he thought.

"Let me guess, FBI?"

"Special agent Cooper, Mr. Wainwright. We need to talk," answered the suit and tie. Cooper showed Randal his identification without even being asked.

Oh boy, thought Randal, just what I need. My boss will be really pissed about this. "What can I do for you?" he asked.

"Mr. Wainwright, we've been keeping an eye on you and your organization. Today I saw you at the plaza with a woman. She answers the description of a woman who was seen at the site of a recent bombing. Who is she?"

"Let me ask you a question. Did J. Edgar Hoover really wear women's underwear?"

For every action there is an equal and opposite reaction. Agent Cooper's reaction was more than equal. Randal found himself pushed against the wall of his casita with a fury that knocked his sense of humor for a loop.

"Listen, wise ass," growled Cooper, "we have you with the woman and we have her at the bombing, so that makes you an accessory to terrorists."

"Terrorists? They aren't trying to overthrow the government. Just destroying a little property."

Agent Cooper could have quoted the Congressional record of the Federal Bureau of Investigation's definition of eco-terrorism, to wit: "The use or threatened use of violence of a criminal nature against people or property by an environmentally oriented, subnational group for environmental-political reasons, or aimed at an audience beyond the target, often of a symbolic nature." Instead he just pushed Randal a little harder against the wall and asked again, "Who is she? Where do we find her? How would you like me to bring you in, Mr. Terrorist?"

Oh shit, thought Randal. "I don't know her name," he said. "She must have been at one of our rallies. She was asking me about the drilling company."

"What did you tell her?"

"I told her where Toxacon's headquarters are."

"Oh, my Lord!"

Near the village of Agua Fria, a traditional community virtually swallowed up by Santa Fe's modern expansion, the river crossing is not by bridge, but by descending the steep banks to slosh carefully across at low water. The road hardly appears on most maps but the locals use the crossing daily. That evening, Paul had found the road easily and maneuvered the Toyota pickup down the embankment and into the stream bed. Although he had neglected to lock the front axles in case he needed the four wheel drive, he was not concerned with being stuck in the river. He had other concerns. Beside him, riding shotgun (although the only gun in the truck was Paul's six shooter) was Mandolin Dan. In the cramped extended cab space behind them, Jenny squatted uncomfortably on three two-by-fours that served as a rumble seat. In the bed of the truck a small box was concealed under a blue plastic tarp which flapped in the wind like a gigantic Steller's Jay. Paul shifted down to first gear and started up the embankment to the other side.

If this were a Hollywood movie, the three conspirators would plant their explosives and escape while a thunderous crash shook the llano and a glorious ball of fire rose majestically above the piñon trees. They would ride off into the New Mexico sunset, its rosy glow turning the foothills of the Sangre de Cristo mountains a bloody deep crimson. Or, if this were a film noir, the femme fatale of the story, Jenny of the blue eyes, would drop the dime on her compadres and take up with the FBI agent who she would later double cross.

Or, if this were a tragic drama, Mandolin Dan would reveal his tragic flaw (that he's basically a wimp) which would cause him to freeze in fear at just the moment Jenny entered the line of fire unleashed by trigger happy FBI agents. Seeing her bullet racked body would send Paul over the edge revealing his tragic flaw (repressed anger) causing him to pull out his Ruger Vaquero and shoot a rather large hole in Dan's cranium.

Or, if this were a television comedy, our three friends, after many hilarious antics, would move to New York City. Two of them would marry and the other would join a rock and roll band. Which two? Take your pick: Jenny and Paul, Jenny and Dan, or Dan and Paul.

Or, if this were reality, the three desperados would be captured as they entered the Toxacon compound and brought to trial. Randal Wainwright the Third would convince Concerned Citizens for a Peaceful Environment's high-priced lawyer to represent them. The case would drag on for ten years and very probably one or more of them would die of environmentally induced cancer before it ended in a mistrial.

Or, if this were a digitally interactive tome you could simply click on the ending you preferred. But it's not. It isn't any of the above. It's just a simple story of three lonely people striking out against overwhelming odds. One of them, because it is his nature; another because she yearns for adventure; and one because he sees himself as guardian and protector of the frivolous.

The pickup rumbled up the dirt road scattering long-eared jack rabbits and mustering a moonlit haze of dust. Somewhere nearby, a coyote complained about the commotion. Paul slowed the pickup and killed the headlights as they neared the adobe building that served as headquarters for Toxacon, Inc. At the same time, Special Agent Cooper and his partner, Special Agent Roy "Paco" Rodriguez, were ensconced in a black Four Runner situated behind a large Juniper, awaiting the arrival of the eco-terrorists they believed would materialize out of the dark New Mexico night. Agent Cooper hadn't seen any significant action since the good old Vietnam protest days and would love to collar a radical or two. Agent Rodriguez, currently reassigned out of the Four Corners division, wasn't quite as vehemently opposed to ruffling corporate feathers and hadn't garnered much enthusiasm for the venture.

"See anything, Paco?"

"Nada, amigo. Not a creature is stirring, not even a pack rat."

Meanwhile, Paul, Dan and Jenny crept stealthily toward the adobe. Dan carried the box with a delicacy deserving of fine crystal or fresh eggs. Or nitroglycerine. There were no lights on in the building but they could see a soft glow from the indicator lights on several computers. Jenny went around the right side of the building while Paul did the same on the left. Suddenly a fierce barking shattered the silence. Paul came face to jowl with one of the largest pit bulls he had ever seen. Ah, the poor man's burglar alarm, he thought. Time for plan B. Plan B was a generous hunk of chuck roast wrapped in butcher paper. Paul tossed the roast, paper and all at the dog and the barking segued into a muffled munching.

"Paco, you hear anything?" quizzed Agent Cooper.

"No man. All's quiet on the Southwestern front."

"I think we should walk up to the house and check it out."

"If you say so, amigo. You sure this dude gave you the right info?"

"This is the place and this is the time he said they planned their caper."

"Hmm."

As the gastronomically occupied dog ripped and devoured huge chunks of $2.95 per pound of Albertson's finest meat, Dan approached the door of the adobe. Finding it locked he selected a good-sized rock, wrapped it in his jacket and swung it through the door's window. In a few seconds he was inside the building laying the box carefully down, opening it and twisting the dial on a kitchen timer attached with wires to some nasty looking brown cylinders. Two more seconds and he was out the door.

"Let's get out of here," he called. "Fast!"

"Wait," said Paul. "I've got to bring the dog."

Trying to pick up and move a very large pit bull who is busy enjoying a meal is no easy task. Paul threw his jacket over the dog and together with Dan, dragged, pulled, lifted, shoved and otherwise managed to get him down the trail toward the pickup, with Jenny close behind. The three almost outran the explosion. They were thrown to the ground, their ears ringing and blood running from their noses. Dazed, it was several minutes before they realized the adobe was in flames.

About this time the two FBI agents were sauntering up the long driveway to a very fancy adobe house in Las Campañas, a wealthy area north of Santa Fe. The resident of the six-million-dollar home was telephoning the security company he contracted to guard his estate who, in turn, were telephoning the Santa Fe Police. It was just possible that Randal Wainwright the Third had given agent Cooper the wrong address.

It was early September when the Yucca blossoms began to split open. Paul's goats, Jules, Jim and Juliette roamed freely on the mesa by the Tarantula Ranch, eagerly gobbling the seeds. A flock of ravens swirled above them swooping down to claim their share. Moses, the donkey, stood nearby, a stolid sentinel always alert for the threat of coyote packs. Paul and Jenny sat in the shade of an ancient piñon tree, enjoying the morning's serene advance. A handful of hummingbirds spiraled above a plastic feeder, vying for position. The promise of a peaceful day seemed indisputable.

Soon after their last escapade Harmonic Dan left for El Paso. It would be easy to jump across the border should the need arise, as he felt sure it would. Randal Wainwright the Third returned to Madison, Wisconsin. There would be very little to do in New Mexico now that the legislature, prompted by public outrage at the drilling, had recently passed new, tougher restrictions on oil exploration. Toxacon, Inc. had shelved their ambitions and would wait for the inevitable rise of oil prices to make their efforts profitable once again. Agent Cooper was recalled to the East Coast where he would soon become occupied with new concerns. Although he would have preferred to be tracking down Randal Wainwright the Third, that would not be in the cards.

Paul cracked open a red chile-soaked pistachio nut with his thumb and forefinger. "Thank you for bringing Gris back up to the ranch," he said to Jenny.

"No problem. The poor little tike was wandering around town again, trying to beg meals. I know he likes it up here."

"Jenny, I've been thinking. Why don't you move up here with me? You can always get somebody to look after the restaurant."

"You know, Paul, you could just as easily move down to the village and stay with me. You could get Pete or Bob to look after the horses."

"Seems like we've got a New Mexican stand-off here, huh?"

"Certainly looks that way."

"Jenny, I want you in my life."

"I'm in it, babe. It's just a bit of a commute, that's all."

Gusts of wind rolled along the mesa, announcing their progress with the whistling and rustling of the junipers. Close by a mockingbird started its litany of borrowed bird calls that even included the sound of a cell phone ringing. Perhaps the bird didn't realize there was little cell phone reception up there on the mesa. Perhaps it anticipated the ringing of Paul's land line. The telephone had been acquired after a long fight with the phone company who hadn't wanted to run a line all the way to the Tarantula Ranch. It came in handy to have a phone. Especially today.

"Your phone's ringing," said Jenny.

"Hang on, I'd better get it," said Paul.

Paul ambled over to his double-wide. A few minutes later he returned. "That was Margo, at the restaurant. She said to turn on the TV."

Television reception was marginally better than that of cell phones. Network signals rolled easily over the mountains between here and Albuquerque and were rarely disrupted even during the occasional lightning storm. Paul and Jenny sat on the bed and flipped on Paul's set. An unreal series of images began to unfold on the screen before them.

"Is it a movie?" asked Jenny.

"I really hope so," said Paul.

It was mid-morning, September 11th, 2001. NBC was transmitting a picture of one of the Twin Towers of the World Trade Center in New York City. Dense smoke billowed out of a gaping hole in the side of the building. The reporter was saying that a passenger airliner had crashed into the tower. As he speculated about how this could have happened, the picture showed a second airplane careening into the other tower. Al-Qaeda Terrorists had hijacked four US airliners and before long, a third would smash into the Pentagon while the fourth, heading for the Capitol or the White House, would crash into a field after brave passengers attempted to thwart the hijackers. Jenny and Paul watched the newscast in shock as the bizarre events unfolded.

Ambrose Bierce once said that experience is the wisdom that enables us to recognize in an old acquaintance, the folly that we have already embraced. Is it only a matter of degree that separates deep conviction from fanaticism? Is it the magnitude of our deeds that define their relative morality, or is it merely the thought that counts? Certainly, a great gulf divides acts of desperation and acts of hatred. If in heaven some will be rewarded for hate, then what of love? We can safety say the Paul, Jenny and Dan never again blew up anything. What happened to them after 9/11? Well, that's another story.

The Spanish have a saying for it: Así es la vida. Such is life.

NOSTALGIA

Nostalgia is defined as a wistful desire to return in thought or in fact to a former time, home or homeland, or to one's family and friends. It is a sentimental yearning for the happiness of the past. There is something so universal in this yearning that we identify with the remembrances of others, although they be far removed from our own history. When memory is faulty, invention fills in the blanks, true to the spirit, if not to the reality. Sometimes, however, pain must join with pleasure to give perspective to a nostalgic journey. This is a remembrance of a youth of post-war (WWII) Midwest. (It might have been me.)

Doc W____ wasn't the only dentist in town, but he was certainly the oldest. We speculated that he was at least one hundred and two, and his dental equipment was even older. I seem to remember that the drill was powered by foot pedals. Or hamsters. Doc W____'s office was on the second floor: a walk up a high staircase with windows overlooking a narrow, left-over sort of space between buildings where, it was said, a maniacal monkey lived. Although no one had ever seen the monkey we were sure of its existence and that it ate headstrong children thrown there after disobeying the dentist.

The waiting room had hard wooden chairs and old creased and stained comic books we had read a hundred times. Doc would poke his round balding head into the waiting room, smiling his most demonic smile, and would announce, "Next!" in a loud voice that could evoke ripples of terror in the bravest of us. We were almost willing to be fed to the monkey rather than be subjected to the ultimate horror that awaited us.

Entering the room containing the chair and its evil accoutrements was tantamount to visiting a medieval torture chamber, only everything was white. The chair itself was animated by Doc W_____'s series of secret switches and would magically tilt, raise and lower, rendering you prone, helpless and baked by the brightness of the dentist's lamp, a device borrowed from some police department's "third degree" room. A most demonic assortment of gleaming, sharp, and pointed objects was arrayed nearby.

The cotton jammed into the cheeks, the sucking tube under the tongue, the cold flat surface of the dental mirror banging against the teeth, the "Hmm," the "Ah Hah!" the electric jolt of metal probe finding a cavity, the stale smell of Doc's breath: all were nothing compared to the "This may sting a little," and the needle's thrust. Prolonged and excruciating, being pinned against a wall of pure pain by the syringe as the plunger pumped its bitter contents into bulging gums, this particular agony trumped even the drilling that was to come. The deadening numbness brought blessedly to jaws wrenched widely open still could not quiet the scream of the drill.

The Novocain wore off a little before the drilling was done. Doc seemed to lean on your jaw with all his weight as he stuffed the silver filling into the enormous crater he had dug. Then you sat forever with the cotton in your lips and your mouth sucked dry by the gurgling tube. All the other kids were out in the park playing ball or tag or home watching Flash Gordon if they were lucky enough to have a TV. The ritual torture would be repeated again. And again. And again. By my high school years all the fillings Doc W_____ had done had fallen out or had to be replaced. A new dentist would come into my young life. With worse breath.

R_____'s Emporium was on Main Street, one of the last remaining wooden structures dating from the previous century. We were warned never to go there by our mothers, making an expedition to this forbidden place even more desirable. Devoid of paint outside, the inside was a long dark room with a low ceiling that smelled of mold, incense and stale cigarette smoke. There were rows of tables heaped with exotic goods not seen in the more respectable Ben Franklin's Five and Dime or B_____'s Department Store. Madame R_____ herself was usually squirreled into a corner, a hazy, out of focus figure with long dirty hair, draped in strange clothes like a street vender from a far-away land. She seemed to pay no attention to us, but we knew with a certainty, she followed our every move with her all-seeing evil eye.

Some coveted, some actually acquired, the items arrayed on the tables including the Chinese finger trap (a woven bamboo cylinder that tightened when you tried to remove your fingers from both ends), the pea shooter (a plastic straw complete with a paper sack of dried peas), skeleton keys (which wouldn't open anything—we tried), the joy buzzer (a spring-wound metal disk you hid in your hand that produced a buzzing noise and a vibration when you shook hands, simulating an electric shock), extra-large dice (which we believed were "loaded"), and, of course, fake vomit and itching powder, rubber spiders, snakes and rats, and useful non-joke items like the bamboo back scratcher (many things in the Emporium were fabricated from bamboo), the Las Vegas style deck of playing cards (not like your mother's bridge deck with its card backs illustrating Paris, cute little dogs or monogram initials, no—these were genuine Bicycle decks with an intricate and incomprehensible pattern), musical instruments like the Kazoo, the Jews Harp and the Sweet Potato, Yo-yos of every kind, the balsa wood glider, the long cigarette holder (not made from bamboo—probably Bakelite), the cheap ring, bracelet, or necklace (which usually sported oversized gems made of colored glass), and candy.

Candy! What candy! Jawbreakers, Wax Lips, Atomic Fireballs, Licorice Pipes, Tootsie Rolls, Mary Janes, Sugar Daddies, Candy Buttons (stuck to a long roll of paper and bought by the foot), Black Jack Gum, Three Musketeer Bars (that really broke into three pieces), Candy Cigarettes, Necco Wafers, Jujubes, Bubble Gum Cigars, Root Beer Barrels, the Charleston Chew, the Bit-O-Honey, Horehound Drops (nobody liked these), Lemonheads, Red Hots, Tootsie Roll Pops, and Pez!

It was at R____'s that I bought the Rosary. I didn't know what it was. I just thought it was a pretty necklace, with beads and a cross. I had fallen in first love with a little blond girl named Linda. We had sat in the same pew at the Methodist Church one Sunday. Being terrified of speaking to her I thought the perfect way to show my undying love would be to present her with this necklace, and that the cross would remind her of our romantic time together during the church service. I don't know how, but Madame R____ knew who I was and called my mother to tell her I had bought this, forbidden for me, religious item. I was marched back to return it and it was explained to me that since Catholics worshipped the Virgin Mary, they were wrong people, religiously speaking, so any artifacts of that false belief must be shunned. This put a damper on my romantic intentions and I don't believe I ever entered R____'s again. I also became less fond of going to church. What strange relationship there was between my mother and Madame R____ remains a mystery.

Of course, there were comic books. Our mother would not let us buy those "blood thirsty" ones like Superman and Batman. (If she had only seen the some of the others!) We were given a dime to spend at F_____'s Drugstore if we had attended both church and Sunday school, and we were limited to Disney titles. I read a lot of Uncle Scrooge. The other kids around the neighborhood had the more interesting comics, and we had a rotating library of superheroes and the like. I enjoyed the Bob Kane Batmans because of his renderings of very surrealistic backgrounds. But my favorite was

Captain Marvel. Captain Marvel was in actuality a young boy not unlike myself and by uttering the magic words, "SHAZAM" could turn into a beefy and muscular man with a really great costume. He always beat the bad guys.

One summer when we were quite young, my brother J_____ and I invented a game. If it had a name, I don't remember, but the object of the game was for me to prevent my brother from gaining entrance to our house by slamming doors. He would run to the front door, I would slam it shut. He would run to the back door, I would slam it shut. He ran to the side door. It was the kitchen door and had a full pane of glass, not tempered or double glazed as it would be now-a-days. I pushed it closed and continued on through the glass, sending shards in all directions, and colliding with my brother, whose shocked expression remains forever fused in my memory. I had deep gashes along my inner arms and blood was everywhere. Jimmy received a bad cut on his palm. Our mother heard the crash and rushed to us in a panic that struck me as unusual for her normally level-headed mothering demeanor. A neighbor, our "Aunt" E___, was summoned, my arms were wrapped in bloodying towels and we were whisked to Doctor K_____'s office.

Doctor K_____ was the archetypical small-town family doctor. He birthed us, removed our tonsils, injected us against smallpox, treated our chicken pox, measles, and mumps and was pretty much the authority on everything medical my parents needed to know. I remember him always with a black cigar in his mouth and once when I was going into the operating room for a tonsillectomy I asked if Doctor K_____ was going to sterilize his cigar before he operated. His office was on the first floor in the same building as Doc W_____. He had the same comic books in his waiting room. And wait I did. Waiting—bleeding into my towels, while Jimmy was treated for his (relatively) minor cut. When you are the oldest, I guess, you get to go first. But I was pretty faint by the time I watched in horror as Doctor K_____ stitched up my wounds. I still have the scars and the memory of that traumatic event. But it was only one of many near-death occurrences of my youth.

The first time I almost died was a lazy afternoon in the summer of 19__ when I was walking along A_____ Avenue where it bent graciously and sloped gently as it entered town near its terminus at W_____ Street. I was not on the sidewalk, preferring instead to shuffle along in the gutter where I might spot the occasional treasure: a lost marble or a discarded and broken watchband, or maybe even a pair of sunglasses not so destroyed by nature as to still be wearable. A car came careening around the curve of the street.

A car! It was a '32 Ford Coupe whose rancorous rumbling sent a murder of crows flying from the nearby maples and caused several unchained dogs to scratch at screen doors in a futile attempt to escape. It was one of those raked, souped-up chariots we called a "hot rod" and it was driven by a misanthropic entity who we called a "hood." This particular hood—sorry, I don't remember his name, let's just call him Dale—was a legend among we younger boys. Dale was a high school drop out of indeterminate age, rarely seen but always avoided. Dale was skeletally skinny, most likely the result of some incurable malady like polio, and it was said that he hated the world—and especially us. "He'd kill you soon as look at you," was the usual comment. "Don't ever…ever mess with him!"

I heard the blast furnace sound of the glass-packed muffler and squeal of the worn rubber tires against the low curbing. I glanced over my shoulder to see the charging behemoth driven straight at me, wheels aligned with the gutter. I could picture my battered and broken body flung high into the air and landing in a nearby Box Elder tree where it would hang, dripping, like a wet wash rag, unnoticed until it became food for turkey vultures. I leaped, sprawled on the parkway grass trembling, but lucky to be alive.

Another nearly lethal escapade happened to me as a teenager, walking along a favorite short cut. A gravel path ran between the river and the old swimming hole. There was a chain link fence on the beach side and a steep bank down to the river on the other. Blocking the path and chugging like an angry dragon was an electric pump pulling water from the pool and spitting it into the river. Not wanting to back track around to the other side of the fenced-in beach, I valiantly placed one foot on the massive rubber hose, steadied myself on the fence and grabbed onto the pump to pull myself up and over. I succeeded in grounding myself and a jolt of who knows how many volts surged through me, tossing me like a rag doll into the air and back ten or so feet to land limply on the gravel. I came to several minutes later and, trembling, back tracked sheepishly back to the long way around. It felt like I had been struck by lightning. I experienced a subtle shaking for nearly a week. But, being embarrassed by my own stupidity, I never told anyone about the incident and consequently avoided a trip to see Doctor K_____.

Then there was the time we took my father's car for joy ride. It was one of those warm, sunny, summer days when the world seems a wondrous place, but the stupid little town you live in seems the most depressing prison ever invented by adults to plague teenagers. It was getting late and nothing seemed able to relieve our ennui. We were bored to tears. And, of a sudden, there it was. *It* sat there in the driveway, the greatest temptation known to boykind, a shiny, gleaming sentinel to adventure, a forbidden vehicle as alluring as Rocky Jones Space Ranger's rocket ship to the far reaches of the universe—Pop's new car.

And so I sat proudly behind the wheel of my father's amazing automobile, a brand new 1957 Chrysler Windsor. Beside me sat my friend J____ in what they called the "suicide seat." I was only 15 and had just gotten my learner's permit, but J____ said, because J____ was 16, it was legal for us to take the Windsor for a drive. I wasn't sure that my good friend actually had a driver's license himself, but I wasn't going to quibble when an adventure of this potential was in the offing.

The car had a gapping front grill like the mouth of a shark and tail fins that made it look like a Flash Gordon's rocket ship. This car was pink, embarrassingly pink, a concession, my father had said, to my mother, who had wanted a more conservative car for driving to church, school and the grocery store. Perhaps a station wagon…a Buick, of course. But Pop, urged on by a hidden wild streak, had purchased the futuristic looking chariot with its big V8 engine, and still drove it to church. Pinkly.

The interior was also sickeningly pink. The dashboard was a round fish bowl-shaped globe with lighted orange tabs like miniature grave stones sticking up to indicate oil pressure and the like. That completed the spaceship motif. Except for the color and the fact that it was an automatic, J____ approved.

J____ had been one of my best buddies all throughout our school years and I looked up to him as if he were my big brother. It was J____ who had taught me to play draw poker and had shown me how to mark my father's whiskey bottle before stealing a slug so it could be watered to its previous level. It was J____ who had given me the courage to climb the fire escape at that old hotel downtown to toss water balloons at passing cars. And it was J____ who now persuaded me to ease the big car out onto the highway, out toward the country roads south of town.

It was on a strip of straight-as-an-arrow country road about five miles long that we now found ourselves parked, sipping cokes and relishing the outstanding, if temporary freedom of our summer vacation. As the late afternoon sun cast golden shadows across fields of corn that bordered the road, J____ was possessed of a singular idea: why not see if the car could really go 120 miles per hour as the speedometer said it could.

"There are no other cars on this road, and you've got plenty of space to top it out on," J____ said. J____ had never steered me wrong.

"Oh, It will do 120," I said.

J____ nodded. "Take it easy now, don't tromp on it, you'll flood the engine."

I gripped the pink plastic steering wheel and pressed lightly on the accelerator. The car started down the blacktop. 30 mph, 40 mph—I began to increase pressure on the pedal. 50, 60—the car handled beautifully, even piloted by an inexperienced driver like myself with a tendency to over-steer at the wheel. 70, 80, 90, I couldn't believe the rush I was getting as the big car roared compliantly down the straightaway. I glanced over at J____, saw the wide grin.

"OK, now goose it."

I goosed it. 100, 110, the automobile trembled a little but didn't complain. The road was flat and smooth and only a slight vibration of the steering wheel betrayed that our speed was anything but normal.

"It'll do it! It'll do it!"

The needle, glowing red under the glass-globed dash, inched toward the coveted goal: our Holt Grail of 120 miles per hour! We were flying through space. They were Haley's Comet, sprinkling stars in our wake. We were a pink flash across the black macadam road.

"You should start slowing down now."

"Just a little more."

The road was straight as an arrow, but like many country roads it had a sharp right-angle turn at the county line. I heard J____ yell at me…something indistinguishable, but obviously communicating panic. We were sailing at 120 miles an hour toward the right-angle turn.

I stomped on the brake pedal and jerked the wheel. The car, an engineering miracle of Detroit, stayed true, though there occurred a bit of a wobble. The evidence of marks of heated rubber on the macadam would testify to the near tragic event we had narrowly avoided. We stopped at the angle turn where a stand of elm trees formed a sort of barricade should anyone foolishly fail to make the turn.

We sat, panting, sweating, then: laughing that nervous laugh one voices in the most embarrassing manner after a stupid action has come to a risky, but life-saving conclusion. Yet as we sat there, happy that the county sheriff's police were not cruising the county roads today, and that the Chrysler wasn't piled up against the elms, I blinked up a vision of an alternate ending to our adventure:

I had missed the turn. The Windsor flipped, flew through the air, hitting upside down and rolling—one, two, three times—the pink top and black undercarriage alternating—pink, black, pink, black, pink, black—across the green of the field and the darkening blue-gray of the afternoon sky. The driver's door popped open and I was thrown from the car as it continued its pink, black, blue, green pirouette. I heard, rather than felt bones cracking and saw a curtain of blood drawn over my eyes. I bounced between consciousness and the blackness of oblivion. Red, black, red, black.

When I forced my eyes to open I saw a strange pink shape, convoluted and jagged. It no longer looked like a car but like some giant, squashed bug, its pink guts streaming out onto the green field. What is it? Where am I? I can't feel my legs. J____? Oh no, J____! I've killed J____! A crow landed next to me, curious, black against pink and green. The blackness grew and enveloped me. There was no time, no dreaming—only a sudden awakening and a muffled, hallow sound like a voice. I know that voice. Eyes open. Someone standing over me. J____? Is that you, J____? Are you an angel? Black.

The only waiting room that didn't have worn out old comics was the one at the barber shop downtown. It did have some men's magazines which we tried in vain to sneak peeks at and some old copies of Field and Stream. The fascinating thing about the barber shop, though, was the clock. The drive gear for the second hand was missing some teeth. The hand would climb normally from the 6 up to the 12 and then plummet down from 12 to 6, remaining there, swishing like a skinny pendulum until the gear caught up with it 30 seconds later. It was good entertainment while you waited.

The first time I was allowed to choose what kind of haircut I wanted I opted for a flattop. This bizarre haircut (many years before Bart Simpson) was popular in the late forties and early fifties and was possibly inspired by GIs returning from World War II. It was like a crew cut but grown longer on top and then clipped to a level flatness. There was a greasy green gel that came in a small jar that you had to comb into it to force the front to stand up straight. I later abandoned the flattop for a hair style of my own creation, with a curl like Bill Haley's. Other kids claimed to be cultivating a DA, (duck's ass in back and pompadour in front), but mostly their mothers nipped that in the bud.

Mothers were always nipping things in the bud, but sometimes they were intimidated into withdrawing their motherly protection from us. My mother was a substitute teacher in the public schools, as was my aunt. The school authorities took great measures to insure neither woman would have us in her classroom (to avoid favoritism, they said). In truth my mother and my aunt would have been much harder on us than on the other children.

I think I was in fourth grade when one of the teachers noticed some initials carved into one of the wooden desks: B. G. My initials! I hadn't done any desk carving and certainly wouldn't have been stupid enough to sign it if I had. It didn't occur to the authorities that there might be other kids with those initials, so it must have been me. My mother was called on the carpet and, consequently, she reprimanded me. Despite my pleas of innocence, I obtained one of the first black marks to go on my "permanent record."

Was there such a thing as a permanent record, or was that a sort of academic boogie man used to frighten us into behaving? Teachers always seemed uncomfortable around us, especially as we started to enter adolescence. I remember in seventh grade there was a girl we all thought was "pretty hot" who wore short shorts to the last class of the spring term. Our teacher, a large, ungainly but mild-mannered man who had never raised his voice in class became a Mr. Hyde to his usual Dr. Jekyll. He shouted that such a wanton and disrespectful act could not be tolerated. She would have to stay after class. We wondered about that.

Our mothers signed us up for ball room dancing class. It was taught in many of the Midwestern suburban communities by a fellow who, it turned out, also had a Jekyll/Hyde personality. He often turned us loose to practice the four-step while he took one of the girls off to the side for some special instruction. This involved his adjusting her posture with one hand on her back and another on her chest. We wondered about that. Many years later he was convicted of being a pedophile—which wouldn't have surprised us had we known what that was. The dance class was a milestone in our social development, allowing us to "close dance when the teacher wasn't looking. He did, however, teach us to "jitterbug," and I have vivid memories of P____ doing the "rubber-legs" to Bill Haley's "Rudy's Rock."

Good friends. It must have been second or third grade when I first noticed the new kid. He had jet black hair and a handsome face—for a kid. I could tell there was something different about him. He always seemed deep in thought. Or dreams. Every day he would wear a different wristwatch to school. Not real watches. Toy watches. And at least one that he seemed to have fabricated himself.

Our fast friendship didn't start until high school. B___ had invited me to play poker with him and some friends one evening. We had friends in common but we hadn't bonded as yet. That came slowly as we hung out after school in the cemetery where we would smoke mentholated Newport cigarettes and sit on the steps of an old mausoleum (it had Egyptian sphinx statues guarding its doorway) and talk about life and the world.

Once we could drive we would "shoot the loop," which meant driving aimlessly around the one block of downtown until we were bored of that, then we would park on the street somewhere in the residential section, smoke some more, drink cokes from the bottle, and talk about life and the world. Inevitably the police would appear shining a flashlight into the car and the cop would say, "Good evening, Mr. Grush." And to B___: "What's your name? Do you live in town?" This happened often enough that the police should have gotten to know B___ as well as they apparently knew me. I think they just liked the routine.

One of our hangouts was a funky old restaurant out on the highway called the Pine Knot. We'd order cokes or coffees and sit monopolizing a table to the consternation of the waitresses. We also liked the restaurant across from the movie theater. It had taken the soda fountain business away from the drugstore because it had a juke box. We'd get cherry cokes or Green Rivers and dare each other to put a quarter in the juke box and punch "Happy Birthday" five times.

During the high school years, B____ and I often took the train into the City (Chicago) and sometimes took pictures. We had our favorite destinations there: Altman's Camera, Kroch's and Brentano's Book Store, and Wimpy's Hamburgers. One time we wandered down State Street just past the Loop and found ourselves standing in front of The Star and Garter, a vintage burlesque theater turned strip joint. This was the late 50's or early 60's. It was about 11:00 in the morning. So of course, we went in. They apparently had no trouble admitting a pair of teenage boys. The strippers were old, tired, and boring (and thankfully left a lot of it on) except for this one girl who couldn't have been all that much older than we were. We perked up for her act in which she flashed her G-string at us. Some old guy came up the aisles in between acts selling "Tiajuana Bibles," those pornographic cartoon books that are probably real collector's items now.

I guess we were the geeks of the late 50s and early 60s. I had heard that our class had four or five students who had tested in the genius category or near it The group I hung with in high school included D___ G____ who was building a robot. It had a pair of plyers for hands. I don't think it worked very well. But there were soirees at D___'s house in his basement where we listened to his collection of rock and roll records, especially an EP of Bill Haley's *Rock Around the Clock*.

There was a story about M____ brewing up a batch of nitroglycerin in his basement when the mixture began to bubble. He threw the flask out a basement window just as it exploded. He was the person, I think, that introduced B___ and me to the idea of tossing white phosphorus (which we had to steal from the chemistry lab at school) into the college pond to watch it explode.

Cars. Some us were lucky to have access to secondary family cars which we drove as our own. They had nicknames. G____'s '49 or '50 Dodge was called the "Great Gray Whale." Somebody, I don't remember who, had a Studebaker with a rocket-ship front end which we called the "Needle Nose Bug Fucker." We drove, we parked, we smoked a lot in those cars. Once B___ and I were driving out in the country and had run out of matches. The car didn't have a lighter as someone had thrown it out of the window after lighting up. We pulled over, raised the hood, and attempted to make a spark by shorting out the battery. It didn't work.

And there are many stories about P____. For instance, after every Christmas, the city would collect the undecorated Christmas trees and stack them up on a field. On a given evening they would set fire to them creating a gigantic bonfire for the enjoyment of the town. The field was just across the street from P____'s house. So one year P___ lit the fire—the night before it was scheduled to burn. P___ had been with me the day I had dropped a pumpkin from the railroad bridge over the main highway through town. It landed just in front of a police car.

Most of all I remember the sidewalks. Sidewalks covered with spring's first maple seeds or the crisp dried leaves of fall. Sidewalks crunching underfoot with the shells of 17-year locusts. Sidewalks icy in winter so you could slide in slippery street shoes but not in buckled rubber boots. Sidewalks fresh with rain puddles and writhing earthworms, confused by their new cement world. Sidewalks with cracks you couldn't step on for fear of breaking your mother's back. Sidewalks incised with the trademarks of "Goodwin Cement Contractors, 1951." Sidewalks of brick, of octagonal tile. Sidewalks that bent around trees grown too close and too large like the Alligator Tree— an ancient maple I often passed by. Its roots were exposed like a great reptile waiting patiently for an unsuspecting child to pause there on the way home from school. School neighborhood sidewalks littered with candy wrappers or melted ice cream dropped from cones carelessly held. Tiny ants swarming over the ice cream or erupting from cracks in angry waves of some ant-centric ritual dance. The fragile blue shell of a fallen robin's egg or the occasional dead bird or squirrel carcass blocking your passage. The memory of tricycles, bikes with training wheels, then the first two-wheeler you triumphantly maneuvered down the sidewalk in front of your home. Metal skates clipped to your shoes catching edges where the settling ground raised or lowered sections of sidewalk. Chalked squares and numerals of hopscotch. Names and dates, hand prints and dogs' paw prints pressed into wet cement to forever immortalize a moment, a place once lived, a passage. Sidewalks that ended inexplicably as the nostalgic wanderings of these stories must end. Sidewalks that led home.

EDDIE SUGAR

Eddie Sugar was a grifter. Eddie loved women though, and it hurt him to always be working the Big Grift upon the fair sex. But then, that was his life. That was what he was born for. That was his destiny. And nothing could ever change him—or could it?

After all, he was an artist, wasn't he? Picture the dapper, the dandy, the checkered suit and bowler, the spats. Picture the smile; teeth white as new-fallen snow, one prominent in gold capping stage right. He could twirl a cane with the best of them—he *was* the best of them, or so he thought.

He had cut his grifter's wisdom teeth in Kansas City. The old century—the eighteen hundreds—had faded away like the dying embers of a hobos camp fire. For Eddie, the marks got fewer and farther between. The grifter drifted. St. Louis was ripe, for a time. The constables were more vigilant than he had expected, however. Musicians adept at the new trend called jazz seemed to be coming up the big river. Eddie decided to go down it. Down it all the way to where the river was called the Big Muddy. Down to New Orleans to the Vieux Carré, to the narrow streets smelling of gumbo, to where Creole ladies in brightly flowered dresses leaned over the wrought iron balconies and smiled smiles that put Eddie's own beaming countenance to shame. The French Quarter.

The second decade of the new century had just begun. The Quarter, balanced on the cusp of decay, had been discovered by bohemian artists and writers. Cheap rent. Cheap food. Cheap booze and cheaper women. And a lot less expensive than moving to Paris. William Faulkner would come to write *Sherwood Anderson and Other Famous Creoles* based on his experiences living in the Vieux Carré. The same Sherwood Anderson, a hero to many of the would-bes, would move to New Orleans and throw parties for the likes of Anita Loos,

Edna St. Vincent Millay, and John Dos Passos. A social life evolved; the elite moved up to the Garden District.

Eddie had discovered Le Petit Théâtre Du Vieux Carré, a small theatrical venue occupying a Spanish Colonial style building on the corner of St. Peter and Chartres Streets. Under the stewardship of Irish playwright, Lord Dunsany, a small group called the Drawing Room Players had attracted a wider audience, one whose support had enabled them to buy the building. Now the Le Petit had an exclusive clientele, catering to the upper classes who continued to contribute to its financial and artistic success. Eddie Sugar saw it as a steppingstone in his ambition to hob nob with the high rollers of society.

Dues of $10 were charged for membership to Le Petit. Eddie might have had to struggle to scrape that annoying requirement together save that his current "mark," an over-forty-ish creole woman named Adélaïde St. Victoire, was overly generous with his allowance. Eddie would complain that his wardrobe was shabby. "Lamærd!" Madamm St. Victoire would exclaim. But a dollar or two would appear in Eddie's coat pocket. Dollar by dollar, it was going to take some time.

Adélaïde was descended from the French settlers of colonial La Louisiane and was insistent that her heritage elevated her socially. Not socially high enough for Eddie, however. Eddie suspected that she might not be a pure "White Creole," but, as in the terminology of a previous era in which white supremacy was exceedingly more rampant, she could be referred to as an octoroon, a person of fourth-generation African ancestry: one eight Black. It was not that Eddie was strictly racist, in fact, it delighted him that he might be crossing a presumed taboo barrier to dip his brush into an exotic paint pot of color. But his environmental upbringing precluded racial blindness; it would take more than an experimental tryst to wean him from indoctrinated prejudice.

"T'olé vini kouté lamizik?" she asked: "You want to come listen to music?" It was less of a question than a command, so Eddie agreed. "Ça senm bon." She said everything was good...music was a distraction from the monotony of everyday. He would enjoy it. Of course he would.

In the Tremé neighborhood, up North Rampart Street between St. Anne and St Peter Streets, was Congo Square. True, in an effort to suppress the Black population of New Orleans who congregated there, it had been renamed Beauregard Square, after the infamous

Confederate General, but everyone still called it Congo Square. Creoles of Color created musical venues there, concerts featuring brass bands that evolved into what was now being called Jazz. Black musicians, Kid Ory, King Oliver, Sydney Bechet, Jelly Roll Morton, and Louis Armstrong all played there and in nearby Storyville at one time. Many had left by now, journeying to Chicago, enticed by recording contracts. But some had stayed. Ça senm bon.

Adélaïde took Eddie to a small warehouse building used as an ersatz theater on Rampart Street. It didn't have a name nor a sign to signify its internal activities. People just knew. They knew when a band played, singers sang, and food was in the offing. Food that was cooked in the homes and brought to the festivities. Glorious food like an old familiar song sung to the hearts (and the stomachs) of the Vieux Carré.

Oysters, freshly shucked. Crayfish boiled bright red and succulent. Boulli, a beef brisket cooked in a vegetable soup and served with a sauce made from oil and vinegar, horseradish, and Creole mustard. Baba cake dipped in rum or claret or anisette. And of course, Gumbo. Gumbo with seven greens. Started with a roux of flour and lard. Sautéed onions, green bell pepper, okra, parsley. Then the meats: it varied—perhaps today there had been fresh crabs at the market, or shrimp. Maybe chicken. Certainly, andouille sausage. And a stock made by boiling the discarded crab shells. Seasonings might include garlic, cayenne pepper, gumbo filét, bay leaf and thyme. Somedays there were tomatoes. The pot boiled for hours to thicken as the rice cooked and French bread was heated. Ça senm bon.

And booze. Of course, Prohibition was in effect in New Orleans, just as it was all across the country. And, just as it was all across the country, when people wanted a drink, they got a drink. Rum running was rampant in St. Bernard Parish, where the real stuff, imported whiskey and gin, could be had. Home brewing was popular, and beer and wine and bathtub gin flowed freely since the police had little motivation in stemming the tide. Congo Square had its suppliers and the warehouse without a name, the music venue of the night, was well supplied.

Johnny DuMont's Crescent City Stompers was playing. A full regiment of trumpet, trombone, and saxophone gave forth seemingly independent diverging lines of melody which nonetheless merged into a palatable rhapsody as complex, and spicy, as the seasonings in the gumbo. The banjo and piano syncopated with the energetic rhythms of the drum, echoes of the chant and response of the Baptist Church. The dancing, in some other places, might have been considered wild, akin to a vigorous voodoo ceremony, but it was just a celebration of the joy of being alive. Adélaïde wanted to dance; Eddie did not. They stood silently together, Adélaïde tapping her toes to the music, Eddie surveying the room.

And there she was—across the crowded room—the socialite, slumming, drinking in the exotic, taboo ambience of Black Creole culture. Unaccompanied? No, there was an escort. A man not so dapper as Eddie Sugar, but with obvious similar intent to lead astray for profit, the innocent and the well-to-do, those fresh from the Garden District, and ripe for the harvesting.

"Do you know that woman over there?" Eddie asked. Adélaïde scoffed.

"No…why do you want to know?"

"It's just…I'm concerned for her. You see that man she is with? He is a user. I know his type."

"I'm sure you do. Why don't you go over and rescue her? Oh, and don't bother to come home tonight."

Bread buttered on only one side served to inform Eddie of the inadvisability of following his…heart. Oh, he liked his butter. And yet…an opportunity had arisen here, one not to be ignored no matter what the cost. "You don't mean that. You know I wouldn't…"

"Do me wrong? Like the song says, Eddie mò lamòrè: 'Feelin' tomorrow like I feels today, pack my trunk an' make ma git away.' You know that song, don't you? Only *you* be doin' the packin'."

"Okay, Addie, I hear you."

Some days later, Eddie was waiting on Royal Street for a taxi driver he knew who distributed bootleg liquor from the trunk of his cab. Under the balcony of the Old Sazerac House near what was known as Monkey Wrench Corner, the traditional meeting place for itinerant sailors, the dapper grifter leaned against a dark green shutter. The building now housed a barber shop, but in the earlier days of the Vieux Carré, the Sazerac Coffee House had opened on the Exchange Alley side. There, in the mid-nineteenth century, the Sazerac Cocktail was first concocted of absinthe, Sazerac-de-Forge et Fils cognac, Peychaud bitters, and a sugar cube. Eddie desired nothing so elaborate, a simple bottle of imported whiskey would do.

The smell of bananas from the docks off Cannel Street mingled intrusively with the fragrance of oleander and bougainvillea. Arrogant autos added exhaust fumes and the occasional, anachronistic horse-drawn conveyance dropped abundant ordure: nostalgic fetor ripening under the New Orleans sun. Over all of this, the cooking odors of gumbo and jambalaya persisted. Soon a sweet rain would wash it all away.

Eddie was about to call it a day; Adélaïde would have to head for a speakeasy in order to imbibe tonight. He decided to walk up Royal street toward the St. Louis Cathedral and Jackson Square where perhaps another bootlegger lurked when he saw her again. The woman from the dance. Saw her emerge from a horse-drawn carriage as if time-traveling from the not so distant past. Saw the swish of auburn hair not bobbed but full and unrestrained, whipping in the gentle city air as if mimicking the horse's mane. Saw her smooth out her frock—not a flapper's, but the dress of a demure divine dilettante dressed delectably for slumming. She looked lovelier in the daylight. Also more vulnerable.

He crossed the street, approaching this new mark. "Good afternoon, Mademoiselle," he chortled, tipping his bowler and flashing his best ivory-white and gold smile.

"I'm not a Frenchy," she chuckled. This response, framed within a nasal midwestern accent, did somewhat diminish Eddie's anticipation of a sophisticated Southern Belle (this was his original vision of the lass). Still, there was potential here. She certainly was from money. Whether old money or nouveau riche mattered little to an adventurer of Eddie's caliber. He could get past a certain klutziness when need be.

"I'm so sorry, Miss, I took you for a high-born Creole lady."

"I'm also not Black," she retorted.

"Of course not. Creole just means descended from the original Spanish or French that settled Louisiana. It's a compliment."

"Oh, well…that's different. I'm not from here. I'm from Dubuque, Iowa. I'm visiting my aunt and uncle…why am I telling you this?"

"Because I have an honest face? I couldn't help but notice you, and it seemed you might be off in an area, unaccompanied as you are, where you might encounter certain…unsavory types. I was concerned, of course."

"I can take care of myself. You needn't be concerned. Now if you will excuse me…"

Eddie was not one to give up so easily. He gave, instead, a shallow bow. "Please, Miss, let me at least escort you to your next destination. My name, by the by, is Edward Mumford Zukofsky...my friends call me Eddie Sugar. The Mumford is from an English grandmother. Zukofsky is...well, just call me Eddie Sugar."

She suppressed a giggle with an expertise learned, Eddie suspected, at many a cotillion. Her smile, the only remnant of her amusement, told Eddie volumes about his chances. It seemed they were good.

"I'm Alice Bea Gowen. And don't make any jokes about 'Alice Blue Gown.' I've heard enough of them."

"That song was written for Teddy Roosevelt's daughter—an American princess. I hear she is a real beauty. Nothing to be ashamed of, I'd say. So, where can I take you to? Home? Sightseeing along the bayou? Jackson Square? Café du Monde for a cafe au-lait and a beignet?"

Eddie hadn't noticed the man watching them from under the balcony across the street that day of their first meeting. In the following days Eddie saw Alice often. Once or twice he did notice the man—always lurking nearby, pretending not to be watching them by using the most feeble ruses Eddie had ever seen: tying a shoelace, following the flight of a gull or a crow beneath a shading hand, hailing a nonexistent cab, or quickly disappearing around a corner. A cop from the vice division? One of the new Prohibition detectives down from the East Coast? A cheap gumshoe hired by Alice's aunt and uncle? Or one of Adélaïde's deadbeat friends keeping an eye on him? He preferred it not be the latter.

He still depended on Adélaïde's good graces. She supported him, even if it wasn't in the manner he desired and deserved. He had to stay with her for now. And he had to make up excuses to get away so he could see Alice. But Alice wasn't yet a profit center. Slow and steady was the watchword with Alice. Sneaky and stealthy was his technique with Adélaïde.

He hadn't considered confronting the watching man. His boldness in physical encounters with women didn't translate into an enthusiasm for fisticuffs with men. Even verbal disputes were to be avoided. When it came to fight or flight, Eddie Sugar was swift as the wind and just as insubstantial. He ignored the man and hoped he'd just go away. As Alice brought Eddie more and more into her own social circle, the watching man appeared less and less.

Alice took him to a performance by the Drawing Room Players of Mary Roberts Reinhart's mystery, *The Bat*, at Le Petit Théâtre Du Vieux Carré. At last! Entrance to that selective theater where the Eddie hoped to mingle with the elite. Alice's aunt and uncle, being at least peripheral to that elite (which Eddie imagined embodied New Orleans' extraordinary wealth and power), had a season membership. The Bat, the play's title character, was a masked criminal who terrified a group of people in an old mansion during an electric storm. Eddie found it humorous and unrealistic, but entertaining. Near the end of the third act, when the real identity of the Bat was about to be revealed, someone in the audience screamed.

The little theater, it seemed, was haunted. More than one supernatural entity was said to reside there. This night, an audience member had seen the specter of Caroline, an actress who, after a torrid affair with one of the theater's stage workers on the catwalk, had fallen, naked, off said catwalk to her death. Her spirit was often seen roaming the theater along with the ghost of Sigmund, the stage carpenter, and the "Captain," the deceased lover of another of the theater's actresses. These stories, which Eddie heard later, made the incredulous grifter chuckle. Tonight, the scream simply added a little drama where, to Eddie's thinking, a little drama was sorely needed.

Eddie showed Alice the town—on her dime. All his money was temporarily tied up in some investments, he claimed. Couldn't take the money out now for fear of losing a substantial profit, he explained. She was eager to provide funds for the interim. Eddie was such a knowledgeable escort.

They ate at La Restaurant de la Louisiane under crystal chandeliers in a big private room with mirrored walls. There they devoured bisque Écrevisse de Louisiane, redfish courtbouillon, filet de truite marguery, and baked Alaska. Or they dined in the garden at Broussard's, enjoying the oysters al la Broussard among the chrysanthemums, calla lilies and hibiscus. There was a new restaurant they wished to try called Arnaud's on Bienville Street. The menu in the window listed shrimps Arnaud, filet de truite Amandine, breast of turkey en papillate, oyster Whitney, langouste Sarah Bernhardt, stuffed crab Rejane, and crepe suzette Arnaud.

"Tomorrow night, shall we come back here?" Eddie suggested as they strolled past the restaurant. An evening walk through the Quarter.

"Oh! Didn't I tell you? Uncle's business partner invited us all out on his boat tomorrow. Have you a bathing suit?"

"I can get one."

"And pack a bag for the whole weekend. You'll meet some interesting people. Should be fun."

"The weekend? Sleeping on the boat? It must be a big boat!"

She was a big boat. More properly, the *Queen of the South* was a steam yacht. Over 800 tons, 205 feet long with a nine foot beam and a ten foot draught. She had three decks with a saloon for dining, all done in mahogany and brass, and six staterooms on the lower deck. She could make 16 knots at full steam and had a cruising range of 3,000 miles. Her owner, Nathaniel Eberhardt, had her brought down from Bristol, Rhode Island, where she had been built only two years ago, and now she was anchored just off the long pier at the Southern Yacht Club at West End on Lake Pontchartrain. The boat's skiff was docked at the pier ready to transport the weekend guests to the floating palace.

The Southern Yacht Club dated to 1846 and had built an elaborate clubhouse out over the water in 1879. A race had been held by the SYC across Lake Pontchartrain, through The Rigolets to Lake Borgne and into the Mississippi Sound each year since the club's beginnings. The clubhouse always had hosted fancy social events in its grand ballroom and it now provided a venue for many of the emerging jazz musicians from New Orleans. Eddie and Alice sat at a table on the clubhouse veranda sipping Sazeracs as they waited for Alice's aunt and uncle. It was an afternoon that Eddie would have described as golden—or, had he been up on his Mark Twain, as gilded.

Surely, the Gilded Age was winding down to be replaced by the Jazz Age, and Mark Twain's colloquial wisdom and its celebration of the human spirit was to be usurped by F. Scott Fitzgerald's generation of the lost and its eloquent pessimism. Eddie Sugar, not much for literary philosophy, was mired in a worship of Lady Luck and oblivious to the consequences of self-serving modality. The excesses of the Flapper era were, at best, a means to an end for Eddie. That end being the pursuit of easy living. And what better place for such a pursuit than the Big Easy? And what better place to shine a gold-toothed smile in anticipation of good fortune than the Southern Yacht Club?

A waiter came by with a plate of freshly shucked oysters on the half-shell. Eddie waved him away. "Those may be an aphrodisiac," he joked to Alice, "but some of us are so attuned to life that additional inspiration is ultimately unnecessary." As soon as he had prattled this crass decree, he regretted it. "A jest," he followed up with, eager to correct his faux pas. Alice just smiled, eternally demure—or perhaps she had not understood the meaning of the term, "aphrodisiac."

"Oh, here are Aunt Bea and Uncle Thad," she said as the couple approached their table. Eddie had met both Beatrice (the source of Alice's middle name) and Thaddeus Blackburn on several previous occasions, although these had been casual and fleeting. Eddie hoped to be able to spend more time with the uncle during this cruise across Lake Pontchartrain. Getting in the man's good graces was essential to Eddie's ultimate goal: not to marry the girl, but to hop-frog from her family's only slightly stellar social status to a more celestial set of celebrities within the cosmos of the down-right filthy rich. There were stars in his eyes to match the sparkle of his gold tooth.

"We can board now, children," said Mr. Blackburn. "Captain Lenox has sent the skiff to collect us. Elena Whitaker is waiting on the pier with Arlene and Travis Sommer. Oh, Eddie, did you pack some deck shoes? Those spats are a bit impractical for nautical adventures. Slippery from the spray, you know."

Eddie wasn't planning on spending much time on deck. He had brought his own pack of playing cards and intended to start up a nice game in the saloon, if possible. The fact that the card deck was marked gave him an advantage, but he would lose judiciously. It was a good way to assure invitations to future games—games with players from the circle of the elite to which he aspired.

Alice was sharing a stateroom with Elena Whitaker, a widow from Baton Rouge and a good friend of Nathaniel Eberhardt, the *Queen of the South's* owner. Eddie roomed with Ashley Harris, another single guest, and like Eddie, one new to Eberhardt's aquatic galas. Harris was present at the request of Elena Whitaker—an old school chum, she said—and this served to raise a few eyebrows. Two more couples completed the inventory of stateroom inhabitants, Margery and Kingston Grey, and Kathryn and Victor Glenn.

The yacht had gotten up a head of steam and had begun its Pontchartrain odyssey with pomp befitting its imposing size. Flags and banners flew in the breeze and the bright red and green stripes freshly painted long its gunwale reflected unevenly in the brackish water. They passed along the shoreline peppered with fishing shacks and crudely constructed piers where pirogues were tied loosely and rocked with irritation in the *Queen's* wake. Then the yacht turned out toward the deeper water, into the Okta-ta (which meant "Wide Water" in Choctaw).

The steward had brought out some deck chairs for the passengers. They congregated on deck, some sitting, some strolling, while the *Queen* chugged slowly along. Eddie was introduced to the others and he flashed his usual smile until the corners of his mouth ached.

Kingston Grey, Eddie learned, was an author of romantic novels which, Grey explained, illustrated the human condition—greed, lust, jealousy, etc.—for the average reading public. Kingston Grey, Eddie figured, was not the man's real name. It takes one to know one, thought Eddie. The wife, Margery Grey, was almost pretty and seemed to defer to her husband in an unattractive manner. This couple, thought Eddie, had little potential as stepping-stones for social climbing. Victor and Kathryn Glenn, however, were another matter. Glenn was on the board of directors of the Crescent City National Bank of New Orleans. Kathryn was bubbly and flitted from guest to guest like a hungry butterfly in a garden of fading flowers. Perfect, thought Eddie. Now if only the Mister likes poker.

Arlene and Travis Sommer were wild cards in Eddie's current game of vertical mobility. Sommer was a real estate mogul, and as such, should have piqued Eddie's interest. Which he did, but the man was stand-offish. For someone used to glad-handing strangers, Travis Sommer's limp and reluctant handshake with Eddie told much to the grifter about his chances of access to the man, even if he played his cards right. The wife, Arlene, ignored Eddie completely. So much for the Sommers!

After a late afternoon meal in the saloon, Eddie and Alice stood looking over the rail at the sea gulls circling the boat. "Probably think we're a fishing boat," said Eddie.

"You know what that Whitaker woman said to me?" said Alice. "She wants me to trade rooms with your roommate, that Ashley Harris. That takes a lot of nerve!"

"Hmm…that's an idea."

"What?"

"Just kidding, Alice. I respect you, you know."

"Well, thanks. But don't respect me *too* much."

The game began around 8 o'clock in the dining saloon. Eddie had managed to recruit his prime mark, Victor Glenn, and Kingston Grey for an evening of Seven-Toed Pete, also known as Seven Card Stud. At the last minute, Alice said she wanted to play as well. "You can coach me," she said. "Hmm…not a good idea," Eddie said. "Well, tell me the rules, anyway," she said. And so he did, as Glenn and Grey poured drinks from the more than adequate bar.

And so it began. After the cut, not unexpectedly, Eddie won the first deal. Antes of one dollar each were proffered. Eddie set aside the "burn card" which lowered the odds for a perfect hand just slightly. Eddie then dealt left to right around the table, two cards down and one card up. He watched the markings on the cards closely.

"You see, Alice," Eddie said, "the two face down cards are called the hole cards. The one up is the door. You can look at your hole cards, but don't show them to anyone. Now we bet."

The rotation, starting at Eddie's left, was Victor Glenn, Kingston Grey, Alice, and then Eddie. The door cards, in this rotation, were: Victor…five of clubs, Kingston…six of diamonds…Alice, two of hearts, and Eddie…four of spades. Alice, having the lowest door card, was to add the bring-in to the pot. "What do I bet?" she asked.

"You have to put in at least four dollars for the bring-in. You can raise that if you want to," answered Eddie.

"Oh…I don't think so. I've only got a lonely little two!"

No one else raised or called. This could mean someone with an excellent hand was holding back, or that no one had anything decent. Only Eddie knew for sure. Eddie began the second round dealing one more card face up to each player.

"Here comes the fourth street," said Eddie. "Six of clubs to Victor…a possible straight flush, the Jack of diamonds for Kingston…watch this hand closely, the two of spades for Alice…a neat pair, and a ten of hearts for me…no joy there!"

Now the betting was more interesting. Victor Glenn raised to the table limit agreed upon before the game began: twenty dollars. Eddie folded. Two more rounds were dealt face up, followed by more betting. Kingston Grey's cards showed little hope and so he folded, leaving only Alice and Victory Glenn still in the game. The final card was dealt face down. There was a substantial pot in the center of the table.

Eddie scanned the two sets of cards (of course he could read the values of the downturned ones just as well as those face up). He grinned. Glenn's upturned cards showed the five, six, eight, and nine of clubs. Did he have a straight flush, or was he trying to bluff? Alice's upturned cards showed the two of hearts, the two of spades, the three of hearts, and the queen of diamonds. She might have three of a kind, or a straight, or just the pair. Still, one pair would beat Victor's shown cards. So she bet the limit. Victor raised. Alice called.

Victor had failed to achieve a straight flush, but he had two more fives which gave him three of a kind. He started to reach for the pot. "Hold on," said Alice, as she turned over her cards revealing another two twos. "Four of kind beats three of a kind, doesn't it?"

Eddie turned over the burn card. It was the seven of clubs: the card that would have completed Victor's straight flush. Clearly, Eddie was having fun and enjoying his own cleverness. But he knew he must be careful lest he be discovered as a cheater. He would let Victor win a few hands during the rest of the evening.

"Must have been beginner's luck, said Eddie. "Victor, it's your deal. Everybody in?"

As Victor began the second round of stud, Alice chatted with Kingston Grey. "You're a writer!" she said. "How marvelous. Of course, I haven't read any of your books…I will…but that must be a wonderful profession. What are you working on now?"

"Well, I…I just finished a romance that takes place in Paris during the Second Empire. Now I'm starting something a little different. A murder mystery. It takes place on a sea-going yacht, by the way."

"Oh! I bet you're here on this cruise to collect material."

"Well, you never know."

"Let me guess," interjected Eddie Sugar, "the murder takes place during a poker game. It is solved by a sweet little old lady who…"

"Nothing that obvious," answered Grey. I'm thinking someone will get pushed overboard. To make it look like an accident, of course. And no sweet little old ladies, please!"

Breakfast the next morning was served in the saloon promptly at 7:00 AM. The yacht's chef, Émile Côté, had once worked for Hypolite Begue in his restaurant on Decatur Street, an establishment famous for its six-course Bohemian breakfasts lasting 3 to 4 hours. Foie de Veau Sauté à la Bourgeoise, or sautéed calf's liver in a black butter sauce, had been one of his specialties. Today there was Eggs Florentine—

poached eggs on dumplings with sautéed spinach, chopped tomato, sliced ham, and Hollandaise sauce, served with roasted small potatoes.

Alice had indeed traded rooms with Ashley Harris and a new chapter in the storied relationship between her and Eddie had begun. Eddie hadn't considered Alice as an objet d'amour, but he was glad for the company. If Harris and Elena Whitaker had enjoyed a clandestine histoire d'amour, he could be happy for them as well. It was all in the game.

One by one and two by two the guests came to the saloon. Nathaniel Eberhardt, the *Queen of the South's* owner, escorted his wife, Edith. Ashley Harris came in by himself—Alice had expected Elena to be with him, but she entered later, separately from her paramour, an unnecessary gesture as the tryst was well known on shipboard. Margery and Kingston Grey and Kathryn and Victor Glenn had been strolling the deck as the steward set the table. They came in as a group. Beatrice and Thaddeus Blackburn, Alice's aunt and uncle, were next. Last to appear was Arlene Sommer. Her husband, Travis was not at her side.

"Isn't Travis coming to breakfast?" Alice asked Arlene once they had all taken seats around the table.

"He isn't feeling well. He wanted to stay in the stateroom. Rest for a while."

"A little seasick, perhaps?"

"Perhaps."

Coffee and tall flutes of champagne with fresh squeezed orange juice in which floated ripe strawberries were placed in front of each guest. Eberhardt proposed a toast to the day ahead, one, he said, which would be filled with gaiety and conviviality. We will, he said, be traveling through The Rigolets to Lake Borgne today. It looks as if, he said, the weather will cooperate. Perhaps, he said, some of you may wish to swim before we raise anchor. The waiter brought plates of Eggs Florentine and potatoes, a platter of smoked Andouille, and another platter of the ubiquitous shucked oysters that Eddie, this time, would not avoid.

"Well, Mr. Grey," said Alice, provocatively, "there's your story. The wife has poisoned her husband and come to breakfast alone. She hopes no one will discover the body right away."

"Alice!' scolded Aunt Bea, "that's horrible of you to say. You apologize to Mrs. Sommer."

"Of course. I'm sorry…I didn't mean…"

"Anyway," said Kingston Grey, "poison is not the avenue to a perfect crime. As I said last night, she would have pushed him overboard."

"Please!" shouted Arlene Sommer. "That's my husband you're taking about! Will somebody pass the Andouille?"

Later, four did swim off a dingy lowered over the side of the yacht for that purpose. The water was cold and, to Alice's surprise, a bit salty. Eddie had opted out of swimming to spend time with Victor Glenn in the saloon over morning coffee laced with bourbon. He had managed to obtain an invite to an evening of poker at Glenn's penthouse the following week. Success!

"We prefer Texas Hold 'Em over Seven-Toed Pete," Glenn told him. "Well, I'm going back. Enjoy your coffee."

As a rule, Eddie wasn't much of a drinker. He was on his second cup now and beginning to feel the liquor. It felt nice and warm. He'd have another, this time without the coffee. Outside on the second deck, Alice found herself alone with Ashley Harris, sunning themselves on juxtaposed towels. Elena Watkins, like Eddie, had opted out of the swimming. The other swimmers, the Greys, had returned to their stateroom to shower. The warmth of the sun had chased the chill of the lake from Alice. She rolled over onto her stomach.

"Thank you for changing rooms with me," Harris said.

"Oh, I never would stand in the way of true love."

"True love? What about you and Eddie Sugar?"

"Eddie? He's a sweet man. Exciting and handsome. I wouldn't say I loved him. Say…you look a bit like him, you know? Same rugged build, same dark curly hair. All you need is a gold tooth and you'd be a dead ringer for him."

"If he sees us together like this, I *would* be a dead ringer! Gee, I hope you aren't getting too much sun."

"There's some lotion in my bag. Would you put some on my back? I can't reach there," Alice said.

"Like I said, a *dead* ringer."

As Harris stroked Alice's bare back applying the suntan lotion, a man watched from the deck above. It was a man who had been hired to the crew at the very last minute before the *Queen of the South* had embarked. The man had been hired to replace a crew member who was missing. The man had made sure that the crew member would be missing. He had been following Alice and Eddie for days now, waiting for an opportunity. There was his quarry, Eddie Sugar, with the girl. From this distance, he could not tell that the man was not Eddie. But an opportunity was just about to present itself.

"Well, it's been fun," said Alice, "but I'm going in now. A nice warm shower and some stylish clothes are waiting. Oh, and Eddie."

The girl had left and the quarry was lingering by the rail, watching something in the lake. Sharks perhaps? Were there sharks in Lake Pontchartrain? The watching man hoped so. Better be sure that the quarry can't save himself. Hit him over the head with that steel bar he found in the boiler room. A quick glance to ensure no one was looking. I'm doing this for you, Dear Sister, the man thought to himself. No one two-times Adélaïde St. Victoire and gets away with it!

A blow to the head from behind sent Ashley Harris to the deck. The watching man no longer needed to watch. Now he hoisted Harris up and over the rail. The body hit the water with a splash but didn't sink immediately. Now the man disappeared below decks. Now the First Mate, hearing the splash, surveyed the surface of the lake from his post on the top deck. "Man overboard!" he called.

Eddie Sugar's muse had always been Lady Luck. Lady Luck had saved Eddie from being thrown overboard, but the Lady was fickle and not above jealousy. Would the Lady remain true to Eddie?

The *Queen of the South* had docked at Milneburg on the southern shore of Lake Pontchartrain, this being the closest port with a long pier extending into the lake. Captain Lenox sent for the sheriff and had admonished the crew and passengers to remain on board until the law arrived. Already, having assembled the passengers in the saloon, the Captain had begun questioning each to determine who was where and who might have had the motive and the opportunity to assail the hapless Ashley Harris. Been reading too many detective stories, thought Eddie.

Ashley Harris hadn't drowned, although he was considerably waterlogged after being pulled up onto the skiff and hauled aboard the *Queen* and laid out on the deck where attempts at artificial respiration by pounding on his chest and pulling up his arms proved unnecessary and only added more trauma to his body. Harris hadn't seen his assailant, but he had an idea about whom it might have been. The finger of guilt pointed at Eddie. Eddie, Captain Lenox determined, had been alone in the saloon at the time of the attack. And drinking. His motive? Harris had been carousing with Eddie's girl.

"Nonsense," Eddie complained. "If she wanted to go with Harris, well...more power to her."

The Captain wasn't convinced. Mr. and Mrs. Blackburn were not convinced and forbade their niece to continue any relationship with Eddie. Alice was torn between wanting to believe Eddie, although his indifference to a possible affair she might have with another man irked her, and the strong circumstantial evidence that painted him in the colors of a jealous boyfriend capable of murder—colors which might soon be replaced by the black and white stripes of a convict's attire. Alice came up with an alternate theory of the crime.

"Kingston Grey," she said, "predicted the attack. He has been writing a murder mystery in which a character is thrown off of a ship. You all heard him talk about it. Maybe he needed to do some realistic research."

"Preposterous," retorted Grey. "More than likely Eddie Sugar got the idea from my describing the plot of my story. Unfortunately. I am sorry if that is the case, but I could hardly know what was to happen."

"Perhaps," answered Alice. "But you've certainly been given a wonderful model to follow when you put it all into print." Then to the Captain she asked, "Captain Lenox, have you grilled your crew the way you are grilling we poor innocent guests on this 'marvelous' (sarcastic inflection) boat?"

"Yacht. And no, I have not, but I suspect the sheriff will do so. I suggest we all wait quietly now until he arrives."

No one had noticed at this time that one of the crew was missing. Once Sheriff Dolan did arrive with two deputies, however, the absence was discovered. That the man had jumped ship just as an investigation was beginning was attributed to a fear that some criminal record he had might be revealed during examination. That was the theory. No motive for murder could be applied to the man, anyway. Eddie was the prime suspect. Eddie was taken into custody.

Eddie Sugar was a grifter and a gambler and a two-timing philanderer. Eddie had a record back in KC as well as in Saint Louie. Sheriff Dolan really liked Eddie for the crime. But, wouldn't you know it, Lady Luck smiled on Eddie once again (perhaps she had some gold teeth of her own). Ashley Harris declined to press charges against him. Perhaps some other lady had persuaded Harris: name of Alice Bea Gowen? Perhaps a new love affair was afoot. Perhaps, thought Eddie, it is time to move on. Miami sounded like an interesting place. And anyway, Alice had decided to bob her hair. Eddie couldn't stand bobbed hair. So he hopped aboard the Pontchartrain Railroad, the train they called the Smokey Mary, and once back in New Orleans, found a boat sailing across the Gulf to Florida. Ça senm bon.

Byron Grush

THE YELLOW KID MEETS HIS MATCH

It was always as dark as a cavern under the "L" tracks on Wabash Avenue. And windy. This wasn't why Chicago was nicknamed "The Windy City," that was because of loud-mouthed politicians, but somehow, what people called "The Hawk," the hash wind off the lake, managed to swing ruthlessly down Wabash like its namesake after some doomed prey. Bits of paper and indeterminable artifacts of that crepuscular realm swirled up in dust-devils to strike the lurking figures of panhandlers and the occasional adventurer lured to the South Loop by the prospect of refreshment or illicit entertainment. Here were blatantly undisguised venues for drink—and this at the height of Prohibition.

The establishment known as the 226 Club, after its address on Wabash Avenue, was one such gin-joint, or speak-easy if you will. But there was no back room or hidden entrance here; your drink of choice was served up front in the restaurant proper in coffee cups. Rumor had it that the infamous Alphonse Capone, who stayed just a few blocks away at the Lexington Hotel, had a financial interest in the 226 Club. Certainly, he frequented the bar—and the brothel located upstairs, where Art Deco chandeliers dimly illuminated nefarious exploits. An innocuous wooden door at the front of the club led to a series of underground tunnels: an important escape route during raids and a necessary access to the restaurant for bootleggers delivering the booze.

Edison Riley was an infrequent patron of the 226, preferring the more upscale Green Mill Gardens on North Broadway. There was always good live jazz to listen to at the Mill and the décor was more to Edison's liking—velvet curtains and colored lights. Lately, however, the atmosphere at the Green Mill was getting a bit too tense. Capone had a private table there, not far from the trap door that led to the tunnels. Also, the owner had leased the bar to a mobster named

Vincenzo Antonio Gibaldi, who was better known as Jack "Machine Gun" McGurn. When a favorite performer of Capone's named Joe E. Lewis decided to leave for a better paying venue, Capone ordered McGurn to shoot him. At least that was the story. True or not, Edison Riley sought a new watering hole. The 226 club would do.

Riley's first encounter with the Yellow Kid was at the 226. One day he was seated at the bar when a well-dressed man slid onto the stool next to him. The man had a neatly trimmed goatee, round, horned-rimmed glasses, a bright yellow vest, a homburg hat that looked two sizes too small for him, and he carried a pair of yellow chamois gloves which he laid on the bar in front of him. He introduced himself to Riley as Joseph Weil, a real estate investor. That was his real name, but he was also known as the Yellow Kid.

The Yellow Kid was a notorious con man, focusing on bankers and other wealthy persons who were not only greedy, but gullible. Someone who wants something for nothing, he once said, usually winds up with nothing for something. His nickname was given to him by an allegedly crooked Chicago alderman, "Bathhouse John" Coughlin, who was referencing a popular comic strip by Richard Outcault called "Hogan's Alley and the Yellow Kid." Weil hung out with a man named Hogan.

Riley and Weil were chatting about the weather, the White Sox, and the sad state of affairs brought about by Prohibition, when a rough-looking man took the stool on the other side of Riley. The man leaned in closely to Riley and opened his palm to reveal a flashy ring with a large red stone.

"She's a ruby," said the man. "A real beauty, ain't she? Well, I have to admit she's hot...given me by an associate just before he went on vacation down in Joliet. I'm willing to let her go at a reduced price, say, $50. Now, that's a real steal!"

Almost immediately, the Yellow Kid jumped up and grabbed the man by the collar. "You crook!" he yelled. "Get your ass out of here before I get angry. And take that relic from a crackerjack box with you."

The man left in a hurry. The Yellow Kid grinned at Riley. "Can't be too careful," he said.

Riley responded, "I thank you for getting rid of that grifter, but I saw through his ploy. That ring was as phony as a three-dollar bill."

"Oh? You mean one of these?" said Weil, pulling out his wallet and retrieving from it a folded bill which he laid face up on the bar. It was a three-dollar bill. It certainly looked genuine, but of course, it couldn't be real, could it?

"You probably think this is fake," said Weil. "Most people don't know that these were issued very briefly, then recalled. Only a few exist. The two-dollar bill has always been popular, especially at the racetrack, so the Treasury Department decided to try a three-dollar domination as a follow-up. They made a mistake however in placing the image of President James Buchanan on the bill, as you can see here. Buchanan was controversial because of his support of slavery, what with the Dread Scott case and the Kansas-Nebraska Act. They had to destroy all the bills they could get back."

"That's very interesting," said Riley. "Would you consider selling it?"

"Oh, No, I couldn't ever! This is my good luck piece. Whenever I'm in a situation where I place a bet…at the track or at a fight…I hold the bill and concentrate. I'm very good at picking a winner. Of course, there are other ways of assuring a win."

"What do you mean?"

"Oh, nothing. I shouldn't have said anything. Dear me, look at the time. I really must be going. It was nice talking with you. Don't take any wooden nickels!" Pocketing his three-dollar bill, the Yellow Kid left the 226.

Riley was dumbfounded. He had expected Weil to hustle him to buy the phony bill. Well, maybe it wasn't phony. He would have to go look that one up at the library. But not today. He placed a few bills on the bar to pay for his "coffee" when he noticed that Weil had left behind his yellow gloves. He slipped them into his pocket. He thought to catch up with Weil out on the street, but that didn't happen.

He returned to the 226 several times in the next few weeks, always bringing the yellow gloves with him. No one there had seen a man of Weil's description, nor did they know who he was. Riley tried the Green Mill with the same result. He perused other venues. It was at Bert Kelly's Stables on Rush Street that he learned that Weil's nom de guerre was "the Yellow Kid." The Kid was elusive, he was told. Impossible to track down. That was how he stayed out of jail.

Riley also found a book on US currency at the library. In it he learned that, of course, there was no such thing as a three-dollar bill. He learned other interesting facts about folding money. For instance,

George Washington's was not the first image to appear on the one-dollar bill—that was of Salmon P. Chase, the first Secretary of the Treasury. Alexander Hamilton had appeared on the two-dollar bill before Thomas Jefferson. Hamilton then replaced Andrew Jackson on the ten. Jackson replaced Grover Cleveland on the twenty, and Cleveland ended up on the one-thousand-dollar bill. Oh, and Salmon P. Chase? He was relegated to the ten-thousand-dollar bill. He wasn't much seen. But this president switching gave Riley an idea. What if you could manufacture one of those obsolete bills? What would a collector pay for such a rarity? He'd give it some thought. Meanwhile, there was the Yellow Kid to locate.

If Edison Riley was having trouble tracking down the Yellow Kid, the Yellow Kid had not had trouble finding where Riley lived, what he did for a living, who his friends were, and, importantly, how much he was worth. All of this sleuthing had taken place well before the supposedly chance meeting of the two men at the 226 club. The Yellow Kid left nothing to chance, and he was very good at sizing up his mark.

Riley had come to Weil's attention by way of a suggestion given him by Doc Meriwether. Meriwether was one of Weil's early associates during his introduction into the world of what he called "honest crime" (referring to the fact that it was impossible to hoodwink anyone not thoroughly greedy and dishonest at heart). Doc Meriwether, like Weil, sported a neatly trimmed goatee. He wore **pince-nez glasses and dressed in black trousers and a black frock coat with extra-long tails.** Doc Meriwether had met Riley during a high-stakes poker game and through close observation of him determined he had at least two of the three prerequisites of a perfect mark: he had money, and he wanted more of it. Now it was necessary to learn if he had the third quality—was he gullible? Doc Meriwether turned the task of finding out over to Weil. The Kid began his investigation.

He traced Riley to a stately American Foursquare style house on North Sheridan Road in Edgewater. The large, landscaped lot reached back to a coach house of the same style. Although not presumptuous in design, and often considered "affordable," albeit only for the well-to-do, the location indicated that Riley was indeed well-to-do. The Kid followed Riley to an office building in the South Loop, the Monadnock Block on West Jackson. There he watched Riley enter an office whose glass-fronted entrance displayed the words, "Gordan and Riley

Brokerage." Satisfied that he had confirmed that Riley had access to the type of funding that Doc Meriwether and Weil enjoyed pillaging, the Kid engineered the meeting at the 226 Club.

Weil gave some thought to exactly how he chould scam Riley for the most money. One his early scams involved horse racing. He would convince the mark that he knew of a race that was fixed; the jockey and the judge were in on it of course. Weil would usually have something of apparent value to offer as collateral so that the mark would loan him a sum of cash to bride the jockey and the judge, as well as to bet on the horse. There wasn't really a fix, the horse wouldn't even place, the collateral would prove to be worthless, and Weil would abscond with the money.

There was another variation on the horse racing scam. It was complicated and involved hiring a great number of people as actors. Betting on the horses was often done at betting parlors called "handbooks." Information on the winner was transmitted to the parlor by a Western Union hookup. This scheme involved the pretense of having an insider at Western Union who worked on the line used for the races. The race results could be told to the mark and the transmission could be delayed so that the mark could have time to bet heavily on the winner. At least, this was what the mark was told. He could not actually win because the betting parlor was fake, and he was given the name of the wrong horse. It was quite a elaborate hoax but worth the trouble. The mark could not go to the authorities since he himself was implicated in a crime.

While the Yellow Kid set about arranging for the fake betting parlor and hiring actors, Edison Riley was busy with his own scheme: creating a counterfeit bill or two. He had decided on Treasury Notes designed in the 1890s. The larger denominations were of interest to him due to their rarity and the probability that almost no one would be familiar with them. There was a 500-dollar bill which pictured the Civil War general, William Tecumseh Sherman which had never been issued, but existed in proof form. And there was a 1000-dollar bill that preceded the current bill that pictured Grover Cleveland; this one showed Major General George Meade. The year of issue for the Treasury Notes, 1891, soon saw a redesign of the very elaborate reverse side to a more simplified form in order to make the bills more distinguishable from counterfeit ones. Ironically, the simplified form would be easier to counterfeit.

One month later, Edison Riley found himself knocking on a painted wooden door at the top of the stairway in a three-floor walkup apartment building on North Broadway. The door opened just enough to allow a watery eye to peek through. "Oh, you're back," said a voice. The door was pulled open by a stooped man of uncertain age (although seemingly ancient) who gestured for Riley to enter. The apartment within was shabby, with little furniture and faded wallpaper on which the blooms of a once bright floral design seemed to have shriveled and mildewed. Angled across one corner of the room was a worn, overstuffed davenport draped by an old quilt upon which slept a cat mangy enough to fit in perfectly with the rest of the depressing environment. A metal table of the type used in kitchens was in the center of the space. It was piled with old newspapers.

"I've brought the photographs," said Riley. They should be good enough for you to work from."

"I'll be the judge of that," said the man.

His name was Edward Brotz. He had been a member of a counterfeiting gang back in the days when the Treasury Notes had first begun to be replaced by modern designs. He knew how to imitate the intricate flourishes of the older designs. He knew where to obtain the right kind of paper. And he knew how to avoid capture. He was retired, the major portion of the counterfeiting gang having been sent "up the river," as the expression went.

Riley had located him with great difficulty. Convincing Brotz to make some bogus bills for him had been nearly impossible. The man was adamant that his days of skirting the law were over. Then Riley mentioned the Yellow Kid. He told him that the Yellow Kid would be his mark. Brotz brightened.

"That bastard nearly got me arrested," said Brotz. "Yes, if we can take him down...I'll do it. But I must have a good sample to work from. My eyes aren't what they used to be."

Now Riley showed him the photographs he had taken of a real thousand-dollar Treasury Note. One with the picture of Major General George Meade on the front and the simpler design on the back.

"Ah," said Brotz, "the so-called 'Grand Watermelon' note. See, the oval shapes that hold the numbers? But where did you find one to photograph? They are very rare."

Riley related his quest for the bill which began by a search through back issues of *The Numistmatist*, the premiere coin-collecting magazine. In one issue he found a personal ad placed by a collector seeking obsolete paper money. He called himself "Colonel Green," and could only be contacted through the magazine. Riley learned that Colonel Green was one Edward Howard Robinson, a wealthy businessman with political connections and the son of the notoriously stingy investor, Hetty Green, who was called the "Witch of Wallstreet." He was as famous as Hetty was, but in his own circles.

Riley located Green at his mansion in Round Hill, Massachusetts and approached him, representing himself as a photographer for *The Numismatist*, working with a writer on an article about Treasury Notes. He told him needed a good photo of the Grand Watermelon for the article. Green agreed, provided that he would not be mentioned as owning the note, as he was worried about theft. Green was a large man, well over six feet tall and heavy. Riley noticed that Green limped as he showed him into his study where a display of rare coins was arrayed in velvet-line cases on long oak tables.

"My leg," Colonel Green explained, "had to be amputated when I was just a child. I've lived with this damn prothesis all this time."

Riley felt somewhat guilty about deceiving the man. But only somewhat. He went about the business of setting up his camera on a tripod and angling lights at the bill. When he was finished, he asked Green if there had ever been such a thing as a three-dollar bill. "Of course not," came the answer.

Joseph Weil, aka the Yellow Kid, was satisfied with his arrangements. On the corner of Randolph and Wells Streets stood the Briggs House, a prominent hotel originally built in 1855, destroyed in the Great Chicago Fire of 1871, and rebuilt in 1873. Weil and his associates had rented a banquet hall at the hotel and fabricated within it a pool hall outfitted as a betting parlor. They had installed a cashier's cage where bets would be placed, a large board on one wall where the odds for the horses in the various races would be posted, a telegraph apparatus which was hooked up to another located in an adjoining room, and a big wall clock, set back fifteen minutes to allow for the necessary delay between the finish of the actual race and their own reported results.

In legitimate betting parlors, news of races was transmitted through direct lines from Western Union. An operator sat at the telegraph desk in the pool hall, listened to and decoded the clicks, and would announce the moment when the race began: "They're off!" At this time, betting on the race would be closed. The operator then called out details of the race and the final finish with the names of the horses that won, placed and showed. At the Yellow Kid's bogus betting parlor, all of this would be acted out for the benefit of the mark who would, of course, not be allowed to win.

The first mark they brought to the phony betting parlor was Marcus Macallister, owner of the Macallister Theatre, and one of the principal backers of the proposed amusement park, the White City. Macallister was bilked out of $7,500.00 through an elaborate scheme which the Yellow Kid was eager to use on Edison Riley. He had to meet Riley again, accidentally, of course, and persuade him, as he had Macallister, to come to the financial aid of an actor posing as the Kid's brother in law who supposedly was in serious debt to some loan sharks.

"Lend my brother in law the money he needs," the Kid had told Macallister, "and I'll show you how to make some easy money." It was easy money all right, easy money for the Yellow Kid and his associates.

Edison sat at the bar at the 226 Club one overcast afternoon in April. A tap on his shoulder caused him to turn and see Joseph Weil standing beside him. "Come with me to that booth at the back," said Weil. "I need to talk privately with you."

The booth had high wooden-backed seats that shielded them from the view of anyone in the front of the place. Edison did not think this was suspicious. He was expecting some kind of con to come from the Kid. He kept his facial expression neutral and waited for it. They had gotten drinks at the bar before retiring to the booth: teacups filled with Canadian "coffee"—the real McCoy, not something brewed in a bathtub. Edison sipped his slowly. Then he said:

"Nobody coming to try to sell me a phony ring, is there?"

"No, no," replied Weil. "That's not what I'm worried about."

"Well, you do seem to be worried. What's the problem?"

"It's my brother-in-law. He's up to his ears in debt to some loan sharks. Real nasty fellows. If he can't pay up…"

"And you want me to lend him the money. How much are we talking about?"

"He needs $2,500.00," said the Kid. "But I would not ask that of you. He would get off the hook, all right, but he'd couldn't pay you back. No…I've got a better idea, but it does require a small outlay of capital. It is only a couple thousand dollars and if you can front that much, I can show you how to make a great deal more in return."

"I'm listening," said Riley.

"You know about handbooks, don't you?"

"Betting on horse races in a pool hall or some such place."

"Right…perfectly legal. But what if I told you I could guarantee you the name of the winning horse in advance of the race?"

"You've fixed the race? Then why don't you bet your own cash. What do you need me for?"

"Simply that I am known at the betting parlors all over town. I admit…there was a time I did fix races. That was risky. But not this time. This time it will be fool proof. Do you know how the handbooks get the race information?"

"Radio? Telephone?"

"Western Union. Through a direct hookup. It just so happens that my brother-in-law works for Western Union. He has just been promoted to the Gold Wire. That's the racing wire. He gets the word from whatever track is running a race and relays the message to the handbook. All we need to do is to convince him to give us the winner's name and to delay that relay long enough to place a large bet on the horse. See, it's fool proof."

And I'm just the fool to prove it, thought Riley. But he played along and accompanied Weil to the Western Union building to meet the actor playing Weil's brother-in-law, who was introduced to him as "Billy." Billy put on a show of reluctance when the plot was presented to him, but once the Kid reminded him what the loan sharks could do to him and his family, he agreed. The Kid then took Riley to the bogus pool hall at the Briggs House. There was a pay phone in the lobby. They waited for Billy's call.

"I've only got about a hundred dollars," said Edison Riley.

"That's okay," answered the Kid. "This is just a test run to see if it works like I think it will."

The telephone rang. The Kid answered it. He nodded. "Okay," he said. "The winner is Colorado. He's 4 to 1! Hurry, let's place your bet."

But when they got to the window it was blocked by several men engaged in a heated argument. The Kid pushed his way through this, yelling that he had to place a bet. The angry men shoved him so hard he fell to the floor. Just as this happened, the telegraph clerk shouted out, "They're off!" The cashier shut the cage's window. "No more bets," he proclaimed.

The telegraph operator narrated details of the race, making it sound as exciting as if they all had been at the racetrack. The winner was, indeed, Colorado. It had been a real race with a real winner, but it had happened fifteen minutes before. The fight had been staged to prevent Riley from being able to bet. The whole charade was intended to make him a believer.

"Damn!" said the Kid. "You would have won some good money. Well, we'll have to try it again another time. That was the last race today."

"I'm convinced," said Riley. "We might want to ask for a bigger delay next time, however. I would be willing to bet a great deal more money than just the twenty-five hundred your brother-in-law needs. But I don't have instant access to large amounts of cash. I'd have to raise it."

"How long would it take you?"

"Say, why don't you meet me tomorrow back at the 226? About 2 PM. I may need your help raising the cash. I'll explain it to you then."

The Kid had no choice but to agree. Riley was obviously on the hook. But now he had to be reeled in.

Capone had been in earlier to check on things, so the place was unusually vacant. Just as well, thought Riley. When the Kid arrived, Riley motioned for him to join him at the same booth they had occupied the day before. Its surface was sticky from spilled beer. Along the top of the wall were Art Deco features with a middle eastern flair. Above their heads swung Moroccan-style lighting fixtures. The decor gave the speakeasy an exotic look. They might have been at the Casbah negotiating the sale of a camel.

"This is what I have to work with," said Riley, showing Weil the counterfeit thousand-dollar bill.

"Say, that's an old bill, isn't it? Is it still any good?"

"If you took it to a bank you would get $1,000.00 in cash for it. Then they would destroy it. But it is worth much, much more than that. Collectors seek after these kinds of rare bills, just like they do for rare coins. This one could go as high as six or eight thousand. Maybe more."

The Kid whistled. "Can you sell it?"

"That's where you come in. There is a Numismatists' convention coming to town next week. I happen to know that one of the major collectors is already here at one of the hotels. He would love to get his hands on this before any of the other collectors."

"So? What is my role in this?"

I can't approach him. It has to do with how I obtained the bill a few years ago. It wasn't altogether legitimate. That's all I will tell you about it. I think you should be the one to approach him."

"Okay. So, you give me the bill and tell me his name and location, I get the money and we put it on a sure thing with my system. For a split?"

"That's acceptable. However, I really don't know you, do I? I can't just give you the bill without worrying that you might skip town. Tell you what though, you advance me, say… $4,000.00. It's like I'm selling you the bill and you are reselling it. If we don't end up doing the racing deal, I would still have my money and you'd have your share, which would be a whole lot more than the four thousand. Don't forget, we could double or triple it at the handbook. You'd need me to place the bet, so it would make sense to follow it through to the end."

Weil didn't like the idea of investing that much cash up front. But the more he thought about it, he realized that if Riley was right about the bill's worth, he could make a killing, racetrack scam or no racetrack scam.

"But how do I know this collector will value the bill so high? Or if he even would want to buy it?"

"I'll give you his name and a picture of the bill. You can go talk to him, show him the picture, and if you're satisfied, we'll go ahead."

And now it was the Yellow Kid who was hooked. "I don't have $4,000.00," he said.

"You can get it. I'd be willing to bet that you can. Meet me here again tomorrow and let me know one way or the other."

At Michigan Avenue and 7th Street stood the 21-story Blackstone Hotel. The first story of pink granite featured high arches which supported the red brick building which was trimmed in white-glazed terracotta. Some called its style neoclassical Beaux-Arts, others said it was Second Empire. In either case it was impressive. Warren G. Harding was selected as the Republican candidate for the presidency at the Blackstone, and it was known as the "Hotel of Presidents."

Now it was the temporary residence of a man calling himself Dale Nossinger. Joseph Weil had looked him up in the *Numismatist* just to make sure he was really a collector. He was there all right, but there was no physical description. All that the magazine had said in its profile of Nossinger was that he was an avid collector of paper money. Weil worried somewhat about this sparse identification. Perhaps his innate con man instincts had come into play. He proceeded cautiously.

Nossinger's suite on the 19th floor had an excellent view of Lake Michigan. Weil looked out the window while he waited for Nossinger to fetch two drinking goblets and a hip flask from the adjoining bedroom.

"I hope you like Scotch," Nossinger said. "It's from my private stock...pre-prohibition."

"Oh, that will do fine," returned Weil. "Have you ever seen one of these?" he asked, taking his bogus three-dollar bill from a vest pocket and placing it on the table in front of Nossinger. It was the only test he could think of to see if the man was legitimate.

"Ha, ha! That's funny," said Nossinger. "I saw one of these at the World's Fair in St. Louis back in oh-four. It's fake, of course, but it might be worth something. Maybe ten dollars. Is this what you want to sell me? Hardly worth your while to trek all the way up here from...where did you say you were from?"

"Milwaukee. No, I don't want to sell it, it's sort of a lucky piece. This is what I wanted to show you. Just a photo, but I have the real thing if you're interested in seeing that. I just want to have it appraised. Is all." Weil then produced the photograph of the thousand-dollar Treasury Note.

"Ah ha! A Grand Melon. Yes, I'm interested. But tell me, what color is the seal on the front?"

"What color should it be? Is there a difference in value?"

"Yes, of course. The blue seals are worth...oh, a few thousand at most. But the ones with the red seal, can go as high as ten grand. There are very, very few of them in existence. If you have one..."

"Um, I guess I should bring it to you to examine. Condition and so forth. How about tomorrow?"

"I'm going to be at the opening of the Numismatists' convention tomorrow. All day. Can you come back later tonight? With the bill?"

"Yes," said Weil. "I had thought I might sell it at that convention. Of course, I could give you first crack at it."

"I had one once upon a time, but it got away from me. In a sort of swindle. I don't like to talk about it. I'll consider making an offer once I see it. Come back about nine o'clock."

"With bells on."

The Yellow Kid kept his appointment with Edison Riley at the 226 Club after stopping first at his own apartment to retrieve four-thousand dollars in crisp new one hundred-dollar bills, part of a recent take from the horse race scam. It was going to be hard to part with it, even temporarily, but he would get it back along with the money from the sale of the Treasury Note, once he arranged for another sham race at the betting parlor.

"It seems probable that Nossinger will buy the bill if it happens to have a red seal on it," Weil told Riley.

"It just so happens…it does," said Tyell, producing the bill. "Have you the money?"

"I do. The deal is, I sell the bill to Nossinger, then we invest that money and the money I am giving you now in a bet on a sure thing. We split the profits fifty-fifty. Does that sound okay to you?"

"We are going to become very rich indeed," said Riley.

Now, the Yellow Kid was an expert scammer: a con man's con man. He had learned from the best of them, from Doc Meriwether, Fred "The Deacon" Buckminster, Frank Hogan, "Fats" Levine, and Colonel Jim Porter. He once traded a chicken to an old prospector for a gold nugget. He took the Italian dictator Benito Mussolini for two million dollars. He sold Andrew Mellon's brother a nonexistent silver mine for half of a million. He fixed horse races and prize fights, sold phony stock certificates upon which he had forged the signature of J. P. Morgan. He knew all the tricks of the trade. And he knew better than to trust another con man or to let his own greed get in the way of his good sense.

So he was in a bit of a quandary when he returned to the Blackstone to learn that Dale Nossinger had checked out leaving no forwarding address. The next day he attended the Numismatists' convention and did find Dale Nossinger—the real Dale Nossinger. Nonplussed, he attempted to sell the Treasury Note to the real Dale Nossinger only to be told that it was an excellent forgery, but nonetheless, worth slightly less than the paper upon which it was printed. He knew it was useless to brace Edison Riley about the matter, assuming he could even locate Edison Riley. When he went to the Monadnock Block, the office he had followed Riley to no longer had his name on the door. It now belonged to a building maintenance firm. Riley's house on the North Side was closed up and vacant. The Yellow Kid had met his match. But now he began to wonder if the real Dale Nossinger ever bet on the horses.

THOMAS HARDY
AND THE BATTLE OF CHERBOURG

June 19, 1864, aboard the USS Kearsage

Thomas Hardy leaned over the rail of the Kearsage, a three-masted, steam-driven, Mohican-class sloop-of-war now paused at the harbor entrance to Cherbourg, France. He watched the waves lapping at the wood-and-chainmail armored hull and mused upon the long journey that had brought him here. The USS Kearsage had been searching from the Canaries to Madeira, to the Outer Hebrides, and all over the coast of Northern Europe for the elusive Confederate raider, the CSS Alabama. Now she had located her prey in the harbor at Cherbourg. Now she prepared to do battle.

Twenty-some years ago, Thomas Hardy had sailed up and down the Mississippi on side-wheelers like the Messenger, hauling cotton bales, riverboat gamblers, fancy women, and hard-worked slaves. He had crewed on the showboat, Spelling and Ross' Floating Palace, where minstrels in blackface entertained the local citizens from Memphis to Cairo. He had helped a runaway slave seek asylum with the Underground Railroad.

He had become the first mate on the Witch of the Winds, a clipper ship deemed the fastest, smoothest, and cleanest on the seven seas by its Captain Stoughton, a man with whom he would nearly come to blows over another race-related incident. He had sailed on that vessel around the horn and upon reaching the coast of the Yucátan Peninsula in 1860, he helped a cargo of slaves Stoughton had taken aboard to escape, inadvertently running the ship aground in the effort. Stoughton had fired him once they reached port at New Orleans.

Hardy had come to hate the paddle boats that steamed up the Big Muddy, but he had no choice but to crew on another of the glorified barges or face dock work or worse. He had an idea to help more fugitive slaves get to Canada, but that would require two important things: a boat, and an obliging captain willing to risk breaking the law. He found a boat, but not an agreeable captain.

Hardy walked up the levee of New Orleans. The smokestacks of paddle wheelers thrusting upward into the hazy sky extended for miles like a forest of leafless trees. The docks were bustling with the loading of cotton. Rivermen stood smoking clay pipes outside the seedy bars and brothels that lined the wharves. Gulls dipped into the impossibly red-brown river to scoop up minnows, then landed on pilings already stained white with their droppings. The air was filled with acrid smoke from fires set to counteract the poisonous city vapors believed to cause the recent yellow fever epidemic.

He walked up a gang plank past sweating Blacks carrying bales of snow-white cotton. He had just boarded the Alonzo Child, a 500-ton sidewheeler with a 36-foot beam. He sought out the captain, a man named David DeHaven, to solicit a position. DeHaven replied that his striker had succumbed to the yellow fever only a week ago. Did Hardy want the deceased engineer's job? He did. DeHaven introduced Hardy to his pilot, Sam Clemens, and to his co-pilot, Horace Bixby. The Alonzo Child was about to embark upriver to its home port of Saint Louis.

It was November of 1860. The Alonzo was about seventy miles upriver near the Houmas Plantation. The plantation, owned by John Burnside, consisted of 12,000 acres devoted to sugarcane. Burnside ran his sugar mills with the labor of 750 slaves, the largest slave holding in Louisiana. Sam Clemens, piloting the Alonzo, was racing another boat when they encountered a heavy fog, the result of sugar cane waste burning on the shore. Clemens ran the Alonzo aground on the banks of the plantation. The sidewheeler was to be stranded there for two weeks until the river rose enough to float her free. Each day Hardy and Bixby tried to entice Clemens into joining them in a game of cards, but Clemens decided to write in his journal instead. Hardy noticed that the man did a lot of writing that trip.

In December, as a reaction to the election of Abraham Lincoln, South Carolina seceded from the Union. But now the Alonzo was stuck once again, this time off the shore of Cairo, Illinois, where the ice-clogged river was too low for navigation and no goods could be had for transportation. Clemens had left the steamboat to seek work elsewhere, and Captain DeHaven had come down with the fever.

Thomas Hardy considered leaving the ship as well. Packets steamed up the Ohio every day. Hardy jumped ship and joined the crew of the Marengo.

President Buchanan's Secretary of War, John B. Floyd, ordered a shipment of 124 cannons to be sent from the arsenal near Pittsburgh to New Orleans where the government was building forts along the Gulf. The Marengo, along with the steamer Silver Ware, was commissioned for the shipment. The war hadn't started yet, but Thomas Hardy saw the possibility of the South seizing the cannons. Others saw it too. In Pittsburgh, crowds protested as the loading began. Pittsburgh, after all, would be the city that invented the labor strike. Only about 2 dozen cannons reached the decks of the steamers before Floyd, reluctantly, rescinded the order for the shipment. Hardy jumped ship once again and sought work as a dock hand in Pittsburgh.

In February of 1861, Jefferson Davis, a former officer of the U. S. Army, was sworn in as President of the newly formed Confederate States of America. On March 4, Abraham Lincoln, a lawyer from Illinois, was sworn in as the 16th President of the United States of America. Then, on April 12, General Pierre Beauregard and Confederate troops opened fire on Fort Sumter, a Federal stronghold in Charleston, South Carolina. They captured the fort and the American Civil War officially began. Lincoln immediately issued a Proclamation of Blockade against Southern ports, planning to cut off trade by the South with Europe and the East.

The Union Navy, however, had only about 40 ships to cover the Southern coastline which included over 2,500 miles. It also needed ships to control the inland rivers and support the troops. The South was in even worse shape. Both adversaries began commandeering privately owned steamboats on the Mississippi and Ohio Rivers and began an intense program of ship building as best they could. The South, under Confederate Secretary of the Navy, Stephen Mallory, began attacking Union merchant ships on the high seas.

It might have made sense for Thomas Hardy to join the Union Navy at this juncture. He did not. Hardy wasn't exactly a pacifist, although he had a deep disdain for war. But the divisiveness of the people around him, the pro-war and anti-war demonstrations, illustrated for him the uselessness of the prospect. So many would die for the benefit of the few, and in the end, there would be no solution for the hatred, the exploitation, the suppression of man against man—men whose blood, Hardy knew, was all the same color. So he worked the docks on the waterfront.

Pittsburgh, the City of Steel, the City of Bridges. Smelter to the nation and supplier of armament for the Union Forces. Where the Monongahela joined the Allegheny and became the Ohio. Where the Fort Pitt Foundry would turn out the castings for the 20-inch bore Rodman Gun, one of the largest the world had ever seen. Where the Allegheny Arsenal would produce bullets and cartridges that would reap havoc on the battlefields. Where the mills would roll out thick sheets of metal for the ships they would call the iron clads, including the USS Manayunk, the USS Marietta, the USS Sandusky, and the USS Umpqua, all locally made. Pittsburgh would be protected by trenches, earth works, and small forts.

Yes, Pittsburgh was very important to the war effort. Major General William T. H. Brooks arrived to organize the defense of the city. He ordered the closing of saloons and bars but most refused. The public liked to tip a few now and then. Thomas Hardy like to tip a few to stave off the depression that dock work brought. He frequented a bar called O'Hara's on Pike street near the Fort Pitt Foundry in the Strip District, an industrial area along the Allegheny River shore.

One day when Thomas Hardy sat in O'Hara's at a wooden table sticky with dried spilled ale, a man he had worked with on the docks but rarely had spoken to approached him. "May I sit?" asked Joseph Butler. Butler was ten years Hardy's junior, in his twenties, lean, muscular, and seemed eager to please. Hardy and Butler began a fast friendship that day. There was no hint that a tragic incident affecting them both was just around the corner.

Butler introduced Hardy to his sister, Mary Ann. The 18-year-old girl with the light brown hair and the radiant smile captivated Hardy. In spite of their age difference, Hardy began taking the girl for walks. Soon the depression that had plagued Hardy ebbed; a new joy had entered his life. Even the persistent desire to return to the sea lessened. It was not yet love, but an honest infatuation that would blossom—if time allowed.

Mary Ann Butler worked at the Allegheny Arsenal in the part of Pittsburgh known as Lawrenceville. The wartime need for munitions had swollen the work force at the plant to nearly 1,100 souls, most of whom were women and many of whom were children of 12 years of age or not much older. Mary Ann worked in the main lab with about 150 others loading cartridges with black powder and shot. Hardy would sometimes meet her there during her brief lunch period.

Pittsburgh in the 1860s was a very large city: almost 50,000 hard-working individuals who made the most of the sparse leisure time allotted to them. It wasn't a city of great parks like Paris or New York or Chicago, but it had a splendid river on both sides. Couples strolled along the Allegheny or the Monongahela to watch fishing boats scurrying about and water birds soaring aloft. Perhaps not as romantic as the gardens of the Tuileries or Central Park, but it was adequate for Thomas and Mary Ann. Today they had a picnic lunch of sandwiches and fruit and they sat on a pier dangling their legs over the side as they ate.

"Do you worry about the war?" Mary Ann asked. "I worry my brother Joe may wish to join the fighting."

"Joe and I talk of it, of course. It is a senseless war. I've lived in the South and seen first-hand the brutal treatment of the Negroes, and certainly there is a need to end slavery. But Southerners will never change. They are willing to leave the Union in order to preserve their way of life. We would have to kill them all to bring about change in the South!"

"Surely not. Do the common folk in Georgia and Mississippi really believe in the secession? It only benefits the rich landowners."

"And the landowners aren't the ones who do the fighting. No, I would not worry about Joe or myself entering the army…or the navy. We agree it is not worth the sacrifice. Besides, it will be over soon. The South has no industry to support them as we do. Of course, you may be out of the job of making bullets."

"That would suit me," answered Mary Ann. Her eyes seemed to be taking on a certain sparkle.

"I wonder if it is too soon for you and me to think of the future. Mary Ann, you know how much I admire you."

"A little soon…yes. But something to think about."

"I'm glad of that," said Hardy. "We'd better get you back to the arsenal before you are late."

The war wasn't over soon. It dragged on and got bloodier. The Battle of Big Bethel in Virginia, then the Battle of Bull Run. Wilson's Creek in Missouri, Fort Hatteras in North Carolina. Lexington, Ball's

Bluff, Mill springs in Kentucky, Fort Henry in Tennessee—battle after battle after battle, and a mounting death toll on both sides. The Battle of Roanoke Island in North Carolina, the Battle of Pea Ridge in Arkansas. Then in March of 1862, in Hampton Roads, Virginia, a naval battle between two ironclads, the USS Monitor and the CSS Virginia (previously the captured USS Merrimack).

In April, the Battle of Shiloh. In June, the Battle of Seven Pines near Richmond. In August, the second Battle of Bull Run. And then, on September 17, 1862, two tragedies. The first, the South's first invasion of the North at the Battle of Antietam in Maryland, a horrendous blood-letting which would be followed by Lincoln issuing the Emancipation Proclamation. And the second, the deadly explosion in a munitions factory called the Allegheny Arsenal which killed 78 civilians—men, women, and children.

It was nearly 2 o'clock on Wednesday, a payday. Thomas Hardy had dropped Mary Ann off at the arsenal after a brisk walk along the waterfront. He was three blocks away when he heard the blast. Turning back toward the arsenal, he could just see the columns of smoke above the treetops. He ran. The main lab building, where Mary Ann worked, was in flames. There was debris all around the grounds: burning shards of wood from the building and ungodly things that later would be identified as body parts. There was a second explosion, then a third.

Inside the lab, the lucky ones were killed instantly by the blast. Others were incinerated or were overcome by the toxic smoke. In the intense heat, cartridges the women and children had been loading went off and later their bodies were found filled with hundreds of lead balls. Outside, severed limbs flew through the air and landed hundreds of feet away. Women jumped through windows, their clothing aflame or burned off entirely.

A man named Alexander McBride, who was Superintendent of Operations, had jumped from a window. His daughter, a 14-year-old girl named Kate, was trapped in the building. McBride was unable to rescue her. He began carrying buckets of water to pour on the burning bodies of people who had managed to get out of the lab. McBride, a former cooper, a builder of barrels, had warned against the arsenal's practice of accepting gunpowder which Dupont shipped in previously used barrels. The covers of these barrels, he maintained, could not be fitted properly. The gunpowder could leak. There was danger that a spark could set the gunpowder off. It is possible that this is what had happened.

The Commander of the arsenal, Colonel John Symington, would eventually be investigated for incompetence, but would be exonerated by the military board of inquiry. Just an accident, it was said. But Colonel Symington had paved the drive in the front of the lab with stone. And he had not allowed it to be scattered with the wood shavings which would retard sparks as suggested by McBride, claiming that it would be unsightly. Powder, spilled from the loosely closed barrels did accumulate on the drive, creating a hazard. Colonel Symington, in spite of his own fastidiousness, had not ordered the powder swept up. Thus at 2 o'clock, when Joseph Frick drove his wagon up to the lab to deliver more barrels, the steel-clad wheels of the wagon scraped against the stone road and caused a spark. The spark ignited the powder on the drive and the flames spread quickly to where other barrels of gunpowder were stacked. Boom. Just an accident.

"It was sabotage," Joseph Butler told Thomas Hardy as they stood in the Allegheny Cemetery where 39 black, military issue coffins containing, in some cases, only parts of bodies were being lowered into a mass grave. Fifteen other caskets were being buried at the nearby Catholic Cemetery where a priest was saying some fine words; these victims had been identified by teeth or swatches of hair.

"Colonel Symington's son joined the Confederate Army, did you know that?" continued Butler. "His daughter wears the Confederate rosette to church, for God's sake."

"You think they had something to do with this?"

"Someone did. There are Confederate sympathizers everywhere. If you were the enemy, wouldn't you try to blow up the arsenal?"

"Why would the Symington boy endanger his father like that?"

"Maybe he hates him for being in the Union Army."

"I'll avenge her death," said Hardy, "one way or another."

Thomas Hardy, with a new-found enthusiasm for the destruction of the Confederacy, investigated. He found out that Colonel Symington had two sons. William Symington was studying mining in Europe and was thus beyond suspicion. But John Symington Junior, had indeed joined the rebels. He was a member of Company A of the 38th Battalion, Virginia Light Artillery, known as Read's Battalion. Junior had been at the Battle of Gaines' Mill at the Chickahominy River where Lee had defeated McClellan, and at the Battle of Cedar Mountain, another Confederate victory. Had he been with Lee at Antietam on that fateful day? Had he been able to give strategic information to Confederate spies about the workings of the arsenal? The theory of conspiracy suggested to Hardy by Butler was inconclusive: it seemed to be at a dead end. Perhaps it had only been an accident after all.

*　　*　　*

This is a tale of two ships. One came into being in a British shipyard at Birkenhead, Wirral, near Liverpool in July of 1862. Although the British government had vowed neutrality with regard to the American War Between the States, it was legal to build the sloop-of war without its armament. Secrecy surrounded the 1,050-ton vessel, originally launched as the Enrica. Later, in international waters, she was outfitted with six British-made, muzzle-loading, 32-pounder smoothbore cannons, and two pivoting cannons, a 100-pounder with a 7-inch bore and 68-pounder with an 8-inch bore. She was 220 feet long and had a 31-foot beam. She could move under sail or by steam-driven propeller and could make 13 knots. Captain Raphael Semmes took command of the CSS Alabama with 24 officers and 83 crew members, many of whom were British. Her mission was to disrupt Union shipping in port or at sea. She became the most feared and most elusive Confederate raider of the war.

The other ship was built at the Portsmouth Navy Yard in Kittery, Maine and launched in September of 1861. She sported two 11-inch smoothbore Dahlgren guns, four 32-pounders and a 300-pounder Parrott rifle. She was both steam and sail driven with a top speed of 11 knots. The USS Kearsarge was named after Mount Kearsage in New Hamshire; like that daunting mountain, she was formidable. Captain Charles W. Pickering took command of her in January of 1862 and began the hunt for Confederate raiders such as the CSS Sumter. He was later replaced by Captain John A. Winslow. A year later, while at port in the Azores, the Kearsage was outfitted with hull armor of single-link iron chain to protect her engines and boilers. This chain mail would come in handy when she eventually engaged the Alabama.

. The newly commissioned CSS Alabama sailed the shipping lanes southwest and east of the Azores, capturing and burning merchant ships and whalers. Her score for the first two months of her career was ten vessels that would never again aid the Union effort. Then she headed for New England and Newfoundland and ranged as far south as Virginia. Ten more burned ships were added to her score. By December of 1862 she was in the Gulf of Mexico, raising havoc. There she sank the Union side-wheeler, the USS Hatteras.

By December of 1862 Thomas Hardy was in Baltimore, having traveled to that city first by train from Pittsburgh to Philadelphia, then by steamboat on the canal. His thought was to take passage by steamboat to New York City where he might find work on an ocean-going Merchant Marine vessel. He deboarded the boat at the Light Street wharf. Unfortunately, the daily packet for New York had just left.

He wandered up Calvert Street for a few blocks until he came upon the Barnum's City Hotel. The building was impressive, its jutting balconies and Italianate details spoke of luxury. He looked in the window of the first-floor restaurant at a menu posted there. The leg of mutton with capers sounded good, or the corned beef and cabbage, or the chicken with oyster sauce. But...my God! He thought. Three dollars for a bottle of Madeira? This place was too fancy for the likes of an out-of-work dock hand. (It would eventually be the meeting place for a group of conspirators led by John Wilkes Booth.)

On Front Street in the section known as Old Town he passed along a narrow street lined with two-story wooden houses tucked tightly among a series of odd business establishments. Next to the St. Thomas Infirmary he found a tavern and rooming house that looked to be more in line with his financial situation. The sign read, "Bull's Head Hotel, Jehu Young Proprietor." He would spend the night there waiting for his ship which was leaving in the morning. Certainly, for the price of a Madeira at Barnum's he could stay here for a week and still have food and drink money left over.

At the bar he surveyed the glass jars of pickled eggs and pickled pig's feet. He ordered a pig's foot and a beer and picked up a newspaper someone had discarded. He thumbed through it. An advertisement caught his eye. It read:

SLAVES WANTED!
We are at all times PURCHASING SLAVES, paying HIGHEST
CASH PRICES. Persons wishing to sell will please call at
282 Pratt Street
Communications addressed to
B. M. & W. L. CAMPBELL

Hardy brought the ad to the attention of the bar keep, jabbing at it with a finger dripping pickle juice. "What's this?" he said. "I thought the President freed all the slaves. This isn't the South."

"This," answered the bar keep, "is Baltimore. You will find both sides of the argument in our fair city…and good people on both sides of it."

"I didn't realize…"

"Most people here voted for Breckinridge, although they had no love of slavery. Many were sympathetic to the Confederate cause though. The Know-Nothing Party was ousted by the Dems and when Lincoln was elected all hell broke loose. The state militias from Massachusetts and Pennsylvania marched through the city at the beginning of the war and they were attacked by a mob of the rebels. We are now known as 'Mobtown.' Now, I'm not sayin' who's right and who's wrong, but Baltimore is an occupied city…federal troops everywhere. You just passin' through?"

"I'm headed for New York. Looking for work in the Merchant Marine."

"Best keep a low profile on the streets around this part of town. Someone might ask for your views of the war. Any answer you give will probably anger somebody."

The following morning, Thomas Hardy hefted his duffle bag over his shoulder and started for the harbor. As he walked down Pratt Street he noticed a crowd gathering in front of a two-story brick building with barred windows. An alley led to the back of the building. Glancing down the alley, Hardy could see a brick-paved courtyard enclosed by a tall stockade fence. In the courtyard were a number of Blacks, milling about. He approached a man in the crowd and asked, "What is this place?" The man answered, "It is the Slatter slave jail. There will be an auction today, if you are interested." Disgusted, Hardy walked briskly away from the scene.

At the harbor while he waited for the New York packet, he saw a large, three-masted sloop anchored a few piers down. He had several hours to wait so he went to inspect the vessel. It was taking on cargo and some of the crew wore the uniforms of the Union Navy. Would it be sailing the Atlantic, or just up and down the coast, he wondered. Then he noticed the big cannons and saw the name of the ship: the Kearsage. He had a sudden desire to board her.

*   *   *

June 19, 1864. Thomas Hardy stood at the scuttlebutt, the cask of drinking water that sat next to the mainmast. With him was Joachim Pease, a twenty-year-old Black man who had been with the Kearsarge practically since its launch. Pease told Hardy he was born in São Filipe on Fogo Island in Cape Verde, under the shadow of Pico do Fogo, the island's active volcano. The volcano erupted in 1857, prompting Pease to relocate to Long Island, New York. Now he was principal loader of the big gun number 1.

Joining the two men was an Irishman, Michael Ahern. Ahern had come aboard in November of 1863 when the sloop-of-war was docked in the Queenstown harbor of County Cork to take on coal. Captain John A. Winslow, who was short-handed of able-bodied seamen, went ashore to recruit anyone he could find. This was strictly illegal, but 16 men were signed up at 12 dollars per month. When British authorities became aware of the recruitment, Winslow characterized them as stowaways and returned them to shore—all except Ahern who was somehow overlooked.

"Them's came to 'merica in chains," Pease was saying, "needs freein'. "I's here to hep free the slaves best way I can. Boat's a good thing. An' I likes the sea breezes." He chuckled.

"We Irish know a thing or two about oppression," said Ahern. "You heard of the Potato Famine? And anyway, it's an adventure, isn't it? What about you, Bo'sun?" he said, addressing Thomas Hardy.

"Bo'sun's *Mate*...junior officer," corrected Hardy. "And only because of my experience at sea which most of you land lubbers don't have. I'd like to think I was here because of a fair lady that the war killed too young. Wasn't the love of my life, but it affected me in the most terrible manner. I can hate the Rebs. But I also hate the war! Anyway, I wanted to return to seafaring. If I'd gone Merchant Marine

I'd a been sunk by now."

The Chief Mate was calling to hove the anchor. Now he came to the three idlers at the scuttlebutt and sent them to their duties. Except:

"You, Hardy, wait amidships for a bit...the Cap'n wants a word with you."

Hardy walked the gangway to the rail as the Chief Mate called to raise the tacks and sheets. They were moving into the harbor under sail instead of by steam. Hardy leaned over the rail and watched the waves lapping against the side of the ship. Captain Winslow approached.

"Hardy, you be coxswain for the longboat," he said. "Take three with you. Deliver this message to the captain of the Alabama. Be quick about it!"

As they lowered the longboat the Chief Mate called, "Let go and haul!" Up went the sails. Hardy looked at the paper the captain had given him. It was an order for an unconditional surrender by the CSS Alabama.

The CSS Alabama had been busy. She had taken 29 ships off the coast of Brazil in July of 1863, had cruised off the coast of South Africa and into the Indian Ocean where she had taken 3 more prizes, and then more in the South Pacific in the Strait of Malacca. By the time she arrived in France for repairs and a well desired rest she had been at sea for 534 days, boarded 450 vessels and captured and burned 65 Union merchant ships. She had taken over 2,000 prisoners.

Her captain, Raphael Semmes, was among the first commissioned commanders of the newly formed Confederate Navy. He had begun his career on the CSS Sumter, named for the Revolutionary War hero, General Thomas Sumter of South Carolina. He had captured and burned 18 Union merchant ships in the West Indies before sailing to Gibraltar for coal and repairs. There the Sumter was met by Union blockade ships including, ironically, the USS Kearsage. Semmes was forced to abandon the raider. He managed to reach England where he was assigned to the newly built CSS Alabama. Now in the harbor of Cherbourg, his ship and crew showed signs of fatigue, but he would have a chance to try to avenge himself upon the Kearsage.

The four men in the longboat had tied off its painter and had climbed a ratline over the gunwale of the Alabama. They were escorted to the quarterdeck where Captain Semmes stood with a glass looking at the Kearsage.

"Captain Semmes, Sir," announced Hardy, "I have the privilege to bring you greetings from Captain Winslow and to relay to you the terms of your surrender. You and your crew will be treated admirably as prisoners of war. You ship will be scuttled."

"What is your position?" asked Semmes.

"Bo'sun's Mate, Sir."

"He sends me a bo'sun's mate to make this pitiful demand? You and your fellows, Bo'sun, are now *my* prisoners. I will give your captain his answer. Master of the watch! Ready the fore cannon! Prepare to come about!"

Captain Winslow had trained his own glass on the Alabama and watched as his crew members were marched from the quarterdeck. Then he saw the big guns being loaded. "So she wants to fight, does she?" he said to no one in particular. Then he called: "Come about to the weatherboard. Reef the jib and strike the mainsail. Prime the stokehold and get up a head of steam, boys. We're taking the fight to international waters. Ready all guns!"

On shore, French citizens, aware of the two enemy war ships in their harbor, had come out to watch. Some waved Confederate flags and a band played Dixie; the French always appreciated a revolution. As the CSS Alabama came about to follow the USS Kearsage out of the harbor, a French iron-clad named the Couronne escorted her, intending not to engage in the battle herself, but to aid survivors, if any. Also following the Confederate raider was an English yacht, the Deerhound, owned by John Lancaster, a textile merchant vacationing in France. "What luck to witness a sea battle," said Lancaster to his wife and daughter who accompanied him on the holiday cruise.

At seven miles from shore, Winslow turned around and headed for the Alabama. From the Alabama a puff of smoke indicated that a broadside had been hurled at the Kearsage. A second and third volley came quickly but Winslow did not return fire. Not yet. The Alabama's gunnery was less than accurate and the powder she was using was old and dry. Winslow knew he had the advantage.

Winslow closed to within 500 feet of the Alabama and began firing. The Kearsage's gunners were well trained, rested, and ready. Shells brought down the Alabama's rigging. The boats began to circle each other, each trying to cross the other's bow. The Alabama loosed twice the amount of ordnance as the Kearsage, but many of her shells proved to be dubs and many missed the mark, falling short or overshooting.

Some of the rigging of the Kearsage was hit and fell to the deck. Shells found the sides of the Kearsage, but could not penetrate her chainmail armor.

"My God!" uttered Semmes, "if I'd known she was armored, I wouldn't have engaged her!" But he persisted. A 100-pounder shell lodged in the Kersage's sternpost but failed to explode. Now human carnage littered the deck of the Confederate raider. Holes appeared near her waterline. Broadside after broadside crippled the Alabama and she began sinking by the stern.

In the hold, the prisoners Thomas Hardy and three of his crewmates, huddled together, fearful of the bombardment they could feel and hear, and they were now conscious of the tilting of the ship as it began to sink. Water rushed into the hold. "This is it," Hardy said to his fellows. "You have been exemplary in your duties. I only wish this war…"

Then the hatchway opened and Hardy heard a voice calling, "Get those men out from there. We're not savages to let them drown like rats." Once up on deck he saw that it was Captain Semmes who had ordered their release. He also saw that Captain Semmes was wounded; shrapnel had struck him and blood stained his uniform. Semmes then pulled his sword from its scabbard.

"I'll not surrender this sword to that Union devil," he said, and flung it into the sea.

Semmes's First Lieutenant, John McIntosh Kell, ordered the colors to be lowered, thus signaling the surrender of the CSS Alabama. Captain Winslow on the USS Kearsage, however, noted that the white flag had not been raised. Two of the Alabama's light gunners were still firing on their enemy. Winslow sent a salvo of five more lethal shells at the Alabama, an act that would bring him criticism and official chastisement. A shell exploded on the deck near Captain Semmes and Thomas Hardy, knocking them overboard into the freezing water. Now the white flag was raised.

The English yacht, the Deerhound, was near the Alabama as she went down. Hardy grabbed Semmes, who was struggling in the water on the verge of drowning, and swam with him to Lancaster's vessel. The Deerhound took aboard a dozen men at that time, and in all rescued nearly 40. The Keasage lowered lifeboats and also rescued as many as she could. Others were not so lucky. On the Alabama, 21 were killed by shot or drowning, another 21 were wounded, 70 were made prisoners, and others escaped. On the Kearsage, three were wounded, one died from his injuries.

As the Deerhound neared the Kearsage, Captain Winslow yelled to Lancaster asking if he had seen Captain Semmes. Lancaster replied that Semmes had downed, although he was hidden beneath blankets on the yacht. Hardy lay on the Deerhound's deck, delirious, attended to by Lancaster's daughter, Catherine. He would wake up, not on the victorious USS Kearsage, but in the port of Portsmouth, England, just across the English Channel.

Byron Grush

Some Afterthoughts

In the lead story, "The Cabinet of Curiosities of Barnaby Cannon," the character Cannon makes reference to Ole Worm, a famous 17th century physician and naturalist who assembled an astounding collection of oddities. Whereas Cannon is fictitious, Ole Worm was a real person named Olaus Wormius (1588-1654), whose collection reportedly contained a fictional creature which was half plant, half animal, called the Scythian Lamb (actually an exotic fern), and an unicorn's horn (actually the tusk of a narwhale). Frederick Ruysch (1638-1731) did display, besides rare butterflies and birds, preserved -body parts which his daughter dressed in collars and strings of pearls, and an assortment of small animal skeletons posed with musical instruments or weapons of war. These bizarre collections were the antecedents of our modern museums.

In the story, "Tempus Teapotus," the Antiquarian Bookstore, and, to an extent, its proprietor, is modeled after a used bookstore I frequented during lunch hours when I worked in Chicago's Kinzie Street neighborhood in the '70s. Charlotte Anne Moberly and Eleanor Jourdain were real people who experienced the sensation of traveling through time while visiting the Palace of Versailles. They wrote a book describing their adventure, first under pen names, then reissued it under their own. They faced extreme ridicule. My story follows theirs closely.

Milton G. Norton, the photographer in "After Banking Hours," did work for the *Chicago Herald and Examiner* and did ride in the ill-fated *Wingfoot Air Express* which fell into the Illinois Trust and Savings Bank in one of the least known and most bizarre disasters in Chicago history. Norton, the White City's publicity director Earl Davenport, the blimp's pilot Jack Boettner, Harry Wacker, and Carl Weaver suffered fates described in the story. White City, an amusement park located at 63rd Street and South Parkway on Chicago's South Side, was the location of one of the few airship hangers used to build dirigibles for the U. S. Government's war effort.

George Holland and Rose Dockrell were circus folk extraordinaire, presenting unique equestrian acts in many early twentieth century circuses. If George ever knew or worked with Little People is unknown. The story of Dolores the elephant is based on a real incident that happened in 1883 to an elephant traveling along the Missouri River with the Stickney's and Cooper Jackson Circuses. The tent fire in the story is based on a terrible fire at the

Ringing Brothers & Barnum and Bailey Circus in 1944 in Hartford, Connecticut. It killed 167 people.

I greatly enjoy writing about New Mexico where we lived for 11 years. Santa Fe, the City Different, is a wealth of visual and historical images. Visitors may learn about the tradition of the burning of Zozobra, aka Old Man Gloom, and perhaps witness the event. They may eat a Frito Pie at the Five and Dime or travel up the High Road to Taos. Returning from Taos on Highway 68, they would be skirting the Rio Grande where kayakers and rafters brave the white water Race Course rom Pilar to Embudo.

Another day trip for tourists is a drive down the Turquoise Trail to Madrid, once a coal mining town, then nearly a ghost town, and now a vibrant community of artists, musicians, and just plain folks living the kind of life they prefer, sometimes difficult, sometime idyllic. In my story, "The year the Yucca Bloomed," Madrid appears in disguise as the town of Magarona (named after a dubious cocktail involving a glass of margarita into which has been placed an upside down 6-ounce bottle of Corona beer). The sad story of the young woman skateboarding through town carrying her dead baby is true.

We lived on a mesa up in the Ortiz Mountains near Cerrillos and Madrid for a time. The Tarantula Ranch and its unusual and wonderful occupant (and dog pack) were our neighbors. The threat of fracking was a very present danger. However, no one ever set off a bomb, as far as I know. Jules, Jim, and Juliette were our goats and Moses, the donkey, lived next door. Goldmine Road, our access road, continued up the mountain to the mining town of Real de Dolores (now totally disappeared). Thomas Edison did live in Cerrillos for a time trying to separate gold from ore electrically at Dolores Gulch.

No less colorful was Eddie Sugar's New Orleans. It was America's Paris in the 20s, before Americans left for that more famous City of Light. The Sazerac Coffee House, Broussard's, La Restaurant de la Louisiane, Le Petit Théâtre Du Vieux Carré, The Southern Yacht Club on Lake Pontchartrain, The Garden District—all haunts of the rich and famous, the would-be-rich, the would-be-famous, artists, writers, jazz musicians, and maybe a few grifters like Eddie.

And speaking of grifters, Chicago's Yellow Kid, unlike Eddie Sugar, was a real person. His nickname was given to him by "Bathhouse John" Coughlin after the comic strip by Richard Outcault called "Hogan's Alley and the Yellow Kid." The 226 Club on Wabash Avenue, possibly financed by Al Capone with a brothel upstairs, still exists. Today it is called The Exchecker. They serve there one of the best pizzas in town which, considering this is Chicago we're talking about, says a lot. Colonel Green aka Edward Howard Robinson was a famous coin collector and the son of the notoriously stingy investor, Hetty Green, who was known as the "Witch of Wallstreet."

The Battle of Cherbourg was a critical naval battle of the American Civil War in which the Union's USS Kearage finally caught up to the Confederate's CSS Alabama. The deadly explosion in the Allegheny Arsenal munitions factory in Pittsburg took place in September of 1862. Alexander McBride and his daughter Kate, Colonel John Symington, and Joseph Frick were real people. Slave trade did take place in Baltimore even after the Emancipation Proclamation; the Slatter Slave Jail was on Pratt Street. My character, Thomas Hardy, first appeared in *All the Way by Water*, and again in *Once Upon a Goldrush*.

Byron Grush

Muse Image, A Memoir
Our First Three Years in an Art Gallery In New Mexico
Episode Thirteen: Madrid!

Madrid (MAD-rid), New Mexico, sits in a shallow valley in the Ortiz Mountains, about 25 miles south of Santa Fe, on what has become known as The Turquoise Trail. It was a major coal mining town in the 19th century, owned and operated by The Albuquerque and Cerrillos Coal Company, and had 2500 residents in its heyday. Now they number under 200! It is a fascinating story of a "company town" where the miners lived and worked and shopped and played under the auspices of the superintendent of mines, a man named Oscar Huber, an entrepreneur and a sort of benevolent monarch. There was a ballpark, which still exists and is now used for jazz and blues festivals. The town was famous for its Christmas decorations, an early and unique use of electricity for the time, which is said to have influenced Walt Disney in later years.

It nearly became a ghost town once the demand for coal, particularly by the railroads, dropped in the 1950s. In the early 1970s, Joe Huber, Oscar's son, owned the whole town and all its buildings. These consisted of miners' cabins, small wooden affairs which had been built in Kansas, cut in half and shipped on railroad cars to Madrid, as well as stores, a hotel, a church, a tavern and, of course, the ballpark. The town was put up for sale: the entire town could be had for $250,000. No one bought it. Joe started renting out the miners' cabins and an influx of creative types (some called them "hippies") and other brave souls began revitalizing the town.

We enjoyed hanging out in Madrid. I remember one 4th of July parade down the main drag in which one of the locals dressed, or should I say, undressed, as Lady Godiva and rode *his* horse through town. The same parade featured a lady we saw at many events who had a pet boa constrictor hanging around her neck, and a fellow who had parakeets perched on his shoulders and head. And Elianne and her troop of belly dancers, and local musicians, and people who just simply liked to dress up and relished any excuse to do so.

And so when the time came to exit Santa Fe and relocate our gallery, we naturally investigated Madrid. After all, we now lived only 5 miles out Goldmine Road, which itself was only a mile or two up the Turquoise Trail from Madrid. In 1998, the main road through town was lined with shops and galleries, restaurants, a grocery store, a "board walk" with more shops, a bed and breakfast and coffee shop, the Mineshaft Tavern, Mining Museum, and at any given time was patrolled by errant dogs, scruffy-looking people, and bus-loads of tourists. We knew we'd fit in.

After a bit of searching we found a vacant house right in the middle of town which hadn't been rented yet. Its owner, Big Mike, was renovating it. He was an interstate trucker alternating his time between Madrid and another interesting funky town, Vega, Texas, right on Historic Route 66. He stayed in the basement while he worked on the house and we negotiated with him to reopen Muse Image there. The only condition was that we could not use the two back rooms until he was finished with them, which included sanding the floors. Oh, and don't drink the water, he cautioned. This was because the drinking water in Madrid contained about 10 percent coal dust. It also made washing the floors a real challenge.

The house was the former residence of Oscar Huber, himself. And although nobody seemed to care, we put up a plague identifying it as such. It was the largest house in town and perfect for our needs, with a sweeping front porch and large windows. We called the phone company and requested a phone. In a few days we received a letter informing us that, as there were no longer any free lines coming into Madrid (somebody had to die before one was freed up), they would be happy to install a phone for us for the nominal fee of $20,000. I am not making this up. I still have the letter, somewhere. A few days later, we saw a phone company truck coming up the road and flagged its driver down. We explained our problem. The building had once been an office of some kind and three phone lines were sticking out of the floor. Within minutes, the phone guy had us hooked up. No charge.

Madrid was like that. An enchanted place full of contradictions. We made many friends and only a few enemies. One day as I was sitting at my desk in the gallery an individual came in and sat down to chat as if around the classic cracker barrel. The conversation began to get a little strained as he began a tirade on the subject of people who opened up businesses in this nice little residential community. People who put up signs and attracted tourists, disturbing the tranquility and (my word) lifelessness of Madrid. When he began foaming at the mouth I began to get worried. I'd heard that a large portion of the town were returning Vietnam Vets and some were a bit shell shocked. But he calmed down and left, I smiled and wished him a good day.

Another time, again seated at my desk, my feet propped up and my vintage Stetson hat resting on the open windowsill, I was visited by a man who looked uneasy and a bit haggard. He had been sent, he explained by his lady friend, who had a display of her work in the gallery next door and who had seen my hat in the window. "Tammy," he said, "Wants your hat. She told me not to come back without it." Tammy, I should explain, was Tat2 Tammy, a sort of folk artist who specialized in creating art from the bones of deceased animals. She made some miniature sculptures of motorcycles that I thought were quite exquisite. She had a reputation, and I can't testify to this, as being a sort of "scary person." Certainly, my visitor gave the impression that he might die if he failed to obtain the hat. He offered twenty bucks and, although I really liked that hat, I didn't want to cause any undue strife, and so Tammy had a new hat. She wrapped an animal skin around it for a hat band and wore from that day on.

Our grand reopening, we decided, would be our tried and true Haitian art show. We got in some small iron sculptures and paintings to add to the drapos (sequined vodou flags). We contracted Kaffou-Karré, the Haitian dance troupe to perform and hung a large sign out on the porch. The Sunday before the opening, around the parking lot at the Catholic church in nearby Cerrillos, there was much conversation about the evil Vodou people who had just opened a gallery in Madrid. No one confronted us, however, and we were totally unaware of being seen as controversial, especially in a hippy, new age, extroverted town like Madrid.

The dancing was spectacular in our new space. The drumming miraculous. The crowd left something to be desired, however. Another gallery was having a party up the street and the loud blues band had attracted almost everybody in town. Still, we created some interest, sold a few items and started on the second part of our journey into this brave new, incredible world

About the Author

Byron Grush was born and raised in Naperville, Illinois, just southwest of Chicago. He is a third generation native of that town. Grush studied art and design at the University of Illinois and filmmaking at the School of the Art Institute of Chicago. At the Art Institute he was a student of Gregory Markopoulos, one of the originators of the New America Cinema movement in the 1960s.

Grush then taught at The School of the Art Institute of Chicago, creating a course in film animation in the mid-seventies. He later became an Associate Professor at the College of Art at Northern Illinois University in Dekalb, Illinois, where he taught in the Electronic Media area. He is the author of a book on hand-drawn animation techniques entitled *The Shoestring Animator.* Becoming interested in genealogy, he wrote a trilogy of historical novels based upon what he had learned about his early ancestors.

He and his wife moved to New Mexico in the late 1990s, and opened an art gallery called Muse Image which featured Outsider and Visionary Art in Santa Fe. They returned to the Midwest to retire in the small town of Delavan, Wisconsin, a place that reminds them of their roots. Grush's films are in the collection of the Chicago Film Archives. Grush writes, paints and studies Tai Chi.

Other fiction by Byron Grush

All The Way By Water

Once Upon a Gold Rush

Road of Stars

Dance Beneath A Diamond Sky

Violet at The Breakers: a novella

The New Unwritten Law: a novella

The Scrapple Eater: a novella

1954 or Just press the I Believe Button

Luncheon at the Dead Rat

The Death of Time

Romeo's Revenge and Other Wisconsin Stories

Nonfiction by Byron Grush

The Shoestring Animator

www.ingramcontent.com/pod-product-compliance
Lightning Source LLC
Chambersburg PA
CBHW032148020726
47496CB00003B/766